Gorgeous
misery

new york times bestselling author
ja huss

Gorgeous misery

new york times bestselling author

ja huss

About the book

Wendy Gale isn't the kind of girl you marry. She's not even the kind of girl you date. She's not a friend with benefits, she's not a one-night-stand, and regardless of what she thinks, she has never been a rebound.

Wendy Gale is kind of girl you kidnap and lock in your basement so she can't ever escape. She's the kind of girl you tie up. You put a collar on her. A leash. Handcuffs. You chain her to things and gag her mouth. A blindfold isn't a bad idea, either.

Because Wendy Gale is the kind of girl you grab on to—any way you can—and you never let go.

Wendy. Babe. You only need to know one thing about me, OK?

I will *never* let go.

Gorgeous Misery is a dark romantic thriller about one man's desperate desire to save the woman he loves at all costs. It is the third book in the Creeping Beautiful series and must be read in order.

PART ONE
the wild

"Whosoever is delighted in solitude is either a wild
beast or a god."

— Aristotle

CHAPTER ONE

CHRISTMAS #21
2 ½ YEARS AGO

Majestic, lovely, delightful, glorious, powerful, heavenly...

Wendy Gale isn't the kind of girl you marry. She's not even the kind of girl you date.

She's not a friend with benefits, she's not a one-night stand, and regardless of what she thinks, she has never been a rebound.

Wendy Gale is the kind of girl you kidnap and lock in your basement so she can't ever escape. She's the kind of girl you tie up. You put a collar on her. A leash. Handcuffs. You chain her to things and gag her mouth. A blindfold isn't a bad idea, either.

Because Wendy Gale is the kind of girl you grab on to—any way you can—and you *never* let go.

She is *that* special.

Wendy... you only need to know one thing about me, babe. Just one.

No matter what happens, I will never let go.

Today she is pouting in her truck as I watch her through the cabin's living room window. Her lower lip even sticks out a little bit. Her sky-blue eyes aren't angry or anything. There are no thunderclouds in there. But they are tired. Even from here, I can see that weariness she carries inside her.

It's Christmas Eve. We have a thing for Christmas. Birthdays, too. Hers, not mine.

This cabin is home—hers, for sure. But even though I only started coming here on any kind of regular basis four years ago it's starting to feel like home for me as well. Before that the open road was my home. My truck rambling along just to the right of that endless dotted-white line in the middle of the pavement was the only constant I could count on. I needed it back then. I needed that lie I was selling pretty bad. The lie that I was free. That I was running from something that could be outrun. That I was protecting them, even though I always knew I wasn't.

This is my major problem with Wendy these days. Somewhere along the line I failed miserably and she has gotten old enough now—hard to believe she'll be twenty-two this year—but she has gotten old enough now that ways have been set and everything I've been ignoring all these years is starting to become glaringly obvious.

She is who she is and the thing that bugs me most about that is that I missed it. I mean, I was there, ya know? I have been there since she was five years old and if I really want to emphasize my involvement, I could even say that I helped raise her. In the same way that I might claim I raised Lauren.

I was there when they were little, but we all went our separate ways. Wendy first, of course, because I wasn't her father, or her brother, or anyone, really. And Chek needed her for jobs, so her time with us was always temporary. But if you add it all up over time, Wendy spent about thirty percent of her life with me until she was fifteen.

Then Lauren was gone, I was officially dead, and Wendy was a seasoned professional.

I needed them the same way I needed the road back then. Wendy and Lauren were the only two people I had left to love. But it's been just Wendy for so long now. This is why she thinks she's the consolation prize.

Fuckin' saddens me.

Wendy is at home on the road as well. That's also my fault. I'm the one who taught her how to ramble through life. I'm the one who was running and I'm the one who took her along for the ride. She settled into the wanderlust way too young to ever have a chance of escaping it later. It's in her bones now. But... this cabin has always been here. It has been her true home since she was five. This is where Chek brought her for downtime. This place in the woods surrounded by birdsong, rivers that burble, and the kind of stillness at night one only finds in tucked-away places is her one true place of peace.

Even though my time here started with anything but peace.

The first time I came out to this cabin was seventeen days after Chek's death. That was four years ago.

11

Of course, that's not our beginning, Wendy and me. Because I have known her since she was a five-year-old child and I was a filthy drug lord's eighteen-year-old prisoner. But that first time I showed up for her seventeenth birthday, seventeen days after Chek died, that's when she stopped being on my side and I started being on her side.

But back to that very first meeting that night of the massacre, after I was taken to the Fenici superyacht just off the coast of Santa Barbara to meet the man who would dictate everything that would happen next. That was just a casual glance at a little blonde girl in the corner with a dirty face and a long scowl.

It would be another four years before she came to stay with me and my new baby girl, Lauren. Wendy was... well... Wendy was *supposed* to be my babysitter when that happened. My little helper. Someone to keep me sane, on loan from Chek to help me get through those rough early days when all Lauren wanted to do was wail in protest about her early bad luck.

But Wendy was way more than that.

And look, I'm not saying it was the ideal situation or anything—I mean, relying on a nine-year-old to be your best friend is the epitome of selfishness—but it was what it was and I have no regrets.

Wendy Gale has been my best friend for almost thirteen years now.

She has been more than my best friend for two years.

We are a team. We work well together. We get shit done.

And I get that part too. This isn't your typical love story because Wendy and me, we're not your typical people.

But make no mistake, this *is* a love story.

We were just born into something beyond our control and we've spent our entire lives trying our best to break it apart.

But here's the problem with breaking things... in the end, they're broken.

And yeah, I know. I know what you're thinking. I'm stating the obvious. *This is how shit works, Nick.* We all know that when you drop a piece of glass it shatters. And we all intuitively understand that things are very, *very* messy when it's over.

Fine. Agreed. I get it.

This is a fucking mess.

And there is no real way to put broken shit back together without lots of cracks.

But I don't mind the cracks. Wendy doesn't mind the cracks, either.

That's why we're so good together. We kinda love the cracks.

Wendy still hasn't gotten out of the truck and I haven't moved from the living room window. There's a chance she just backs up and drives away, but she's here now. And it's been a while, so I think she's staying. She's just having the same pointless internal monologue as me.

Wondering if this is... what? Normal? Satisfying? Enough? As good as it gets?

That's not what I'm wondering, obviously. Every time we see each other after a long absence like this I replay how terrible I am. How she needs anyone else

13

but me. How I don't deserve her, how I'm going to ruin her, and how it'll probably be me who gets her killed in the end.

And yet here I am. Every single time.

But that's not what *she's* thinking about. She has no baggage when it comes to these visits. It's all very in the moment. Temporary. You know, like… a salve. I'm something soothing to her. Tea, or comfort food, or a warm blanket.

She thinks she's using me. She's told me this. But that's not why she hesitates in her truck.

She hesitates because she *thinks* she is my number two. Or three, maybe. Sasha, in Wendy's mind, will always be my one true love. And in a different way, Lauren will always be my second.

Wendy hesitates because she thinks she is the only thing I have left.

She hesitates because she thinks that I would walk away from her if I could have Sasha and Lauren back. And the fact that Sasha and Lauren are together—that Sasha has raised my daughter as her own for all these years—that's just something Wendy can't get past.

If she invests her heart with me, she could lose it so quick. So fast.

In her mind, I am one easy decision from walking out on her for good.

She really thinks this. And yet here she is.

Because I'm all she has left too.

But unlike her, I don't take this personally. If I *wasn't* all she had left, she wouldn't be here.

And anyway, we're not just best friends and occasional lovers. We're a real fuckin' team. And when we do a job, we do it right.

I meet her here so we can hang out. We kick back, we cook some food, maybe go out to dinner a couple times, we laugh—or cry—and we sleep together like we're normal. We lie in bed and talk, and fuck, and sleep. It's all very normal.

But it's also all very temporary.

You see, we can't be together. Not for any length of time.

It's all so very complicated.

Her truck door opens and she steps out, leaning back into the cab to grab something, which I see is a backpack once she closes the door. She pauses and her eyes find mine in the window. She sucks in a deep breath, then walks towards the porch. I meet her at the open door and I have the same thoughts every time this happens.

I want her to fall into my arms.

I want her to melt into me, and kiss me hard, and admit that she has been miserable since our last meeting.

Sometimes it almost happens that way. The first time we met out here, seventeen days after Chek's death, she kinda did fall into me. But that's not how it happens this time. Or any time after that one time, to be honest. Because even though we both show up here and do what we do, it always ends with a fight.

She always hates me when she drives away.

My heart hurts when this happens, but my brain— the rational side of me? That part is always OK. Because even though she walks out, she takes the job I offered with her.

She doesn't want to do the jobs, but Wendy is a lot of things. She is moody, bitchy, mean, ruthless,

15

deadly. But she's also a professional. And she always comes through for the jobs I give her.

Hold on, I know what you're thinking. You're thinking—*Damn, Nick. That's harsh. You're using her for jobs?*

And if I was really using her for that kind of job, I'd agree. It would be way more than harsh. It would be... unforgivable. But I am not asking Wendy to kill people when I send her out. It's busy work. That's it. She digs info for me. She keeps an eye on shit. And maybe she knows these jobs are fake, or maybe she doesn't. It doesn't matter. These jobs are just how we keep in touch between Christmases and birthdays. I hand them over, she does them, sends me back the info I ask for, and we pretend this is all normal.

Wendy and I are very, *very* good at pretending.

I'm blocking the front door when Wendy approaches—and I do this on purpose. It's a way to make her choose.

Does she want to hug me? Kiss me? Push me aside?

She pushes me aside. Squeezes past me and keeps walking deeper into the cabin. I turn and I'm just closing the door when she drops her backpack onto the counter. Then the pause.

There is always a pause.

A moment she takes to ask herself things like, *Do I want to be here? Do I want to do this? Why, why, why do I even show up?*

But it's Christmas, not her birthday, and that means that if she wants to have a fight when she arrives, it will be a small one.

She turns, a smile on her face, and she says, "Hello."

It's always been about 'hello' with us.

I nod my head at her, cool like that, and walk into the kitchen. "Hello, yourself. Did you have a nice drive in?"

She shrugs. "It's the road, ya know?"

Yep. I do know. "Are you hungry?"

She doesn't answer me right away. Instead she looks around, spots the tell-tale signs and then sighs as she leans against the kitchen island and crosses her arms. "How long have you been here this time?"

I could lie. But I don't want to lie. I want her to know. "Two weeks."

She scoffs out her words. "Two *weeks*?" She blinks at me. "Why?"

"I like it."

She goes quiet for a moment, then just shakes her head. "Well, I'm not staying. You told me to come, so I came. But I'm not staying."

"Then where *are* you staying?"

"Your house." She says this with a total straight face.

But I can't stop my smile. "Is that right?"

"Mm-hmm. I figured… fuck it, right? You're gonna stay at my house while I'm gone, I might as well stay at yours while you're gone."

I press my lips together and nod. "Seems fair to me."

"So what do you want?"

"You."

Her eyes go lazy. Almost a look of indifference or boredom.

But it's not indifference or boredom.

It's a challenge.

One I am definitely up for.

Making love to an assassin should always come with caution, and making love to Wendy Gale comes with a lot more than that. But I'm careful as I walk towards her and place my hands on her hips. She smiles at me. That's the best part of every time we reunite. She's so happy.

I love Happy Wendy.

"Why are you looking at me that way?"

I reach up and drag a stray piece of hair away from her eye and tuck it behind her ear. She shakes her head, removes the carefully placed strand of wayward hair, and cocks her head at me. "Why are you looking at *me* that way?"

It comes out snappish. But she's not being mean and she's not angry. She's just uncomfortable because we're at a point now where decisions have to be made.

What are we?

Where is this going?

How in the hell will we ever be able to get there?

"You think way too much," I say.

She grins and cocks a hip now. "At least I'm careful."

Both of my hands rise—slowly—so I can cup her face. She stares up into my eyes, black pupils shining, and I see our past in my own reflection. "I'm careful."

It comes out serious. More serious than I intended, but she gets it and her body relaxes. "So kiss me then. Let's get on with it."

I can't stop the smile, and neither can she, so when our lips touch, this smile exchanges between us. It's like a happiness transfer. That's what I give her. But she gives me trust.

When I back away, I take her hand and lead her into her bedroom. I bought a ton of candles for this reunion. Three-foot-tall pillars. Candelabras. Several dozen votives. It's magical.

Because that's what Wendy deserves.

If ever there was a girl who needed the happily ever after—*deserved* the happily ever after—it is this one right here.

"Stop looking at me."

I can't. I can't stop looking at her. I will never want to stop looking at her. And I don't even know how this happened. I don't even know how I fell in love with her.

Am I in love with her? Or is this just our predetermined inevitability?

Is she just the only girl left? Is she just the default love interest?

She thinks so, but I know better. That's not what this is.

It's not the job, either.

Wendy Gale is lying in bed next to me, naked. It's five am on New Year's Eve morning and we have made it seven full days in the same place.

A record.

We haven't spent this many consecutive days together since she was in her early teens and I like it.

The white bed sheet is only half covering her small, lean body. And the curve of her back is calling to me. I trace my finger down her spine and her skin prickles up at my touch. Not in a creepy way, but a shivery way.

Her reaction is anticipation.

"Stop. Looking at me."

She's lying on her stomach, her face buried in the pillow, her gorgeous blonde hair spilling over her bare shoulders in unruly waves, so she can't see me. But she doesn't need to see me. We have known each other for *seventeen* years. She was there the day my first life ended and my second one began. She was only five years old, but she was *there*.

Wendy turns over and pushes her hair away from her face. "What the hell are you looking at?"

She's almost always like this. Snappish and testy. But I don't mind.

"You love me," I say simply. And it comes with a knowing smile.

She doesn't smile back. It takes more than a little flirty joke to make her smile, at least on the outside. But I know how she works. I know how she processes things. So her mind is whirling, looking for a comeback.

"I love nothing," she says, smug now.

"Not true."

"Why are you being weird?" She props herself up on her elbow and squints with disapproval at the snow glare infiltrating its way through the curtains.

"Why is it weird? I'm just appreciating you."

20

She makes a face. It's kinda like a wince and it comes with a crinkled nose. This face is adorable, but it's not meant to be. And that just makes it even more adorable. "And why are you smiling at me? For fuck's sake, Nick. Don't start with me today. I'm not staying here and there's nothing you can say to change that."

I know she's leaving. I also know she's right. There aren't enough words in the universe to change her mind once it's made up. Besides, until I come up with a better plan, this is just how it has to be.

I trace my fingertip down her arm and she shivers again. Her hand comes up to push me off.

But I was anticipating that. My palm collides with hers and then our fingers are laced together. I climb on top of her, my inner thighs gripping her hips just in case she gets edgy. Then I grab both her wrists and pin them high above her head.

She doesn't know what to do. She wants to be in a bad mood. She wants to get up, pack up her shit, get in her truck, and leave. She wants to push me away.

But things are changing and she can feel it. Not only that, she likes it.

I shake my head at her. "It's not working anymore, and you know it."

This makes her huff. "I'm in control of what works."

"Don't fight it. Just give in."

Now she smiles, her eyes drifting down to stare at my mouth. They slowly migrate back up and I can see all the little flecks of color in there. So many blues. But her eyes are not completely blue, not like most of the Zero girls'. Then again, Wendy never was a typical Zero. Her eyes have flecks of light brown and a little

21

bit of gold. They are the exact color of a blackbird egg, speckled and wild.

Everything about her is speckled and wild.

"Kiss me, then," she whispers.

"Just get it over with?" I laugh. "Not likely. I'm gonna take my fucking time. And you're gonna like it."

That cracks her, because she huffs out an incredulous laugh. But she also wriggles, trying to get free. I'm six foot two and I've got sixty pounds on this girl, easy. She's a tiny thing. Of course, her size has no bearing on her fighting skills. She's better trained than most professional assassins. Nine times out of ten a guy my size has no chance at all of overpowering Wendy Gale. She's that dangerous.

But I'm not most guys. And my danger level is a few notches higher than hers. So all this wriggling gets her is the full weight of my much bigger body resting on top of her chest.

She sighs. Not in frustration, but in annoyance. "I can get out of this, ya know."

"So get out of this," I challenge back.

She huffs again. "Why do you always have to turn it into a confrontation? Why can't you just ask for sex, like a normal guy?"

"Normal guy? What do you know about having sex with *normal* men?" I mean for it to come out easy, like a joke, but it's got an edge.

"Mmm. What's that I hear? Jealousy?"

I pause to think about my answer. Am I jealous? Oh, hell yes, I am. But there's no good reason for it. She's not sleeping with anyone else but me. She's never slept with anyone else but me. "Sure," I say. "I'm jealous. But you're mine, Wendy. You know you're mine."

She sighs. Closes her eyes. Relaxes her body. Gives in. "Fine. Let's fuck."

My laugh is a guffaw this time and I roll off of her, settling at her side. She leans her body into mine and then we're wrapped up together. We fit in all the right ways, my arm around her, her cheek on my chest, my thigh between her legs.

I love this girl.

And this submissive thing she does? This giving-in thing? That shit just makes me sigh and close my eyes.

"Fuck you." Wendy laughs. "You're not going back to sleep. You woke me up, let's do this."

I don't answer her right away because I'm suddenly thinking about… *things*. All the things. All the fights we've been in—not between us, but real fights with other people. All the times I've saved her, all the times she's saved me, all the sex, all the kisses, all the love. And all the mornings after when we had to go our separate ways.

"Do you have any idea what I would do for you, Wendy?"

She doesn't answer right away. Her body goes still. It takes her about ten seconds to find the right words. And they are simple ones. "Thank you."

"You don't have to thank me, Wen." I play with her hair because I love her hair. "I don't need anything in return for this. But I would literally blow up the entire fucking planet to save you."

"That's diabolical."

"Yep." I nod in agreement. "And I don't care. I've lost—" I pause here to reconsider my words. "*We* have lost so much, ya know?" I shake my head. "Never again. I will never let them get you."

She props herself up on her elbow and smiles down at me. It's a real fucking Wendy Gale smile. Not the kind that says, *I'm gonna kill you now*. And not the kind that says, *You just underestimated me, motherfucker. And that will be the last mistake you ever get to make*, either.

No. It's a genuine I-love-you-back smile.

And that means it's a sad smile too. This part of her has always broken my heart. Because to Wendy, happiness and sadness are the same thing. Because she cannot be happy or appreciate anything she has without first thinking about what she had to do to get it.

She sighs. "You're the one hunting *me*, Nick. Don't you think that's kind of ironic?"

"What the hell? That came out of nowhere."

"Come on. Are you, or are you not, making plans with Nathan St. James to kill the Zero girls?"

"Those aren't Zeroes. They're Zero two-point-oh. They need to go."

"You say this like"—she pauses, lets out a breath—"like they're different than me."

"They are."

"They're not, Nick."

"So what? They're dangerous."

"I'm dangerous. You're dangerous."

"Why are we even talking about this now? I thought we were having morning goodbye sex?"

"Yeah, well, you took too long. Got all sentimental and shit. You should've just got on with it and then we wouldn't be having this argument right now. We'd be moaning with ecstasy."

I reach for her, but she pushes my hand off. And it's a serious push. Not playing. "Come on."

"No. I've put this conversation off for too long. Why am I different? And if you don't have an answer for me, then that's a problem, Nick."

"Wendy—"

"Don't." She puts up a hand. "Do you have plans to kill Sasha?"

"What? What the fuck? What kind of question is that?"

"Yeah. That's what I thought."

"Thought? Thought what?"

"She's a Zero too." Wendy throws the cool white sheet off our bodies and gets out of bed.

"Where the fuck are you going? We're having sex here."

"No," she says, pulling on her jeans. "We're not."

I get out of bed too, pull a pair of sweats up my legs. Because she's about to escape and even though I knew she was going to leave me today, I'm not ready for it. Especially if we're fighting. "What did I do? What's your fucking problem?"

She's already got her t-shirt on. Her feet slip into her boots as she scans the bedroom for her purse.

"Wendy," I say, walking towards her. "What—" I grab her arm, but she shoots me a look. It's a dangerous look, so I let go. "What did I do? You want me to stop hunting those girls? Fine. Let's talk about it."

She finds her purse, hikes it up on her shoulder, and turns to me. "You won't stop. You've been doing

25

this my whole life. That's not a throwaway expression, either. You have literally been hunting down girls like me for twenty-one years."

"That's not true."

"No? When did you kill the first one? Hm? When, Nick?"

"I dunno."

"Think. I need an answer."

"Why? Do I go around asking you when you made your first kill?"

"*When*?" Her face is dead serious. She is going to walk out of here no matter what I say. But if she walks out angry, she will stay angry. Wendy Gale knows how to hold a grudge like nobody's business. And I didn't call her here to make her angry. I have a job for us. A long one with the sweetest prize at the end. And if she walks out now, she won't even get to hear my plan.

So I tell her. "I was ten." She takes a step back, like she was not expecting that answer. "But it's not what you think. It was me or her. It was a *hunt*, Wendy. Trust me, I didn't choose to be on that island that night. My father made sure I was. And in the end, it was either me or her."

Wendy just stares at me. And this new silence quickly fills the room and creates a chasm of distance between us. Finally, she says, "What was her name?"

"Her *name*?" My words come out incredulous. "I don't fucking know her name. It was twenty-seven years ago."

"Twenty-seven years ago. Do you hear yourself? I'm twenty-one, Nick. You've been hunting these girls for so long, you wouldn't even know *how* to stop."

26

I take a moment. Breathe. Calm myself. "Question for you."

"Shoot." She tips her chin up, letting me know her word choice is deliberate.

"What do you think we should do with them? Just let them… breed? Let this whole Company shit perpetuate for a few more generations? Let it get all out of control again?"

"Is it in control now?"

This is a trap question. And I don't want to say what I'm about to say, but it has to be said. "We lost a lot of people, Wendy. A *lot* of people gave their lives to get us to this moment."

She pushes both middle fingers up to my face. "Fuck you."

"Do you want to make all those sacrifices meaningless? We are winning. We've practically won for all intents and purposes. They scurried away like cockroaches and now they're hiding in the floorboards. But that's only because we're shining light on them. We're still diligent. If we turn the lights off, Wen, what happens then? Hm? What do cockroaches do when you turn the lights off?"

"So when do you stop?"

"We stop when they're gone."

"What about us?"

"What *about* us?"

"We're them. So I'm confused. How is it that you and me, we get to come out the other end alive yet they all have to die?"

"We're the good guys, that's why."

She snorts. "That's hilarious. There are no good guys. I'm pretty sure you're the one who told me that when I was a kid, actually. We're not the good guys, Nick. And they're not the bad guys."

I just stare at her for a moment, trying to see it from her perspective. "Who are you trying to save?"

"What?"

"Who are you worried about? That's what this is, right? You've got a friend still stuck inside. Just tell me who they are, I'll see what I can do."

"I don't have a *friend* inside. I'm speaking in general terms. I'm a Zero. You're a Zero. We're people, Nick. And so are they. People who did not ask to be born. People who had no choice in who they are."

"That's the point, Wendy. They don't know any better. They think—"

"They think this is normal?" Wendy asks. She shakes her head at me. "That's so fucking stupid. You think hunting them is normal. You don't lose a single wink of sleep at night over this shit, do you? Don't you see it? You're no better than them."

"I never said I was."

"You're worse," she continues. "Because you're a failed Zero. You, and James, and Santos, and Vincent."

"Vincent wasn't a Zero."

"You *men*"—she clarifies by pointing her finger at me—"you men were the problem. And we were the answer."

I don't even know what to say to this. I can't really argue with her because this is all true. All the male Zeroes in the initial program went insane. Only James really made it out. Adam and I don't count. We were both pulled early enough. And Vincent was never in the program. He was being groomed for politics. But

Santos… he was the poster child for what a male Zero was. Even *he* knew he needed to die.

"You all went insane during the Zero training." Wendy is still talking. "Us girls? We're the ones who can handle it."

Now I'm starting to get pissed. "What do you want, Wendy? You want me to quit? You want me to leave them alone?"

"You already leave *some* of them alone. You're picking and choosing, Nick. So let me ask you again. Are you gonna kill Sasha?"

"Don't be a fucking bitch. I'm never going to kill Sasha."

"And she's the worst of them."

I laugh. "No, Wendy. She's not."

"Who is then?" She tips her chin up again. "Hm? Who is? Indie? Angelica? Avery? Daphne? Lily? Hannah? Me?" There is only one girl left that she knows I care about. Only one girl left that I will not kill and for a moment I don't think she'll say it, but she does. "Lauren? How are we different?"

"You guys are…" But I pause here to gather my thoughts.

"We're not, Nick. We're not different."

"So you want me to stop. Just let them all breed like crazy. Let whoever's in charge of them take over the world again with creepy blonde assassins?"

At the word 'creepy,' she cringes. Creepy Wendy, that's what everyone calls her. Not to her face, of course. And it's not even deliberate. 'Creepy' is just the correct word for these beautiful blonde killers. You can't look them in the eyes and not see it. There is something deeply wrong with them.

29

And Wendy is not different in that respect. She's wrong though. Sasha was never even in the running for being the worst of them.

"No, Nick. That's not what I'm saying. I'm saying you can't just pick and choose."

"Yeah. I can. When you win the war, you make the rules. We won. I make the rules." Wendy might not be the worst of them, either. But she's in the running, and she knows this.

"You're not even in charge, Nick. Not for real." I start to laugh, but she keeps going. "Adam is. You think you're in charge because half the Company thinks you're dead and the other half just wants you to keep pretending that you are. They want you to stay on the road forever so they never have to think about you again."

"Damn, you're mean this morning. Can I get you a cup of coffee, Wendy?"

"You're not in charge," she says again. "Adam is."

For a moment, I don't understand where she's going with this. But it's a willful misunderstanding. Because I know exactly what she's saying. We stare at each other, and it's a real standoff. I shake my head. "I know you have a thing against Sasha"—she guffaws—"but you need to stay the fuck away from her. Do you hear me, Wendy?"

Her smile says so many things. But it's not a sad one, so it's not a real smile. "What happened to 'do you have any idea what I would do for you?'"

For a moment I'm speechless again. But if I don't say something she will turn and leave and that's not how this inevitable separation will begin. And then, before I even realize what's happening, she's out of the bedroom and walking towards the front door. "Stay the fuck away from her, Wendy."

She whirls around, laughs. "Sasha. I always knew it. But now I have proof."

"Proof of what?"

"I'm just a stand-in, aren't I? That's all I've ever been. Ever since that day on the beach in Santa Barbara, that's all I've ever been to you, wasn't it?"

"You're being fucking stupid. You were five years old. I didn't even know you. I didn't even *like* you."

She grabs her coat and flips me off. "Fuck you, Nick. Stay the hell away from me or I will show you just how dangerous us Zero girls can really be."

It always ends with a threat.

"You didn't even hear my proposal," I yell after her. "I have a plan for us!"

But she's already in her truck. Already starting the engine.

This is my problem.

No matter how hard I try, Wendy Gale always wants to kill me in the end.

And this fight was just a tease. The previews. And I know what you're thinking. *She's not gonna kill you, Nick. Don't be stupid. You are her best friend. You're all she has left. And besides that, she loves you.*

But you're being stupid. And by you, I mean me. Because I've been waging this war inside my head for four years now.

I started out denying it. She's not like them. She's different.

And she is, of course. But she's not, either.

She knows if we stay together for too long—and I'm not talking two months, I'm talking two weeks—she *will* kill me.

She won't be able to stop herself.

So she picks a fight, and she leaves.

And it breaks my fucking heart every single time.

I can't live like this.

She can't live like this.

And anyway, I was telling the truth.

I would do anything to save her.

Anything.

CHAPTER TWO

PRESENT DAY

Sometimes I look around and wonder where it all came from.

Not the world. Don't be stupid. The fuckin' family.

I need to know how I ever got this lucky. How a guy like me, who came from the Boston slums, who threw away a free MIT education, who joined the army instead and spent the next several years breaking people's minds and hunting down runaway Company girls, could possibly end up a husband and a father.

And then I think, *How long? How long can it last before someone realizes I don't deserve any of this and they try to take it away?*

Thinking is almost never good. And the internal monologue is poison. Because it always comes to this. The inherent certainty that what I have here is temporary.

"What are you so deep in thought about?"

I look away from the pool where Avery, Jacob, and Lily are playing in the shallow end. They are still young enough to enjoy the oasis I built out here in the desert. Lauren and Daphne have moved on to bigger and better things. They are inside, hiding behind the three-feet-thick adobe walls that keep things reasonably cool, talking about boys, and makeup, and all that other shit teenage girls gush about.

Even though we are sitting in a grove of shady palm trees, mostly hidden from the late-afternoon sun, Sasha's face is pink, her eyes hidden behind sunglasses. She and Jax came down with the kids this afternoon. Just for a weekend. We get together often enough, but this isn't a holiday and this visit wasn't planned. It's just some random day in July. Which means Sasha came all the way out to the Palm Springs desert because she has something to talk to me about.

Something she can't—or won't—say over the phone.

"These kids, man." I sigh. "Why do they have to grow up?"

This makes Sasha chuckle. "If you're missing diaper days you can always try for another."

Try for another. Interesting way of putting it. Sydney and I have been together for nearly a decade now and there has never once been talk of babies. These girls—Daphne, Avery, and Lily—they're ours. But we didn't make these kids. They were gifts from Nick Tate. So was Lauren, Sasha's teenager. And Angelica and Hannah, who live with James on the other side of the world.

They are Company girls. The kind I used to hunt down.

34

The irony is borderline sad. It's like the world is fucking with me. And it's all gonna come crashing down eventually. I will have to pay for my sins one day. I see it so clearly. I see what fate has in store for me.

An apocalypse of sorts. That's what it's gonna come to.

Sydney and I won't be having children. I'm not against it, but she refuses to pass her bloodline along. It ends with her. She thinks Sasha was crazy for having a biological child. But Jacob is a boy.

They are different.

"Yeah," I say, but it's a throwaway response to her throwaway idea. "So what's up?"

Instead of answering right away, Sasha looks around the backyard. It's like a fucking resort out here. The massive pool, the water slide, the fake beach, the cabañas, the gardens. Having all this luxury was the only way I could convince Sydney and the girls to live in the desert. I pay a fucking mint for water. We have one legal well plus four more illegal ones. Water is tightly regulated and when the government decides to limit natural resources you have to make sure the whims and decrees of those assholes can't touch you. I bribed the driller who made the wells with a yearly stipend to keep his mouth shut. It comes to about two hundred thousand dollars a year. But it ends with him and he's old, so whatever.

I like it out here though. You can't sneak up on me in the desert. I have this place wired from top to bottom. Hell, I have cameras set up on the highway for five miles in both directions. I have sentry drones to cover the sky and if any uninvited guests make it over my walls, I have four face-eaters who will literally eat

35

off your face. If you get past the dogs—well, you don't get past the dogs, but if you do, then we just shoot you.

Even eleven-year-old Lily can hit you between the eyes.

We have a house in Montana too. Really fucking nice log house with one of those massive stone fireplaces. It's a dream at Christmas. But if a bear can break into your kitchen while you sleep at night anyone can break into your kitchen while you sleep at night.

We don't stay in Montana much.

"I got a call about a week ago," Sasha finally says.

"Yeah?" I ask. "From who?"

"Do you know Adam Boucher?"

"Adam. Boucher." I say it like that. Two words. "No. Never heard of him. Who is he?"

"He runs the Company now."

My eyebrows go up. "No fucking shit?"

"No fucking shit."

"So… what's up with that? He wants to kill me or something?"

Sasha chuckles. "No. He's not like that. I mean"— she pauses—"he *is* like that, but he doesn't care about us."

"So what's he care about? And why is he calling you?"

"Well, that's why I'm here. Apparently, what he cares about right now is a man called Donovan Couture. You ever heard of him?"

I shake my head.

"How about Carter Couture?"

"No. I don't know either of them."

"Well, this is the problem, I think. They are the same person. And Adam is looking for a favor."

"Same *person*? What the hell does that mean?"

Sasha lets out a long breath and averts her eyes to the pool where Jacob is coming down the slide. The kids are squealing and laughing. Then she looks over to the outdoor kitchen where Jax is cooking hamburgers and hotdogs and chatting with Sydney. "He's Company too. Very... what's the word I'm looking for here?" She taps her chin with a finger. "Um. He's... royalty, I guess."

"Royalty?" I can't stop the scoff.

"The Coutures are one of the original families. God, I haven't thought about this shit in so long, I can't even remember what we called them." She pauses to think. "Founders. Untouchables. Remember?"

"No," I say again. "I'm not Company, Sash. I'm not really up on the family jargon."

"Well, that's who he is. Like... major fucking rank."

"OK. What's that got to do with me and this dude Adam?"

"Adam is rank too." Her face darkens, like she just remembered something important. "He's like Nick. He's the same rank Nick was. The Tates, the Coutures, and the Bouchers, they are all Untouchables."

"Oh," I say. A chill runs through my body.

"Anyway," Sasha continues. "Donovan is... well. Fucked. He's fucked. He's a dual personality. He was trained as PSYOPS—"

"Fuck that," I interrupt. "Fuck, no. Hell the fuck no."

"I haven't even asked you the question yet."

"I don't need to hear the rest. My answer is no. I'm not getting involved with any of that shit. Never. Ever. I won't do it."

"Merc."

"Sasha."

"Just listen for a moment. Let me tell the story and then, if you say no, I'll call Adam back and tell him it's just no. I promise."

"And then what will he do? Come fuck with me? Hunt down my kids?"

"No. I told you, he's not like that."

"He runs the Company."

"Yeah, but—"

"Did the Company stop doing Company shit?"

"Not really, but—"

"But nothing. We have a truce here, Sasha. We can't get involved."

"You're the only one left, Merc. You're the only man left on this entire planet who has been trained in Company PSYOPS. Donovan is loved by some very dangerous people. He's not a bad guy, either. He's actually... I mean, I've always liked him. When he was *him*. Carter, on the other hand..."

I turn my head away from her. I don't want to hear this shit. I don't want to know this shit.

"Carter is insane. And there was some kind of... standoff at the Boucher house about a month ago and Adam's daughter... I don't remember her name. She shot Donovan in the back of the head with a psychotropic dart and he slipped into a coma. The Company thinks he's dead, but Adam kept him alive, I guess. Life support or something. And now Adam needs someone to come in and… unfuck him. He wants to save him."

"Why?" It's blunt and cruel, but honest.

"They're friends. They—Adam, Donovan, and another guy called McKay—they raised a Zero girl called Indie. And… well, Donovan has stacked up quite a few loyalty points, I guess. They just want to save him and you're the only one left who can do it. Trust me, Adam would not have called in this favor if he didn't really want to save Donovan."

"Called in what favor?" I ask. "Why do you owe him?"

"I mean"—she chuckles—"he's the whole reason I was able to get those drug lord assholes on board with that Santa Barbara massacre. I knew him from my father's gun-running days. He used to come in to the antique mall a couple times a year. So I called him up and asked him for that favor. How do you think we got that meeting with the drug lords in the desert that day?"

I think about this for a moment, trying to conjure up the memories. Nick left Sasha behind to go do Nick stuff and she called me to pick her up from a hotel room in Wyoming. She was like thirteen when all this went down. But she was pissed off about the Company assassinating her father and grandparents, so there was no way to stop her once she got her mind on murder.

"It was Adam, Merc. He delivered me the drug lords."

"He delivered you…" I pause to think. "That Matias guy?" The moment that name comes out of my mouth I regret it. Because he's the man who took Nick Tate. He's the man who crushed Sasha's whole world when she was just thirteen years old. He's the reason she had to shoot Nick in the head nine years ago. He's the reason she's broken.

And I don't care how happy she is with Jax—and she *is* happy. She won. And every day she thanks her God for what she has left. But when you have to shoot your best friend in the head to change the world, you don't get over that. Ever.

That's the whole problem with breaking things.

You either have to put them back together or throw them away.

When you survive an event like the Santa Barbara massacre you don't get to throw yourself away. You have to just suck it up and put it back together. And no matter how well you match up those pieces—even if the thing you broke still functions—it's just never the same again. But when you have to metaphorically kill yourself to save the rest of us, what's left isn't broken. It's destroyed.

Sasha lets out a long breath. It's packed with weariness. "It's an old debt. But it's a real one, Merc. I owe him. If I didn't feel some kind of genuine obligation, I wouldn't even bother you. I would just tell him no."

"But you don't want to tell him no, do you?"

She shakes her head. "I want to do this for him. I liked Donovan. And yeah, I was just a dumb kid back then so what did I know about it? But we've lost enough loved ones, don't you think? Yes, the Company is still around, but none of those old-school assholes are alive. Adam had something to do with that. He helped get rid of them."

"And then he took over. Don't you think that's a little opportunistic?"

"Of course. But someone has to run things. The Company isn't going away. People are greedy, Merc. They want shit. And some of these fuckers are not only greedy, but evil enough to do whatever it takes to get their money. Adam isn't like that. He doesn't care about money. He doesn't want more, he wants less. He wants to be left alone, but that's never gonna happen. And trust me when I say this, when you've got an organization like the Company that needs leadership, you want a man with no ambition in charge of it. We could do a lot worse than Adam Boucher."

I let out a long weary breath too. She already knows I'm going to do this. I would never tell Sasha no. If she comes to me looking for help it's because she needs that help. For whatever reason, she needs to save this Donovan guy.

"There's something else," Sasha says.

I turn back to her.

She takes off her sunglasses to look me in the eyes for this part. "Adam said something to me when we talked on the phone and I can't stop thinking about it."

"What'd he say?"

"He said… if I help him, he will give me a secret. But I need to be very, very sure I want that secret. Because…" She shrugs. "I dunno."

"It's something bad?" I ask.

"Of course it's bad." She scoffs. "But he didn't have to say that to me. Ya know? He didn't have to and he did."

"So he wants to tell you the secret, but he doesn't want to be responsible for the fallout."

"Exactly."

"And even though you know damn well you should let this go, you can't."

"I can't," she admits.

"What do you think it is?"

Her eyes go distant for a moment. Like she's picturing something in her head. Then they refocus on me. "I think it's Nick."

"What do you mean?"

"I think it has something to do with Nick."

"But why do you say that?"

"Because he's the only one who could ever hurt me. And whatever secret Adam has, it's going to hurt me."

I consider this in silence for a moment. Nick Tate. He's the Ghost of Company Past. The sacrifice so that we could live these good, calm, easy poolside lives.

I've heard rumors over the years too. Rather, I've seen rumors. There's a chat board where guys like me like to hang out to get news of things most people don't want to talk about. It's the details. The behind-the-scenes kinda shit. The up-close-and-personal.

Hell, most people don't even want to know about ordinary stuff. They want to live their lives. They want to work their jobs. They want to raise their kids. They want to eat out at restaurants, they want to watch live bands, and stream TV, and go on socials. They want to take vacations, and make plans for the future.

They do not want to know what the people who run this world are doing to it. They don't even wanna know what those people think of them.

That's all inside baseball, as they say. It's minutiae. Detailed inner workings that affect almost no one directly, so almost no one cares about it.

But the people who hang out on this chat board are the definition of inside baseball. And these guys on the board—it's all anonymous. You're not allowed to have a name on these platforms. You're no one. Or rather, you are what you post. If you post bullshit, you're full of shit. If you post new facts, you're a good digger. But if you can draw straight lines between things across weeks, or months, or better yet, decades? You don't need a name to get respect. You've got rank. For an hour or two, at least.

I've toned my participation down a lot over the years. Sometimes I only visit the boards once a month. But when shit happens, I'm on there dozens of times a day trying to put the pieces together just like everyone else.

There was an incident a couple years ago that got a lot of attention on the boards so I made it a point to lurk. The incident was actually the sudden death of hundreds of elites. Billionaires and their entire families suddenly died. Not all the same way. At least, that's not how it was reported. Some of them suicided. Some of them were in a plane crash, boat crash, weird hiking incident. Others died of an illness. How they died didn't matter because it was all lies. The point was— they were dead. Entire families just wiped out. The board called this operation the Purge. And it had Company written all over it so I was following every fucking detail back then. Over the years I lost interest in the board, but I kept up my diligent lurking. And it paid off a few months back when his name suddenly popped up.

Nick Tate.

Back when he was killed—rather, back when Sasha killed him—there was a lot of chatter about us. All of us. Even me. But it died down to an almost imperceptible whimper because all that happened almost a decade ago now.

But then, during the Purge, there he was. And the people on this board, maybe they didn't know him, but they knew *of* him. And they were intrigued.

It should go without saying that grabbing the attention of anonymous posters on a board like this is a bad thing.

Here's how it works on the board:

All information posted is public. There is no hacking happening on this site. There is no leaking of hacked information, either. That's illegal and if you want to keep your anonymous operation going in plain sight like this and not be relegated back to the depths of the dark web, you keep it all legal.

So these anonymous posters, they wait for some nugget of information to be leaked—on purpose or by mistake—onto socials or in the news. Then they pick it apart. They find connections. And lots of times—not always, but lots of times—they even find the truth.

The diggers had made the connection between Sasha Cherlin and Sasha Aston, FBI agent, way, way back when the news of Nick Tate's death was fresh. But this board didn't exist when that happened. So all that info was put up on random websites, or forums, or on IRC. All of which are gone now.

This board had none of that intel. I regularly do searches of Sasha's name just to make sure no one is getting too close. There was nothing. Not a single mention of the name Sasha alone, or with either surname attached.

So when Nick's name came up a couple months ago he was a ghost from a forgotten past. The FBI Twitter page posted a pic of the house where Sasha killed him with the headline, 'FBI puts unused safehouses on the market for quick sale.'

The weirdos on the board watch all tweets from all government agencies looking for secret comms. It's a level of paranoia that most don't have the patience for, but I've done the comm-watch myself many times and it's real. Agencies around the world all talk to each other by posting seemingly innocent pics and headlines on socials. Especially Twitter.

It took about thirty-five minutes for the first post to appear on the board.

And all it said was... *Is it just me, or does this house look familiar?*

I stayed calm and watched them make connections in real time. And they got a lot of it right. Not all of it—there's always some dumbass who takes the conspiracy theory ten steps too far. But most of us recognize that asshole and just ignore him.

And then the inevitable happened. Just like Nick's name, there it was. Sasha Cherlin. It took them about two hours to re-make that Aston/FBI connection. It took them another thirty minutes to find her address in Fort Collins. Five minutes later they had her picture up and a satellite view of her house.

Of course, they found her socials. Then someone started posting pics of her Facebook and Instagram accounts. It's more suspicious to not have socials these days than it is dangerous to have them. So we all have socials. Even I have one. You gotta be present, man. The government don't like when you disappear completely. It makes their almonds tingle when they find shit like that.

So suddenly, there she was. Sasha in the pick-up line outside Saint Joseph's school. Sasha grocery-shopping. Her and Jax having drinks at the Fort Collins Theatre. Her socials are everything you would find on a suburban housewife's Facebook page.

But my heart was racing as I watched them hour after hour picking apart Sasha Barlow's past. They were seconds away from finding her adopted father, Ford Aston—and her original surname Cherlin—and linking the whole thing back to the FBI/Rook mess and I was just about to start making plans to go kill people when they suddenly gave up.

Except they didn't *just* give up. A board volunteer appeared and started banning people and deleting posts. The diggers came back. VPN fixes a ban like magic and everyone knows how to use a VPN on that board. But the board volunteer stayed up the entire night to make sure the dig on Sasha died a slow, but very final, death.

The dig on Nick went on for several more weeks though. And this was the red flag for me.

It was such an obvious diversion tactic that it had to be on purpose. When you want to bury something on the board, you don't usually have a board volunteer intervene, but it's still easy enough to kill a dig. You just shit all over the facts you want to hide and then skillfully redirect the hunt onto someone or something else. Something far more interesting than the first dig. And sure, the urban legend about a little girl with a gun at the Santa Barbara massacre is enticing—alluring, even. But it's like a ghost story. No one really believes it.

Nick Tate, on the other hand, that guy has a real past. And maybe he's not as interesting as a tiny blonde assassin, but they can find shit on him. And once you find a clue, and then you find another, you're invested.

The anonymous poster who had been seriously tracking Sasha was also the board volunteer using a different IP address to hide that fact. And he was also the one who then refocused the dig onto Nick Tate. His first attempt to kill the dig was to post normal pics of Sasha, trying to prove she's just another Fort Collins housewife, but the diggers on the board that night weren't falling for it. So the redirection was the logical next step. If that didn't work the board would've been attacked. Maybe a DDOS attack to fuck things up just long enough that the serious diggers moved along and did something else. Or maybe something worse. Take down the entire server. Redirect the DNS.

But that wasn't necessary. The Nick Tate bait worked like a charm.

And I knew one thing for sure after watching this all go down.

This anonymous poster covering for Sasha was one of us.

So I called James. I didn't tell him anything about the board. Not a single mention of the dig. All I said was, "Got any news I need to know about?" We do this every once in a while. And if I have something, I let him know. And if he has something, he lets me know. James said no and that was that. He doesn't bother with the boards, anyway. He gets his information with spies in the real. Not a virtual guy at all.

So who could it be? Who was this person protecting Sasha?

I went down the list. Was it Ford? He's the next obvious answer, but I called him and nope. He had no news for me. It wasn't Ford.

Was it Jax? He was FBI, after all. Those clowns monitor this kind of board twenty-four seven. But I asked him if he'd heard any chatter. And maybe he's not allowed to break clearance, I get that, but he's broken it with me like a thousand times. I don't think he would lie. So it wasn't Jax.

This was another problem in and of itself.

Because there was no fucking way in hell that the FBI didn't see that dig on Sasha Cherlin the same way I did. It's a public fucking forum. But they didn't tell Jax about it. Because if they had, he would've come to me before I came to him.

That was another rabbit hole altogether. I had to stay focused on one thing at a time.

And that left just one other person who would have the skills, info, and motive to direct attention away from Sasha and onto Nick, and that was Nick Tate himself.

I was pretty sure of it too. I liked the idea that he might still be alive. That somehow, some way, he cheated death.

But now, I'm not so sure. I didn't know about Adam Boucher or Donovan Couture, or some guy called McKay. It could've been them.

And now this Adam guy wants me to help unfuck a PSYOPS? On a dual personality? One of whom is a PSYOPS agent himself?

Fuck that.

My passive participation in this shit is now over.

"Anyway." Sasha sighs. "I told him I would ask you, but I didn't want his secret."

"Yeah," I say. "That's a good idea if you ask me. No one wants to get pulled back into that shit, ya know?"

"Trust me." Sasha chuckles. "Don't I know it. I'll call him back and tell him you declined."

"Wait," I say, just as she's about to get up and go over to Jax. "Don't say anything yet. Give me a week or two to do some digging on this Adam guy."

Sasha squints her eyes at me. "Why?"

"Because I didn't know about him until now. And maybe my answer is still no, but maybe I also want to meet this Adam Boucher."

She sighs again. This time, she sounds tired. "It's probably a bad idea, Merc. I'm sorry I brought it up. I don't want you getting lost down those rabbit holes again. It's a never-ending tunnel and there's almost no satisfaction at the end."

I ignore this warning. Heard it all before. Instead, I say, "What did you say the girl's name was?"

"What girl?"

"The Zero? Adam's girl?"

"Indie?"

"Full name, Sasha."

"Indie Anna Accorsi."

"OK. And you mentioned a daughter?"

49

"Yeah. Indie had a kid when she was a teenager or something."

"With Adam?"

"No." Sasha shakes her head. "With Nathan St. James."

"And who the fuck is this dude?"

"Company. But he got out real early."

"He's a Zero?"

Sasha shrugs. "I don't know if you could call him that or not. He wasn't mind-fucked that way. He grew up with some old Company man who stole him out of the hunt."

"The what?" I ask. "And how the fuck do you know all this shit?"

She smiles at me as she points to her head. "It's all up here, Merc. Never really goes away, does it?"

I assume she's referring to her life with her father, the Company arms dealer. She met everyone growing up. But she's been out of that business for almost twenty years now. "Right," I say. "But who do you talk to? To get all this up-to-date shit?"

"Well." She glances over at Jax and Sydney to make sure they're still immersed in conversation. They are, so she looks back at me. "I have a little spy network in place."

I laugh. Loud. Loud enough to make Sydney and Jax look over at us. They both smile back, assuming Sash and I are having a good time. I lower my voice and growl, "Since when?"

"Since… oh… right before grad school, I guess. I smuggle girls every now and then."

"You *what?*"

50

She nods. "Company girls. Of course, there aren't very many of them left. So it's been a couple years since I had to get one out."

"Wait." I put up a hand. "Back the fuck up, Sash. You're still *in*?"

"In? No." She chuckles. "Trust me, we're all out. One hundred percent out."

"Who is this *we*?"

"A few other girls who found me after I went to live with Ford when I was a kid."

"Sasha. Are you telling me you've been in contact with Company girls this whole time?"

"Merc. Don't be naïve. They're never gonna stop needing me for something. I figured, if I have to keep talking to these people, I might as well do something good with it." She smiles. Big. "When these girls found me, I wasn't really into it. I did it for them, mostly. They were the ones who needed the project and I was the one who had the money to see it through. Funny enough, Jax was on to me when we first met. I came home early from Peru because we had a girl in a safehouse who needed a new identity. But he was there at the Denver International Airport and he took me right into one of the interrogation rooms. Then he followed me for months. And I kinda got sidetracked with everything that happened next and forgot about the girl. That whole operation just continued without me. Must've seen the headlines and realized the FBI was all over my ass. So it took those contacts about two years to get back in touch because they weren't sure I was legit anymore. Jax, ya know?" She wiggles her ring finger to show off her wedding band. "But they needed me. And I needed them, to be honest. So. I help out when I can."

"I can't believe you never told me this."

"I take care of myself, Merc. You should know that by now. I'm glad I have you, and Ford, and Jax, and James. I appreciate it, I do. But I'm not the kind of woman who lets the men take care of things. I have kids now. I have a family. I love my husband and I know he's capable and smart, but I'm in charge of my life, not him. I'm responsible for my past. And there is no way in hell I'm going to spend the rest of my days pretending it's all good. Because I've seen that dirty underbelly. I know it intimately. I know everything that's going on in the Company and that's never going to change as long as I'm alive."

Ah. I get it now. This whole thing about Adam's secret and why she doesn't want it. She thinks Nick might be alive too. She's heard rumors already, same way I have. And she has decided he's better off dead.

"Gimme a name," I say.

"Of who?"

"One of these women you work with. Gimme a name."

"Why?"

"Because I need a place to start, Sasha."

"Don't—"

"No," I cut her off. "You do not get to tell me 'don't' when you just admitted to secretly smuggling Company girls for the past two decades. Give me a fucking name."

My tone has changed and her expression hardens with it. So I expect a little fight. But she takes a deep breath, composes herself with grace, and then says, "Tell me what you're gonna do."

"You know what I'm gonna do."

She weighs her options. If she wanted to say no, she could. I mean, realistically, what could I do? Nothing. But after almost a full minute of serious consideration, she must decide she wants me to look into things, because she gives up a name and I commit it to memory.

"I've heard some other rumors," Sasha says.

"Yeah? Like what?"

"How much do you know about eternal life?"

I scoff. "Well, I know it's a fantasy. Does that count?"

"Sure. It counts. It might not be right, but it counts."

"What do you mean 'might not be right?'"

Sasha's eyes dart back over to Jax and Sydney. They're still talking, and laughing, and smiling near the grill. "Well, it counts because belief is a powerful thing. And it works both ways. If you think eternal life is possible—"

"You'll what? Live forever?"

"No. But necessity is the mother of invention, right? If you believe, you look hard, Merc. You try everything for the very simple reason that you think it's possible. If you don't believe, well…" She shrugs. "I haven't made up my mind about non-believers yet. Because on the one hand, if you don't believe, it never affects you. But on the other hand, if you don't believe—if you don't, at the very least, go searching for it—then there isn't a chance in hell that you're ever gonna find anything, right?"

For a moment I can't tell if she's talking about herself and the rumors surrounding Nick Tate or she's simply pointing out the obvious about eternal life.

"I see you are confused."

"OK." I laugh. "I'll admit to that." My laugh carries across the pool to the outdoor kitchen and makes Sydney and Jax direct their smiles at us for a moment. Then they go back to whatever they're talking about.

"Let me explain better." She pauses and her blue eyes roll up as she considers what to say. She's still the same Sasha to me. Same blonde hair. Same pretty little face. She's still thirteen in my mind. She will always be the little girl in braces. She will always be the heartbroken kid crying her eyes out in a hotel room after Nick left. She will always be the empty shell left behind after she shot Nick in the head that day.

It doesn't matter how I see her. Sasha Cherlin-Aston-Barlow writes her own script in this life. She has always been the one in control. She's not a little girl. Those braces are long gone. She has been very happy for many years now and the fact that she has spelled it out very clearly that she is not interested in knowing Adam's secret, even if it's about Nick Tate, tells me all I need to know about her mental health these days.

She adjusted.

She moved on.

She lived.

That's what a good little Zero girl does.

"Sometimes," Sasha says, "ignorance is bliss, Merc."

"Right." I chuckle again. "Yeah. Agreed."

"Because if we don't know what we're missing, do we ever truly miss it?"

"What's this got to do with eternal life?"

"Turns out, almost nothing, actually. But you gotta watch out for the believers, right? Because belief is a lot more powerful than you think."

"You're in a very profound mood today."

She nods. "Yeah. This thing with Adam."

"What about it?"

"I dunno. It's a thread, I think."

"And you don't want me to pull it."

"No. But—" She looks away, but just as quickly looks back at me. "I would like to save Donovan. I would like to save everyone, actually. But I don't have any say in most of that."

"And you have a say in this," I finish for her.

She nods. "A small one. Obviously, ignorance is still bliss. But it's too late to be ignorant now, isn't it?"

I nod my agreement.

Then we drop it. Because she told me what she wanted me to know—she wants to save Donovan but she doesn't want to find Nick and whatever I find when I pull on this thread, she wants it to end with her blissful ignorance.

The next day Sasha and Jax pack up their kids in their truck and I pack up Sydney and our kids into ours. Then I follow them up to Fort Collins, Colorado for a much-needed, impromptu vacation with some old friends.

But I don't stay in Fort Collins.

I call up a good friend with a small plane and he picks me up at an airstrip about forty miles east of Fort Collins like we're livin' in the old days.

So three days later I'm sitting in a truck in front of a cottage in Key West wondering if this is the moment when it all goes wrong.

Because somehow, in the time between my convo with Sasha and this moment right here, I became a believer.

CHAPTER THREE

BIRTHDAY #17
7 YEARS AGO

Where do I come from?

Well. There is a lane in the woods.

The woods are in Kentucky.

I once asked Chek, "Why Kentucky?" And he said, "It was either here or West Virginia. And West Virginia is too close to the assholes."

That was it. That's all I got out of him.

I was young at the time, maybe seven, so I didn't get it. Took me years, actually, to figure out who the 'assholes' were.

He was talking about Washington, D.C.

The lane is crowded on both sides by trees. Buckeyes, and black walnuts, and red maples. The whole place is thick with them as soon as you turn down the narrow gravel lane. Chek liked the overgrown look, the sense that the trees are in charge here. The way their enormous boughs stretch out over the road like a canopy and how traveling down the lane that leads to the cabin is almost a lesson in claustrophobia.

I am seventeen years old today and Chek has been dead for seventeen days.

There is a code in this. These numbers. They mean something. They say something. It's just... I'm not sure I speak that language right now. There are two warring thoughts running through my mind as I pull the truck up to the mailbox at the end of the lane.

One is, *You are a disease, Wendy. You are a sickness.*

The other is, *It's not your fault.*

I believe them both. That's the hard part about being me. It's all true. Everything they say and think about who and what I am, it's simply all true.

Anyway. The mailbox is not a box, it's a pillar of stacked river stone. Smooth, dark gray stones that we actually pulled out of our own river in the woods back when I was six to make this mailbox.

The pillar is five feet tall, two feet square, and it's hollow inside. It's lined with a super-sized trash bag. There is a lock. There are four of them, actually. And a slot on the front side that looks like the slots on real mailboxes that you see at the post office. The kind that keeps the weather out. This is so the mail person can drop letters inside the box. There is nowhere to put packages here. This is not a place you have packages sent. Just letters.

When I open the mailbox there are maybe... I dunno. A hundred of them?

They are birthday cards. All of them. Every single envelope is a birthday card for me.

And I am suddenly very tired of living. I don't really see the point, but I have this overflowing sense of self-preservation, so don't worry. I'm not going to kill myself. Even if I wanted to end it like that, and I don't, I wouldn't be able to.

Now I have no problem going out doing a crazy job. But I've done plenty of those and I'm not dead yet. Plus, no one is gonna hire me now.

Chek is dead.

The jobs are over.

I am just... a *leftover* now. Just one of Adam's leftovers.

I gather up the edges of the bag, pull it out, and shove it into the passenger seat of my truck. Then I lock the box back up, get back in, and crawl down the lane. The gravel crunches under the tires, but this is all very familiar. Only the mail hurts. The rest of it is fine.

It's fine.

The cabin is literal. An honest-to-God log fucking cabin. The kind with the mortar between the logs and everything. It is thirty feet long and twenty feet wide. The front door is a thick slab of wood that could probably stop a bullet if it had to.

On either side are tall, skinny windows. The windows almost break the rules. They come off as trendy, partly because they are. People are so into the farmhouse look these days. But they aren't meant to be trendy. They are original. Each one is split into sixteen tiny panes lined with lead. And when you look through them, you have to bob your head a little to find a clear view because the glass is over a hundred years old and very wavy and distorted.

I like the windows. They give the place a certain kind of split personality. Everything else is all rustic and crude. It's a lot of raw-edge wood, and stone, and tin.

Like the guy who built it was one of those trail-blazing Daniel Boone kind of people but the lady he talked into doing this whole wilderness shit with him was some East Coast society bitch who demanded these extravagant windows so she could hold on to a little piece of her civilized life back in Philadelphia or wherever the fuck she came from.

But the best thing about our cabin is the porch. I think this was the East Coast bitch's doing as well because again, it's more farmhouse than cabin. It's wide, for one. I'm talking a good fifteen feet from the top step to the front door. There are only three steps leading up to it. Cabins aren't elevated. This one just sits a little bit on the side of a slightly rolling hill, otherwise there'd only be one step up.

But the steps are super long. Like ten feet long. Like maybe the East-Coast bitch had a little Southern Belle in her too? Because it's overkill.

You can't hate anything about this look, though. It all works. So I guess she was more of a genius than a bitch.

The only thing I would change about the cabin is the roof because it's tin. So is the ceiling inside, but I don't mind the ceiling. Rain on a tin roof isn't romantic or atmospheric. It's loud as fuck.

When I pull the truck up to my parking spot just to the right of the steps, I get an overwhelming sense of dread. I'm talking normie-people kind of dread. The kind that incapacitates them. The kind they call 'panic' and then attach the word 'attack' at the end.

I am breathing way too fast. Panting, almost. And my heart is hammering inside my chest. I'm shaking, actually. Like I'm cold, but it's probably about ninety-five degrees outside and I don't have the AC on in the truck.

My body doesn't want to go inside but my body isn't in charge here. My head is.

This is what Chek taught me. How to separate the body from the mind. He said, "Wendy, the way you look, or talk, or act—that's inconsequential. The only thing that matters is the way you think. Thinking," he said, tapping my head with a finger, "is the reason we are not animals."

He told me that a lot. Because I really am an animal. I look human enough and most of the time I act human enough, but still, there's something really wrong with me.

Really, *really* wrong with me.

That's why I had Chek.

So I don't care that I'm breathing too hard or trembling all over. That's not important. What's important is the task. So that's what I think about. And the task is to get inside the cabin and close the door. And this is my plan:

One. Turn off the truck.

Two. Grab the mail.

Three. Go inside and read it.

This is all I have right now.

This is all I need right now.

Getting inside to read the mail doesn't have to be the task. Step three is just my reward. That's what Chek used to call it. I could make the reward something else. Turn off the truck, go inside, take a bubble bath. Or go inside and sleep. Or go inside and read. Whatever. Doesn't matter. As long as there's a step three, and it's a reward, I can get things done.

But I want to read the mail.

Because today I am seventeen years old and Chek has been dead for seventeen days. I have spent the last eleven birthdays with him and these bags of cards, and now he's gone.

It ends here.

The last of us is in this super-sized trash bag in my hand.

And that's all very sad, but it's all I have.

So I do this plan. I get out, I grab the mail, but I'm not even on the top step when the front door opens. And then there's this split second, this *eternal* split second when I'm hovering between two realities. One where Chek didn't die. One where Chek opens the door. One where he and I go back inside our little cabin and we open cards, and read them, and laugh, and eat cake, and we're happy.

And then there's the other reality. The real one. Where Chek did die and it's Nick Tate standing in front of me holding a sunflower in his hand.

Chek is dead.

So it's Nick. And it's a sunflower.

We look at each other but we don't say anything. I have known Nick Tate for as long as I knew Chek. Well, in the literal sense, I knew Chek for about eighteen hours more than Nick. But Nick was there right from the very beginning.

The flower is a symbol for us. Nick Tate has been giving me sunflowers for my birthday since I turned six. It was an accident that first time. We were walking through a market in… fuck, I don't remember. It wasn't America. Might've been Peru? But then again, it might've been Ecuador.

We were tailing someone. Chek was on the other side of the market, and the guy we were sent to kill that day kinda knew we were coming. Well, not me. Back then, they didn't really get it. They didn't understand what we were. It's only been recently that people have figured out how to see us coming. But anyway, Nick and I were walking past a flower booth in the market and he picked up a sunflower and gave it to me. "Hold that," he said. "Act like a kid and sniff it."

Sunflowers don't really smell that great but they are super pretty. So I didn't complain. I sniffed.

Two hours later that guy was dead and we were heading back to the airstrip to go home and when I got out of the truck, I left the flower behind. But Nick picked it back up, handed it to me, and said, "Happy birthday."

It was a throwaway comment. Or a joke. I dunno. It didn't mean anything that year because that was the first time. But when I turned seven, there Nick was again handing me a single sunflower on my birthday. When I turned ten, I was living with him and his daughter Lauren while Chek did other things. I was actually the babysitter because Lauren was just a tiny baby back then. We were at a resort on the beach in South Carolina that day. I remember being unsure if I was happy or not because Nick was sending me back to Chek for work. I guess he was OK with baby Lauren by then and Chek needed me for a job. But I had grown used to being part of Nick's little family. I liked it because I didn't have to work, all we did was play.

Nick sent me back to Chek with a little bouquet of sunflowers that year I turned ten, but today, it's just a single flower.

I'm on autopilot right now. Numb. So I don't say anything as I push past him and I don't take the flower. I just go over to the dining table next to the kitchen and dump out my bag filled with birthday cards.

He closes the door and comes over to me, still holding the sunflower. But then he sighs, gets a glass of water, plops the sunflower in it, and sits down across from me and starts opening envelopes.

Because this was my ritual with Chek, and now Chek is dead and all I have left is Nick.

I don't know a single person who sends me cards but they all come with a picture. Sometimes, maybe, it's of the person who sent the card. But sometimes it's a picture of a dog, or a mountain, or a kid, or a balloon. They can send a picture of anything they want, so that's what they do.

I don't actually know how Chek did this whole birthday card thing. Like... is there a service out there or something? Some start-up business in someone's garage where you sign up to get birthday cards delivered and you pay by the dozen? I dunno. But every year, starting at age six, they came. And the people sending them always knew how old I was. They wrote it special just for me. *Happy sixth birthday, Wendy. Happy tenth birthday, Wendy. Happy fourteenth birthday, Wendy.*

Actually, they all start with 'Dear Wendy.'

Dear Wendy. Happy seventeenth birthday. I hope you have a lovely day.

I hope your cake is tasty.

I hope you get lots of presents.

I hope, I hope, I hope.

There was always a lot of hope in the cards. It was slow, and easy, and good.

We sit here, Nick and I, at the table. And we open the cards.

It's nice, I think. That he's here. I like him.

But he can't stay.

Or maybe I can't stay.

I'm not the same girl he knew when I was small.

I'm not even the same species as that girl.

Somewhere along the way something happened to me.

Or maybe it's not that. Maybe somewhere along the way I just stopped pretending that he and I were something special. That we were family.

Maybe somewhere along the way I just came to terms with what I am.

And maybe, somewhere along the way, so did he.

CHAPTER FOUR

THE CURE, PART 1

Our fight on New Year's Eve morning two and a half years ago wasn't a spectacular fight, but it was a serious one. Even now I can picture her leaving in my head. I know what she was thinking. She would've been in her truck, rambling down some back-country Kentucky road, trying to find a highway as she racked her brain about that stupid cure.

I have no idea where she went because she doesn't share things like that with me. Wendy is a loner. And she thinks that she will always be a loner because of her "sickness". She thinks she has a disease so she thinks she needs a cure.

We cannot be together for real until she has her cure.

She is so fucking stuck on this cure.

And that's what I was gonna tell her that morning before she got all pissed off and left. I didn't have the cure—still don't have the cure—but we're on the right track.

Getting this cure has been a big-ass job. It took time, and patience, and perseverance.

But that's what's so perfect. Wendy and I have this in common. We are very, very patient. And give up? We don't even understand the meaning of those words.

Most of the time, anyway.

I've got it all under control like ninety-eight percent of the time. But Wendy is more of a sixty-forty split. Back when Chek was alive I'd have put her at ninety-ten. Ninety percent in control is damn good. And maybe sixty isn't ideal, but we're still above water.

I keep her above water.

This is my job. And I'm calling it a job because it's a serious responsibility, but it's not something unpleasant. I love running interference for her forty-percent-crazy ass. I've been doing it since that very first birthday after Chek died.

She was only seventeen. She and I hadn't even been friends for years. She never really got over me sending Lauren to live with Sasha, even though I'm pretty sure she understood why it had to be done.

Anyway. On her seventeenth birthday Wendy and I were sitting across the table from each other opening up her birthday card envelopes.

BIRTHDAY #17
7 YEARS AGO

"'Dear Wendy,'" I begin. "'The weather here in Nevada has been hot and dry as usual. So hot you could fry an egg on the sidewalk. I tried it out just for you. Happy birthday! Your friend, Jean.'" I chuckle a little. "She really did it." Then I hold the picture up for Wendy so she can see the egg frying on a sunny sidewalk in Nevada.

Wendy's eyes take their time migrating up from her letter to my picture. She squints a little, then manages a small smile. I think that's the purpose of these cards. Just a small smile. Just a connection to the outside world. Maybe even a lifeline. Because regardless of what Jean from Nevada thinks, she and Wendy are not friends.

"Hey," I say, because I want to check this theory. "Do they come from the same people every year?"

Wendy looks at me, momentarily confused. Then she shrugs. "How should I know?" Her eyes redirect their attention to the card in her hand.

Question answered. *Sorry, Jean. Wendy Gale says you are not friends.*

"'Dear Wendy,'" I start reading the next card. "'We got a new truck and a new puppy this past year. Leon says the dog can come inside the house when the truck can come inside the house. But I'm wearing him down. Here's a picture of both. Happy birthday. I hope it's a good one, Dorothy.'" Wendy reaches for this picture because it's got a dog. She likes to take a close look at everyone's dogs. And I look at the envelope for a moment and notice something. "Holy shit." Then I

69

pick up the rest. How did I never pay attention to this before? "They all have a return address." I hold up the envelope for Wendy to see.

She's still engrossed in the picture of the Irish setter puppy. But after a moment, she looks up. "What?"

"Return addresses. Have you ever... you know, looked any of these people up?"

"Why would I do that?"

"Ohhh..." I have to stop and smile and laugh. She's so different from the others. So antisocial and serious. "You know, to say thank you? Or... 'Hey, did you know I'm real?'"

Wendy makes a face. "They're not real, Nick. It's all fake. It's some... service. Chek hired them to send me cards."

I shake my head and hold up the envelope. "I don't think so, Wen. These people are real. We should look them up. Or send them a thank you. With a pic."

"With a pic?" She looks at me like I'm insane.

"Why not? It's not like you're hiding from anyone. Everyone knows where to find you, Wendy. You've lived in this cabin since you were five."

She drops the picture of the dog and pushes her chair back from the table. "I don't wanna do this anymore."

"OK." I get up too. Because I'm not sure what she'll do next and it's never a bad idea to be alert when you're alone with Wendy. "Wanna go out to eat?"

"Out to eat?" Another accusation of insanity in her tone.

"It's your birthday. We should celebrate."

She snarls at me. "Fuck you, Nick." And then she pushes past me, goes into the bathroom, and slams the door.

I let out a long breath of air and ask myself for the millionth time, why the fuck am I here?

But I know why.

Chek is dead.

Seventeen days.

Seventeen years old.

Chek is dead and even though she won't let me see it, she is falling apart and it's breaking my heart.

About an hour later, Wendy comes out of the bathroom wearing nothing but a towel. She doesn't look at me. Just heads straight to the bedroom and closes the door with a quiet click.

I don't know what to do. Leave? Stay? I don't know what she wants, let alone what she needs.

Come on, Nick. That's not true at all. You know exactly what she needs.

Chek.

But Chek is dead and he's all she's ever had.

Wendy's door opens and she comes out wearing a faded maroon t-shirt with some bar logo printed on the front. Bayou something, which reminds me of Adam. But I don't have time for him right now, so I push his face away in my head and focus on this girl in front of me. She's got on a pair of cut-off shorts. Really short shorts. But they are way too big for her and so they are

71

not the sexy kind of short shorts. They are the lazy kind of short shorts.

She's looking for something, her eyes darting around the small room. She wanders over to the coffee table, then the side tables, then the kitchen bar.

"What are you looking for?" I ask.

"My brush. Have you seen my brush?"

"No."

She goes back into her room and I can hear her opening and closing drawers. Her search is all very random. All very distracted. Like she's looking, but not looking.

I get up, go into the bathroom and find the brush in a basket sitting on the windowsill. I come back out, holding it in the air.

She's looking at me from across the room. Somehow, in the five seconds it took me to locate the brush, she has made it all the way back out to the couch. A good reminder of who she is.

"Sit down," I say, using the brush to point at the couch.

I expect a huge argument over this command because that's the kind of girl Wendy Gale is. Aggressive. Belligerent. Combative. Fighting is her one true God-given gift.

But she gives in immediately and that's kinda sad.

I walk over, sit down to her right, then angle myself into the couch arm. She does the same, angling herself into me.

And then I begin to brush her hair.

This is something I've seen Chek do hundreds of times. When Wendy was little, she hated brushing her hair. I think all little girls are like that. Lauren was like that when she and I were still together. I started brushing her hair after watching Chek do Wendy's.

It calms them. The Zero girls. They hate it and I'm not convinced that it even feels good to them the way it might to a normal girl. But it calms them anyway. Don't ask me why, it just does.

So it calms Wendy now. She lets out a deep breath and her shoulders slump a little as she bows her head in defeat. Like she's giving up on this day.

I am careful as I brush. Lauren was always very sensitive about me touching her head. I don't know if this is something all little girls get weird about, or just the Zero girls, but it's a real thing. She would cry sometimes if I wasn't paying close attention when I was touching her scalp. Not just with a brush, but with anything. I tried to get to the bottom of this several times and she never could explain it. She told me brushing her hair hurt her in the teeth. Which was her way of explaining some weird neurological connection between the two things, I guess. The way you can touch a spot on your leg and feel it in your shoulder. Pressure points. Like Chinese medicine. But she also said it felt like bugs crawling, it gave her the shivers, it made her feel sick, and—my favorite—it made her crave ice cream.

This memory of Lauren makes me smile. I don't think about her much. There's no point. I'm never going to see her again and thinking about her makes me sad.

No one likes to be sad.

But anyway. Back to Wendy. She is the same about the hair. "You can't let it get tangled," Chek used to caution me about Lauren's hair when she was small.

"Or you'll have to shave it off. They can't tolerate the untangling. Put it up in braids. Keep it neat."

Of course, Wendy is older now. Practically grown up. So she does tolerate the untangling. And her hair is kind of a mess. But her skin prickles up and she shudders more than once as I work the knots out.

We are silent as I do this. She's sitting cross-legged on the couch in front of me, her forearms resting on her knees. And I don't know why, but I've always hated the silence with Wendy. It means she's thinking and most of the time I hate it because for as long as I've known her, I have been waiting for the day she decides she really doesn't like me any more.

I mean, she's tried to kill me at least five times but it was heat-of-the-moment kind of stuff and happened at the end of stressful situations. She was angry about something, but it was never about *me*. It was something else, or someone else. It just wasn't me.

But right now, seventeen days after Chek's death, on her seventeenth birthday, I'm pretty sure this silence is about me.

Chek. He was all she had.

She's got a lot, that's not what I mean about this statement. Wendy Gale has a cabin, a hundred acres of land or whatever, a truck, bank accounts, a hidden cache of gold coins, and plenty of weapons. Not only that, she has been trained to survive just about any situation imaginable.

Chek was the only *person* she had. And that's worth more than the house, the land, the truck, the money, the gold, and all the weapons put together.

But I could change that for her. I could become the next only person she has.

74

So I decide to do that.

I say, "Dear Wendy." She turns her head, just a little. Just enough to almost side-eye me. "Do you remember the first time I took you to the library?"

I catch a very small smile creeping into the corners of her barely visible mouth. Then she actually chuckles. "That's not how it went."

"Sure it is. I was all, 'Dear Wendy. Have you ever heard of these things called books?'"

Her chuckle becomes a laugh. "Oh, fuck you."

"What? That's how it went."

"That's not how it went. I was..." She stops, realizing what I'm doing, which is distracting her. And I expect that to be that. I expect her to sigh and give up. Sigh and go silent. Sigh and growl at me.

But she doesn't.

She keeps going.

"I was the one who loved books first."

"I know that," I say softly, still brushing her hair.

"I was the one who took *you* to the library."

"Yep. That was all you, Wen."

"I was the one who taught Lauren how to read."

I kinda wanna argue with this one, because the way I remember it, Lauren taught herself to read using that app on my phone, but this is not the time to argue. And anyway, Wendy was there with us in the beginning. She's part of that time and that means she's part of us. So I say, "You sure were."

"Did you ever miss me, Nick?"

"What?"

"When you dropped me off?" She turns all the way around to look at me and I'm suddenly... I dunno.

75

Nervous, maybe. "Did you miss me when you dropped me off?"

When I showed up at the airstrip begging Chek for assistance with baby Lauren, Wendy didn't want to come help me raise an infant. She was nine years old. But aside from her age, she was working by then. Chek had her so well trained, she was already doing important jobs. So this request not only took her out of the game, it left Chek vulnerable.

But he gave her to me anyway. And she came along. It took her a few days to warm up to me, but she took to Lauren immediately.

Our lives changed that day on the airstrip. And we spent the next eight months together. Just me, and Wendy, and Lauren. We lived on the road, stopping in random places to stay a night, or sometimes we'd find a really nice place and stay a week. We even went on a real vacation once, but that was later.

The first time I dropped Wendy back off with Chek she was turning ten and Lauren was about ten months old.

"You want the truth?" I ask her. "Or you want me to be nice?"

She takes a deep breath. Lets it out. "Truth, please."

"OK." I swallow hard and set the brush down on the coffee table. "The moment you got out of my truck that first time my heart hurt so bad, I wanted to grab you. Tie you up, chain you to the door and just keep you forever."

She doesn't respond. Just stares at me with those blue eyes.

"But it was a purely selfish hurt. Because Lauren was still very small and even though things were easier, I wasn't sure I could do it without you."

She actually laughs. "I was ten, Nick."

I smile back, feeling a lightness inside me for the first time since Chek was killed. "I know," I admit. "But even though you didn't know anything about babies—you couldn't change a diaper, you didn't know how to make a bottle, and it took you a month before you even picked her up—it wasn't about you taking care of *her*, right? It was about you taking care of *me*."

She scoffs. "I was ten."

"I know." This time it comes out with a little frustration. "But you got me through. And I have often wondered if you hated me for all the times I stole you away from Chek over the years."

She studies me for a moment, perhaps giving herself time to choose her words carefully. Then she says, "You didn't steal me. He gave me to you."

"Right. But I *asked* him for help. And if I hadn't—"

"If you hadn't asked for help..." Her face goes solemn and sad. "Something bad would've happened."

I know she's right, but I have never admitted this to myself before now. I was twenty-two when Lauren was born. I was four years into a lifelong prison sentence with a Central American drug lord called Matias and my completely insane secret brother. I didn't know about Santos's plan back then. I thought I was on the run with my baby daughter. And Lauren would not stop crying. She was only a few months old and that moment when I stepped out of my truck on the airstrip and closed the door of the truck, and her wailing was muffled by the pouring rain—I can still remember the relief. It was an all-encompassing sense of relief.

Wendy Gale rescued me that day because something bad *was* gonna happen if I didn't get help.

But it was a reluctant rescue. She was only nine years old, but Wendy has a confidence to her. The kind of confidence you can't manufacture. The kind only people who truly give no fucks about what others think of them can possess.

And Lauren could feel this. She was different immediately. Girls need girls. That was my takeaway that morning on the airstrip. I was a good dad for the short time I had with Lauren. At least, I think I was good at it. I grew into it. But girls need girls and Wendy was what Lauren really needed that day.

"Anyway," I say. "I missed the fuck out of you, Wendy. I don't think I have ever actually expressed how much I needed you that day on the airstrip or how thankful I was every time you came back to us."

She looks down at her hands, which are playing with a piece of frayed denim from her too-big shorts. "Is that why you're here today?" Her eyes lift up to meet mine. "Is this some kind of debt thing?"

I'm shaking my head no before she even finishes. "No. That's not what this is."

"Then what is it?"

I smile nervously. "I dunno. I'm not sure. I just don't want you to be alone." I put up a hand because she's about to say something back and what I just said came out wrong. "That's not what I mean. I don't think you're gonna do something stupid or hurt yourself, Wendy. What I mean is, I can't stand the thought of you being alone right now."

She presses her lips together and for a moment I wonder if she will cry. I have never seen Wendy Gale cry. And she doesn't do it now, either. But she does swallow hard and say, with fake lightness in her voice, "Well, they're all dead now. No one's coming to get me."

She's referring to the Company elite. The Untouchables.

They weren't so untouchable in the end, were they?

So she's right about that. No one's after her.

"Yeah." I nod. "You know that's not what I meant either. I mean… *us*. Ya know?"

I didn't mean to say that. Not that way. She's seventeen. But that's not the reason I want to discourage any thoughts of something more between Wendy and me. She might not be a legal adult in the eyes of the law, but Wendy Gale was never a child.

But again. Not the point.

She is hurting right now and the last thing she needs is me sending weird signals. So I add, "I mean… you're all I have left, Wendy. No one sends me cards on my birthday. Everyone I love thinks I'm dead. You're the last bit of family I have."

This is one hundred percent the God's honest truth, but Wendy is not swayed.

The future has finally caught up with her and she knows it.

I want to tell her everything. I want to spell out the last twelve years so they add up to something more than this right here. I want her to understand how much she means to me, but I don't know how to say it without it coming off gross.

79

Loving her has always felt wrong, but *not* loving her, that has always felt evil.

And I'd rather be wrong than evil any day.

So instead I tell her sweet things. That's all it was gonna be. Just a list of very sweet things.

"You are sweet, beautiful, perfect, and whole. You are everlasting, transcendent, exceptional, and extraordinary. You are remarkable, exquisite, priceless, and sublime. You are flawless, marvelous, divine, and sensational. You are heavenly, powerful, glorious, and delightful.

"You are lovely.

"You are gorgeous.

"And I will never let you go."

And then I made her say it with me.

And that was our *real* beginning.

After her seventeenth birthday I wrote her letters and left them at the desk in Mount Pleasant.

Because letters that begin with the words 'Dear Wendy' make sense to us.

They're not wrong or evil, they're just... *hello.*

And I had to make up for the time we were spending apart.

I had to make up for it or she would lose her way.

So my letters were two things at once. Something to guide her and a memory. A nice memory to soothe her soul.

Dear Wendy,

You are sweet, beautiful, perfect, and whole. You are everlasting, transcendent, exceptional, and extraordinary. You are remarkable, exquisite, priceless, and sublime. You are flawless, marvelous, divine, and sensational. You are heavenly, powerful, glorious, and delightful.

You are lovely.

You are gorgeous.

Do you remember that day at the airfield? Because I do. It was probably one of the worst days of my life, and that's saying something because I've had so many bad days.

But it wasn't you who made it bad. I need that to be clear.

It wasn't Lauren, either. Even though she was only four months old and she had been inconsolably crying for nearly six hours that day.

It was me.

I have never been one of those people who thinks about giving up. I would never, ever be my brother in that respect. I would never let anyone put me out of my misery. And I don't care what anyone thinks—he didn't make Sasha shoot him in the head to save her. He didn't even do it because of some misplaced sense of saving himself.

He made Sasha kill him so he could quit.

I'm not a quitter. This is my point.

But that day, out in that airfield, standing in the pouring rain in front of Chek with Lauren screaming in my truck, I wanted to walk out.

No. I wanted to run. Because that's what I do. I don't quit, I run. From all of it. And yeah, I know what you're thinking. I'm no different than Santos then.

But it is different than Santos. Because when I run away, I'm not quitting. I always make myself do something harder. Something more challenging, not less.

81

I was already thinking about going back to San Pedro Sula so I could hand Lauren over to Santos for training and go back to my life hunting down the wayward Zeroes. And if Lauren was eliminated, so what? Right? So what? If she was eliminated that was the best thing for her. There was no happy ending in this baby's future. There was no real way to save her.

It was either train her and make her capable, or kill her.

So in my mind, this wasn't quitting.

I was handing her over to people more qualified than me so I could go back to the challenge of hunting down Zeroes. So I could make this world a safer place.

Yeah. I was pretty fucked up that day. And I was on the verge of this alternative path in life when you came out of the plane slinging a backpack over your shoulder and cussing like a sailor under your breath.

You saved me that day, Wendy.

You saved my fucking soul that day at the airfield.

You were nine years old, you had no clue what to do with a baby, you were unpleasant, and angry, and threatened to kill me three times before we even got to our hotel that night, but the moment you got in the back cab of the truck and looked at Lauren, she stopped crying.

And that's the moment when I decided to stop running.

Your friend,
Nick

Once Wendy became a part of my life she was just *there*. As in, I counted on her being there, even when she wasn't. There were a lot of good times. Maybe we weren't happy all the time, but happy is a strong word if you think about it. Most days people aren't happy.

This doesn't mean they're unhappy, it just means they're having a regular day where one doesn't have to consider the question—*Am I happy?*

It's more like satisfaction, I guess.

Those early days with Wendy and Lauren were almost all very satisfying. And more than half of them were downright happy.

One day when Lauren was a little over six months old, we were in St. Augustine, Florida. We had been visiting libraries and bookstores for about a month now. Wendy was into it. Like, seriously into it. She had a guidebook app about libraries and we were making plans to go on this stupid library tour across the South.

Even now, this still makes me smile. Libraries and bookstores were a big part of my time being Lauren's father.

But anyway. There were some unhappy times. Not a whole day. I can't recall a whole day where Lauren, Wendy, and I were all unhappy together. But there was this one moment. And the weird thing is that I didn't even know it was an unhappy moment until years later because Wendy isn't an unhappy girl. She's not one of those people who needs to be coddled. She doesn't crave attention. She doesn't want anyone to feel sorry for her.

So I didn't even know.

In the beginning, Wendy was pretty pissed off about being dropped off with me and this girl has always been able to hold a grudge like nobody's business. She didn't yell, or talk back, or do lots of passive-aggressive things. But I knew she was mad.

She thought I was a dumbass because I had no home and I had no plan. We weren't technically living in the truck because we didn't sleep in it, but we were basically living in the truck. And she never stopped talking about the amazing home she had with Chek. She didn't tell me where, but she described it. And even I had to admit, it sounded pretty nice.

I decided I needed a way to mitigate this anger and keep her happy. So I told her she could choose where we went each day. Sometimes we didn't go anywhere. We'd hang out at a nice hotel for a few days. But people notice nine-year-old girls who don't go to school. Homeschooling is a thing. Everyone knows this. But people don't jump to that particular conclusion when they see a nine-year old girl with a twenty-two-year-old man who is clearly not old enough to be her father. Especially when he's carting a baby around.

They think the worst so we were almost always on the move and Wendy was put in charge of destinations.

She took this job seriously.

Wendy takes every job seriously.

This is how we spent our days:

Wake up in our hotel room, wherever that happened to be.

Get breakfast—sometimes the free continental breakfast in the lobby if we were staying at a cheap roadside place. Or in the hotel restaurant if we were staying somewhere nice.

Wendy would consult her app, tell me my choices in an A, B, C 'choose one' multiple-choice-type question, then tell me nope when I picked A, or B, or C. She was going with C, or B, or A. The point was, whatever I picked, she picked something else. It was a way for her to be in control. Little Zero girls are kinda bossy like that, so whatever. I let her do this.

After breakfast we'd get in the truck and drive to the new place. I always got to choose the hotels though. Wendy had no interest in the hotels. Sometimes she wanted to stay at the beach—we were almost always near a beach—but accommodations were my domain, and destinations were hers.

Sometimes we'd be in Brunswick, Georgia, and Wendy would say, "We're going to this library in Mobile, Alabama, today, Nick." In the beginning she would narrow her eyes at me when she made destination decisions like that, waiting for me to object. But I didn't. I just drove our asses over to Mobile, Alabama.

But if she did that, the next ten or fifteen destinations would be logical. Maybe logistical is a better word. They would make sense, is what I mean. We'd drive the coast of the Gulf, hanging close to the beach.

So anyway. It was in this particular library in Mobile that Wendy stole a book. It wasn't a chapter book, either. It was a picture book. She tore the security tag off, slipped it into her backpack, and I didn't know about this until that night when we were putting Lauren to bed and Wendy produced her contraband for story time.

I didn't ask about it. Not that day at least. This book kinda plays a major part in our story so it comes back up later. But on this night Wendy just took it out of her backpack, climbed into bed with Lauren, and started reading it to her.

I don't remember who it was by, but it was called *Wild Child*. And it had a nice rhyme to it. Lauren was paying attention to the cadence of Wendy's words. She wasn't really talking yet—six months old is early for that, even for Zero girls. But she understood shit. You could see it in her eyes. And she babbled in her own baby language as Wendy read the rhyme that night.

It was a poem about feral children, obviously. Children who lived in the wildwoods and didn't have any rules, and were happy. And then the grownups came, and they pulled them out of the wild, and they made them go to school, and stop playing, and put on shoes.

The grown-ups stole the wild right out of the child.

Lauren didn't get it, of course.

I don't even think Wendy got it. Not back then. She was the wild child and she was in no danger of ever being pulled out of the woods. She was gonna spend her entire life in the woods.

Wendy showed no guilt or remorse about stealing the book, so I figured there was some logical reason in her head for this act of rebellion. The poem was nice, and lyrical, and beautiful, actually. But it made me uncomfortable. I'm not sure why, it just did. So I never asked her about it. I didn't reprimand her for stealing, either.

She was the Wild Child.

And she didn't belong to me, she was on loan.

It was not my place to pull her out of the woods.

It would be years before I understood why she stole that book.

It would be years before I fully understood what was going on inside her head that night as she read the rhyme to Lauren.

And I'm not the kind of man who cries—hell, I wasn't even the kind of *kid* who cries. But when I discovered that book hidden under the backseat of my truck almost six years later and I read the words she had scribbled inside it—her own poem handwritten alongside the printed one—I did cry.

Because I knew.

Chek didn't save Wendy when he pulled her out of that Mexican orphanage.

No one could save Wendy.

She was never going to grow up to be Sasha. She was never going to be Lauren.

She was Indie. She was Angelica. She was Daphne, and Avery, and yes, even Lily was too old.

It was a mistake.

That's what hit me that day I read the poem Wendy wrote in that book.

Saving these girls was a huge mistake because we got them too late.

The rest of them were already out of my hands, but just because I understood this didn't mean I was gonna give up on Wendy.

When I found that book it was too late to go backward.

There was nothing left but the future in front of us.

Six years later Wendy was almost sixteen and we had stopped being "friends" the year before when I sent Lauren to live with Sasha. We still worked together, but everything was very professional.

Sixteen was also still in the good times because even though I was technically dead, Chek still had a year and a half of life ahead of him. The Company was not gone, but no one was really working for them anymore. It was very scattered because after Kansas happened, Adam was just getting back to normal after Indie tried to kill him.

Seven years later was seventeen and Chek was dead.

Birthday number seventeen was hard.

But by the time birthday number eighteen rolled around, my world was changing. Or rather, my world*view* was changing. Maybe that's not quite right, either. Maybe... *maybe* that's just when I realized that Wendy *was* my world?

CHAPTER FIVE

When did I start living on the road?

I guess I didn't know I was living on the road until my tenth birthday. Before that I always considered home to be home. But after that, I had to find a place to fit Nick.

Because birthday #10 was our first real goodbye.

BIRTHDAY #10
14 YEARS AGO

"Are you awake?"

I snuggle down into the covers and pretend I'm not.

"I know you're awake. We're leaving today."

I flip the covers over my head. "But it's my birthday. I'm ten. Ten is a big fucking deal. We can't leave on a birthday. It's not fair."

Nick Tate is across the hotel room changing Lauren's diaper. She's content and doing that goo-goo thing she does when she's happy, flinging her legs around, biting her fist, and generally acting like a baby.

"I know it's your birthday. That's why we're leaving. We're meeting Chek in Pensacola tonight and it's a drive, so…"

Chek. I blink a couple times. I had kinda given up on him. I thought for sure he was never coming back for me. In fact, I was so sure of this that I started picturing myself with Nick and Lauren in a forever kind of way. Like a family. It's not a bad life. There are no jobs, so it's a little boring, but it could be a lot worse.

This hotel we're in is a big deal. It's like a mini-resort. It's got a pool, and a water slide, and a lazy river, and a beach. And I had already pictured myself swimming in that pool, and sliding down that slide, and relaxing on that lazy river. Like, hello? This is the kind of place where you spend a birthday! You do not pack up your shit, get in a truck, and go somewhere else when you're already at the perfect place.

This is not rocket science. I don't care who's coming back. This is my day.

We're going to leave tomorrow. It's already planned. And we're going to go somewhere interesting. Nick always lets me pick where we go next. Some days I just close my eyes and point to a place on the map. Some days I do research. So I dunno how I'd feel about Chek coming back, even if it wasn't my birthday.

I say, "But we were going to visit the bayou." And I think I'm actually whining a little.

"You're still going to the bayou," Nick says. "I'm pretty sure Chek has a job coming up in the swamp. So." He looks over his shoulder at me, smiles. It's fake. "You don't need me to take you there."

"Hm." That's what I think about that answer. It's not that I need Nick to do anything. I can do everything myself. But that's not the point, is it?

We were supposed to go together. And now Chek just shows up out of nowhere and plans get erased?

It's like… what the hell?

I'm annoyed.

Life with no Lauren? That I would not mind too much. I mean… she's cute and all, but she's a little brat. And she has so many opinions. And a lot of the time, Nick lets her have those opinions. But she looks like me. And people, when we're out places, they think we're sisters because we both come from that Zero bloodline. All of us have blonde hair, but Nick has brown eyes and Lauren and I both have blue eyes. Sometimes they think Nick is my dad, but he's not really old enough to have a kid my age. So I think they probably assume he's my brother. Or uncle, maybe.

The point is, we look like a family.

Chek and I don't look alike at all. He's bald. Well, he shaves his head. And he's got all those tattoos. When people see us together, I'm pretty sure they think he kidnapped me. But he's too scary-looking—and I'm too creepy—for people to care enough to start asking questions.

When I'm with Nick and Lauren, people always want to talk to us. They want to stop and coo in

Lauren's face. They want to smile at Nick because even though they should be afraid of him, no one is afraid of him. If these strangers are young women, they want to flirt with Nick. And they want to talk to me too. They ask me things. Things like where do I go to school, and how old am I, and what is my name.

And then I get to tell them. I say, "I'm homeschooled, I'm nine—until today, now I'm ten—and my name is Wendy." I'm not creepy when I'm with Nick and Lauren. I'm just Wendy.

No one thinks I'm creepy when I'm with Nick.

I'm just a little girl to them. Like every other little girl.

And I have to say, I've gotten used to that over the past however many months we've been on the road together. So this is what I tell Nick Tate on my tenth birthday. "Maybe I don't want to work for Chek anymore?"

Nick picks Lauren up and turns to face me. "What?"

"You heard me. Maybe I want to stay with you."

Nick sucks in a deep breath. Then he comes over to my bed and sits down. Lauren squirms out of his arms and begins crawling over me, which momentarily makes me smile. "I don't think I've told you thank you, Wendy."

"Don't thank me," I snarl. "I don't want to be thanked. When people say thank you it means something is over and I don't want this to be over."

His hand reaches for me. He slides my messy hair away from my eyes. "Don't worry. You're not getting away that easy."

I push his hand away and sit up in bed. "What's that mean?"

"It means I still need you. And I told Chek that. I mean…" He sighs a little and looks at Lauren. "I can do it." He nods his head, like he's talking himself into this idea. "But I think I do it better when you're helping me."

I wrinkle my nose at him. "I barely do anything." Which is the truth. I do not change diapers unless Nick is not here. He does all of it, really. Unless he's not here. "Wait," I say. "You're going back to work too? Is that why you're worried? You need me to babysit?"

Nick actually laughs. "No. I'm not going back to work. I just think… we're just…" He sighs again.

I point my finger at him. "You *like* me."

"Sure. I like you, Wen. I know you're just a kid, but we both know you're not really just a kid. And you have good ideas, and good opinions, and great instincts."

"Hm." I think about this for a moment. "We're friends."

"Yeah," he says. "We're friends. But you have to go back to Chek."

"Because he owns me."

Nick doesn't answer right away. But he doesn't have to. I know that Chek owns me. I was only five when he came and rescued me from that horrible place far away, and that was half my lifetime ago. But I remember what he said. I remember the part about ownership, and duties, and jobs, and training, and listening. And all of that came true. It's not like I even mind much. I love Chek. And I know that once we're back together I will never think about Nick and Lauren

93

Tate again until we're face to face one day and I don't have a choice.

But if I could pick, I would stay here with them.

I got used to the goodbyes.

I don't like them, but I got used to them.

And anyway, there's almost always a chance that goodbye leads to another hello.

And I live for the hellos.

THE CURE, PART 2
Birthday #18

It always comes back to the cure.

Up until I was nine, I didn't think much about who I was. Or, more accurately, what I was. And so I wasn't thinking about what I wasn't, either.

When I was nine, I heard the word 'cure' for the first time. Well, not the very first time. Obviously, I had heard the word 'cure' somewhere else. A school workbook, maybe. Chek insisted that I learn to read the very first month he brought me home. I didn't go to school like other kids, but I always had two or three school books in my backpack at any given time. I'm sure the word 'cure' was in one of those workbooks. 'Circle all the words that rhyme with 'sure,'' or something like that.

But it wasn't until Chek took me to the doctor that I really had a reason to pay attention to the word 'cure.'

There was just so much going on back then. The Company was bad. As in, everywhere. And we were still part of it. Chek and me, we worked for them. This was after Santa Barbara but before Kansas. I wouldn't say I was dwelling on myself or having any kind of existential crisis, but I was beginning to notice that things about me weren't quite right.

I have always had opinions of people. Random people on the street like kids waiting in line for a bus outside a school, men on their way to work, housewives pushing strollers on their way to get coffee. Mostly I felt sorry for them in their predefined lives. The way they had to follow a schedule and were forced to take part in ordinary affairs.

Chek and I were extraordinary in every way. I mean, me for sure. My quiet, introspective nature, that's what Chek called it. He was the same way. He didn't talk much. If we were on a job, we could go a whole day without saying a single word to each other. He could point, or shake his head, or sigh and I would know what he was saying. It's like being psychic, except it's nothing like being psychic because we were just reading each other's unspoken words. And there's nothing magic about that.

Anyway, the first time I heard of the cure I was in the doctor's office getting a psych eval. But it didn't become important until I heard Johnny Boston and his girlfriend, Megan, talk about it many years later. She was the one who was making the cure and this was to save kids, not grown-ups.

"Chek," I said. "What does she mean?"

Chek put up his hand, palm facing me. A gesture he used a lot. It didn't mean stop, either. It meant...

Careful. Be careful, Wendy. Take your time, Wendy. See before you act. And then he said, "It's not about you. That has nothing to do with you."

Obviously, things were tense at the time. This was right before we took those Untouchables down for good and Megan, Johnny, Chek and me—we were all part of the plan. So I couldn't ask any more questions.

And then Chek died and all the answers to all the questions went with him.

Today is my eighteenth birthday and Chek has been dead for three hundred and eighty-two days.

I stop my truck at the end of the lane.

Three hundred and eighty-two days.

How am I still functioning?

How do I get up every day?

How do I bathe, and eat, and exist?

How am I still alive?

I get out of the truck, keys in hand, and walk over to the mailbox.

Don't do it, Wendy. Get back in the truck, drive away, and never come back.

But I did that already. Twice, actually. The first time was the day after birthday #17 with Nick. I had this urge to hurt someone, and he was the only one there, so I left before I did something stupid. Then I came back for Christmas. Nick wasn't there that time. He didn't know about Christmas, so I was alone. I stayed about... four days? When I first arrived, I really thought I would stay forever. This was it. The open road was over now. I was coming home. I would be normal.

It had potential, that day. And it started out OK. But as per usual, nothing in my world lasts very long.

So I got in my truck, drove away, and didn't come back until now.

I'm not driving away today. I've been living on the road for eight months and I'm tired of it. When Nick and I did it together, it was always so fun. But alone?

No.

Living on the road alone is just lonely.

Back out on the lane, I slide the key into the mailbox and open the large lid. It creaks on the rusty hinges.

Then I blink a few times. Because it's not empty. There is a garbage bag filled with cards.

There is no way to stop my smile.

I gather the edges of the trash bag together, haul it out, throw it on the passenger seat, get back in my truck, and start down the lane.

The tires crunch on the driveway and I go slow. Because I want things to be a certain way when I get to the end of the lane and this is it.

The moment of truth.

And when I see the black truck parked in front of the cabin, I make a weird noise. A sob, maybe.

Because he's here.

He came.

CHAPTER SIX

BIRTHDAY #18
6 YEARS AGO

Priceless, exquisite, remarkable, extraordinary, exceptional...

The cabin at the end of the wooded lane is a place I could live.

I haven't spent a lot of time there over the years, but whenever I rolled down that road it always felt like coming home. Which is interesting because if someone asked me where home was, I would not be able to answer. I grew up on a superyacht in the ocean. We would stop places—Bali, Bora Bora, Hawaii, Indonesia, Southern California—but that's all they were. Just stops.

And none of them felt like home. So I guess if I had to choose a home, I would be forced to choose a room on the yacht instead. Not my bedroom. The cabins were nice—it is a superyacht—but they are not home.

I would choose the swim beach, which is really just a platform on the back of the yacht where you can dive off and get back on. This is where my twin sister, Harper, and I used to spend most of our time if the yacht wasn't moving.

I think about her a lot these days. I miss her. And I wish I could be a part of her life. I wish I could watch her raise that baby with James and teach Angelica how to behave.

But I gave her up. I gave them all up.

This is what it means to be me. Nick Tate.

I have no home, I have no family, I have no friends.

Of course, I stay somewhere. I own a legit corporate farm in Nebraska and a small house on the edge of one of the far fields.

Harper is still alive, of course. And she has a family, so yeah. I have that family. But my real family—Lauren—she's been gone for almost a decade now. She was the one who counted.

I know a lot of people. And if I needed something—even something big—probably twenty or thirty of them would help me out, no questions asked.

But they are not friends.

So Wendy Gale and her cabin at the end of the lane in the Kentucky woods smooth almost all of this over. She erases all the asterisks on the words home*, and family*, and friends*. All the qualifiers disappear when I'm with Wendy.

I have been thinking about her a lot this past year. How things between us have changed since Chek died in the last job we did taking out the Company leadership. She is alone now too. But unlike me, she has this place. This home that Chek made for her.

The cabin is old, authentic, and even though there is almost nothing special about it in the traditional sense, everything is special about it in the ways that count. The big porch, the knotty pine, the way the oversized floor boards creak with every step. The woodburning stove, the tin roof, and the woods, of course.

Wendy is the woods.

If anyone asks me from now on where my home is, I will still lie. But in my head, I will be picturing this place. This cabin on the lane in the woods.

I got in last night even though I wasn't sure Wendy would even be coming home for her birthday this year. She's a wanderer, like me. And I guess that's probably my fault. It was the life I gave her when she was a child. So different than the life Chek gave her out here in the woods. When I showed up at the airstrip back when Lauren was just a baby and begged Chek for help, he came through and gave me Wendy.

She made all the difference.

She didn't have to do anything to make this difference, either. She didn't have to change Lauren's diapers, or bathe her, or feed her, or even play with her. It's like Lauren just knew that two kids and one guy was enough. Me alone, though? Even a baby knew that wasn't gonna work.

We needed Wendy.

And I would like to think that Wendy needed us. But I have never been convinced that she does.

And OK, here's a bit of truth for ya. The reason I make such a big deal about her birthday, and, when she lets me, Christmas, is because I want to give her the perfect gift.

Even if you know someone intimately it's very hard to find them the perfect gift and I have yet to do it. I've come close a couple of times. But that one, perfect gift has always eluded me.

One of these days though, I'll get it right.

That's why I show up, even when she doesn't.

The cabin was musty and had that not-lived-in smell to it when I broke in the back door last night. But it only took minutes after opening the windows for that scent to fade.

I woke up early this morning, not really knowing when Wendy might appear, if at all. Maybe she's done with this place? Maybe she's got someone else in her life now? Maybe she doesn't need me anymore?

Maybe it's always been me who needs her?

Wendy didn't show for breakfast. Or lunch. And I was just about to start talking myself into the idea that she might not show at all when I heard the crunch of tires on the gravel driveway. Then I didn't know what to do.

Go outside and open her door, be the first thing she sees upon her return?

Meet her on the porch?

Let her come to me?

In the end, I take too long and when I open the door, she's already climbing the steps with a garbage bag in her hand.

Smiling.

"Happy birthday," I say.

She pauses on the top step. And did she always have dimples in her cheeks when she smiles?

I dunno. But she has them now.

"You look surprised," I say.

"I mean…" She tilts her head at me, cocks it questioningly, like a dog might. "I left pretty unexpectedly last summer and when I came for Christmas, you weren't here. So…"

"Christmas in the cabin is a thing?"

She nods. "It's a thing."

"Huh. I'll make a note of that."

She comes forward, stops in front of me. Leans up on her tiptoes, kisses my cheek, then politely pushes me out of her way so she can go inside.

Wendy Gale has never kissed me before. And now that I think about it, she never kissed Chek, either. Maybe she's getting better at emotions?

Wendy sets her garbage bag down on the table and turns all the way around to face me, leaning against the side of the table as she crosses her arms. "But you're here."

"And so are you."

"And I'm eighteen."

I nod. "Yep. You are."

"So what's that mean?"

"Don't go there," I say. And I mean it too. She can tell because her smile drops.

"OK," she says. "I won't."

"Good. Because that's not why I'm here."

"Why are you here, Nick Tate?"

"I missed you, Wendy Gale. I like you. We're friends, remember?"

"I'm the only thing you have left, right?"

And yeah. This girl hits the bullseye every time. Without fail. But I'm not gonna lie, so I nod. "Yep. You're all I have left. And I don't even care how that sounds, that's not what it is. You're all I have left because you're the one thing I wasn't ever gonna give up."

This makes her laugh and turn away again. "OK." She shakes her head as she opens the garbage bag and starts dumping birthday cards onto the table. "You're holding on to me even though you let Lauren and Sasha go?" She's not looking at me. She's pushing envelopes around.

"I had to let them go. It was for their own good. But you're better with me than without me."

Her shuffling pauses. And I think I can detect a smile, even though I can't see her face. It's the way her shoulders move, ever so slightly. It's presumptuous, but I'm right. Because she turns again and she is smiling.

"If we're better together, why do we spend so much time apart?"

I let out a long breath. "Well. Maybe it's time to fix that?"

This time her smile is different. So different it catches me off guard. I'm very astute at reading people, but so is she. So the two of us together are a lesson in self-control and checked emotions. But she gives it all away when she blushes and I'm immediately reminded that she is only eighteen years old.

"I know what you're thinking," I say quickly.

Her response comes out as a laugh. "Do you?"

I nod. "Yep. You're thinking... what now? Who are we? Where will this go?"

Maybe she wasn't thinking that, but she is now. And it hits because she's back in control of her expressions, any trace of that blush totally gone now.

"And that's OK, ya know? We can do that."

"Do what?"

"Wonder about things. Intentions and shit like that. Or we can just be who we are."

"Haven't we always been who we are?"

I nod. Slowly. "That's why I like you. I have always been me with you."

"Hmm. I'm trying to think if I can say the same."

"And?"

She shrugs. "I dunno. I didn't see you as a man before last Christmas. I saw you as a..."

Her pause kills me. I die waiting. "Don't say 'brother.'"

She laughs. "No." And then she puts up a hand. "You're not gonna like this though, because when I was a kid, and I was with you and Lauren, I felt like we were a family."

"We were."

"I know. But I mean..."

"Father?" I say. "You saw me as a father?"

"No. You were too young for that."

"So it is brother."

"No. Because if you were a big brother, you would not have expectations of me. You would've been all

105

protective the way you were with Lauren. But you always treated us different. You always had expectations of me."

Now it's my turn to pause. "Did I? What kind of expectations?"

"You know. I had your back."

"Oh." I smile. "Yeah. One hundred percent. If shit went down, I always knew you had my back. So that makes us… friends. Just like I said."

"You gotta start somewhere, I guess."

I agree by nodding my head. "Yeah. So. You wanna get some dinner?"

"Like a date?"

I don't want to pause here, but I do. Because this thing between Wendy and me, it's precarious and I don't want to fuck it up. But it is a date. It's meant to be a date. This entire visit is a date. We are something else now and I'm trying to figure out a way to ease us into this new whatever it is we are, without pissing her off too much or forcing the inevitable hate speech as she walks out on me. I can't deny it's a date, or that sends all the wrong signals, so I go with truth. "Yeah," I say. "Like a date."

"Do I need to change?"

She's wearing jeans, a black tank top that has a white skull on it, and her boots. Which can't be the same brown boots she's been wearing since she was ten, but they look exactly like the same brown boots she's been wearing since she was ten. Her blonde hair is long and straight, one side tucked behind her ear. She is wearing no makeup.

"No," I say. "Please don't change."

She walks over to me, leans up on her tiptoes, but this time she does not kiss me on the cheek.

Her lips are soft when they touch mine. She doesn't open her mouth and neither do I.

It's not a make-out kiss. It's not an I-love-you kiss, either. It's not even a promise-of-something-later kiss.

It's just... hello.

CHAPTER SEVEN

THE DAY I MET NICK

The boat is big and it's in the ocean.
The ocean is close to a cliff.
Atop the cliff is a mansion.
And in the mansion is a massacre.
We are on the boat.

Yesterday I was in a place called Mexico and today I am off the coast of a place called California. This is all I know because I am small and no one wants to show me a map.

I'm not sure what to do with these facts, so I do nothing. I sit. I'm quiet. I listen.

The man with me is Chek. He's got a mean face and bald head. But he's not mean. Not to me. Not so far.

Chek is talking to other, meaner-looking people. They yell, they scowl, they pay no attention to me at all. I think it's because I'm wearing a dress. Chek came to my orphanage in Mexico a few days ago. He wasn't there for me—something else was happening. But he

109

noticed me. Everyone notices me, that's nothing new. My pale skin, blonde hair, and ice-blue eyes make them all take notice.

But not the same way that Chek did.

He came over to me, bent down, and asked me, in English, "What is your name?"

So I told him.

Then he just stood up, went over to the priest who runs the place, and started asking questions. They were all about me. He wasn't very careful about this because he was facing me as he talked and I can read lips. So at first I thought, *Well, he's just another customer putting in his order.* I'm never sent to the customers, so this had nothing to do with me, and I was about to turn away and go back to my coloring when he said, "She's one of us and she's coming with me."

I remember thinking, *Oh, shit, here we go. I guess I'm not so special anymore, am I?*

Chek hit the priest in the face, knocking him down, and said, "Keeping secrets from me is a very bad idea." And then he walked back over to me, held out his hand, and said, "Let's go."

That's how I got on the boat.

But we stopped along the way and took the tender boat into a little coastal village, and he bought me some colorful dresses. I liked them. One was dark red and it was made of a soft gauzy material. Another one was bright yellow, like a canary. The third one was white. I was wearing the white one as the men on the boat argued about whatever was happening on the coast of California.

I think this is why they ignored me. A little girl in a white dress. What could be more innocent?

But Chek knew better. He knows I'm not really a little girl.

No one told me this, not until he came along, but I have always known that I was different. The other kids in the orphanage, they were so clueless. They never questioned anything. When the stupid sisters gave us food, it never even occurred to them that it might be drugged.

But I knew better.

And I didn't eat it unless they made me. Mostly, I only ate what was on the sisters' plates after they were finished. That's why I liked working in the kitchen. It was the only way I didn't starve.

Of course, that didn't work all the time. The sisters were all bigger than me, so I spent plenty of nights in my own drugged-out stupor. But at least I was aware that I was being drugged and did my best to minimize it.

I saw the people who came to the orphanage. They were not good people. The kids who left never came back. I asked about them every once in a while. Well, not directly, of course. That's dumb. I asked one of the other kids. "Hey, Rosa. Where did Isabel go? We were just playing with her yesterday, remember?" And sweet Rosa would get all upset. Her face would go crinkly. She would look around. And then, inevitably, she would reply, "Yo no sé." She would look around again and call Isabel's name a couple times. And then she would wander up to a sister and ask my question. "Sister. Where the fuck is Isabel? She was just here!" Curse-word embellishments are all my own in this retelling. And then the sister would say, "She's been adopted, sweet Rosa. She has a new home with perfect parents who have lots of money and give her presents every night."

I would read these lips from across the compound.

The sister would usually see me watching. But people have a hard time looking me in the eyes. They *want* to look at me, I can tell. But then it's like they know better. Most of them make the sign of the cross and turn away quickly.

They have taken to calling me 'espeluznante.'

At first, they would say my name first. Wendy Espeluznante. But then it just became 'espeluznante.'

Creepy. They called me *Creepy*.

I would be lying if I said I was OK with this, but it kept them away from me. So. Whatever.

These guys on the boat, they saw it too.

They wanted to look at me. They wanted to know who the hell I was. They wanted to know why I was there. They wanted to ask all the questions. But they *couldn't* look at me. And they couldn't ask Chek, either. Wouldn't *dare* ask Chek.

Because he's espeluznante too.

This is why I love him.

Who was on the boat that day?

Nick Tate, of course.

That was the first time I met him.

But it would be a lot of years later before I fell in love with him.

THE CURE, PART 3
PRESENT DAY

The day before Chek took me to an airfield and dropped me off with Nick Tate so I could help him take care of his infant daughter, Lauren, I was seeing that doctor in Savannah, Georgia.

I was nine. I was done with the exam. Which wasn't a take-your-clothes-off kind of exam. It was more of a what-do-these-ink-blots-mean-to-you kind of exam. In fact, it wasn't an exam at all. Let's just call it a test.

And I failed.

Chek and the doctor—a tall woman with dark brown hair and a white coat—were standing face to face in her office. Her office was made of glass. I was sitting in the hallway.

Chek had his back to me, but she was facing me the whole time, her eyes darting to me, then him, then back to me. Talking about me.

Lip-reading is my superpower. Well, I have a lot of superpowers, but lip-reading is my *secret* superpower. Not even Chek knows I can read lips. It's something I've always been able to do. If I can see your mouth, I know what you're saying even if you're way across the room. So glass walls were never gonna be my Kryptonite.

She was telling him that I was not well.

She was telling him that she needs to report me to someone.

She was telling him that I should stay the night. The weekend. The week, the month, the year, the *lifetime*.

113

She was telling him I was never going to get better.

I didn't have time to think about this in the moment, but later, I would realize that she was probably gonna report me to Santos. She was Company, obviously. You don't just plop a little Zero girl down onto any old psychiatrist's couch for sanity tests.

I don't know if she did report me, but I think she might've. I think that's why Chek sent me to Nick.

If Nick had me, then Santos couldn't get me. They are brothers, after all. And maybe Nick wasn't in charge, plus he was on the run with baby Lauren at the time, but Santos wasn't gonna mess with Nick.

He needed Nick.

We *all* needed Nick.

Because Nick isn't just a person, he's a requirement. He's an essential worker. A necessity. Not because he's so smart, though he probably is smart. But because… I dunno. There's just something about Nick that feels *specific*. As in specifically necessary.

But back to the doctor.

She said something else before Chek came out and took my hand and led me out of that tall building, never to return. She said there was no cure for me.

Like I had a disease.

No. Like I *was* the disease.

There was no cure for me.

This was why I was so interested in what Johnny Boston was doing down in Key West. Because his woman, Megan, was making the cure.

And hello? I wanted that cure.

I was tired of being the disease. And even if Carter never got me, or Santos didn't kill me before he got himself shot in the head in Kansas, I wanted Chek to know that I was *not* a disease.

That I am not espeluznante.

I am just Wendy.

That's why I did all those things that day.

That's all I was after.

I just wanted my chance to be cured.

If I could do it over, would I do it differently?

Well. Yeah. Of course.

Of course I would.

"Does that mean you feel regret?... Wendy?"

"I'm thinking."

"Thinking about what?"

"The exact meaning of regret."

"Would you like me to define it for you?"

"OK."

"Regret. To feel sorrow or dissatisfaction on account of the happening or the loss of something. As in, to regret an error."

"Oh. Hm. Then no, I don't feel regret about it."

"But you just said you would do it differently."

"I did say that. But I lied."

Anyway.

It's last Christmas.

I go home a day early.

I pay attention to everything.

The lane in the woods is covered in snow. Snow deep enough that my truck barely disturbs the almost peaceful, picture-postcard imagery when I look in my rearview.

I see smooth, white trunks of paper-white birches—their boughs heavy from last night's storm, a smoky-gray sky thick with the threat of another storm off in the distance, and a rabbit scampering from one side of the woods to the other after the danger of me passes by.

It's so perfect.

I miss this place so much. And even though Chek and I never really lived here for any continuous length of time, it was still *home*.

It doesn't feel like home anymore. It feels like a waystation. I only come by here when I'm meeting up with Nick. Christmas and birthdays. Though we've been mad at each other for a couple years now, so there have been no Christmases and birthdays.

Until now.

Well, tomorrow.

If he comes.

I want to be here a day early to get things ready. I have presents this time. I think, after twenty-four years, I might be getting the hang of this holiday shit.

But when I come around the last bend, just before I get to the cabin, I see that Nick had the same idea. Because his black truck sits off to the left side of my little house. In his spot, I realize. He always parks there.

I park on the other side. And that's where I am when the front door opens and Nick Tate appears with a dish towel slung over his shoulder and a wide grin on his almost too-handsome face.

He still looks a little bit like the teenager I met when I was five. He's not as lean as he was back then. He's filled out a lot, his shoulders are wide and muscular. He's taller too, and his hair is darker now. And his face—while perfectly proportioned with a square jaw and those brown eyes that look into my soul—his face is that of someone who knows things. Has seen things.

He is wise.

We've always been almost fourteen years apart in age, and of course that's never going to change, but he's gotten wiser over the years and I've only gotten more confused.

He makes me want to lean on him and that scares me.

I don't get out of the truck. Not yet.

I just need a minute to enjoy him. Because these visits, they always end the same way. With a fight. With us mad at something. Each other, specifically. We're like that scene in *Ghostbusters*. *Don't cross the streams—it would be bad.* All life as we know it stops instantaneously when Nick and I are together. Every molecule in our bodies explodes at the speed of light when we are close.

That's always how it ends.

And usually it's me who causes this rift in the fabric of spacetime.

I love him. Like *so much*. After Chek, Nick has always been my number one. He's my guy. He's my go-

117

to. He's my best friend, and my only boyfriend—like *ever*. And my rock.

But sometimes I just want to kill him.

And that's not like... a metaphor. I get urges when I'm with Nick and I don't know what to do about them, so I start a fight to create the separation we seem to thrive on.

We have spent more time apart than we ever did together. And even though I lived with him on and off for almost six years back when I was a kid and he was raising Lauren, there is still so much empty space between us. Nineteen years. That's how long we've been friends. And there are more angry phone calls, pissed-off voicemails, and fuck-you handwritten letters over that period of time than there will ever be soft, casual, intimate conversations.

And I hate that.

So I just want this one moment. Before we have that fight, I just want to appreciate how beautiful he is. How perfect he is. How... *mine* he is.

"What are ya waiting for?" he calls, loud enough so I can hear him through the closed truck windows. Like I need to hear him to *hear* him. "Get your ass in here. It's fucking cold out."

I open the truck door. It creaks a little, breaking the almost surreal stillness surrounding the cabin. Then I grab the bag of mail from the passenger side and turn to him as I close the door.

"Uh." He's eyeing my bag of mail. "What do ya got there?"

I hold up the bag. "Mount Pleasant mail."

His eyes narrow for a moment. "How long has it been since you picked up the mail?"

I cannot stop the smile. "Why? Did you write me fuck-you letters?"

He chuckles, but it's a nervous chuckle.

"I'll take that as a yes."

He walks forward and jumps down the porch steps with his hand out. "Give me the bag."

"No." I turn when he reaches me, laughing. "I want to read them all. I want to hear all the silent fuck-yous you sent over the past two years."

"You haven't picked up Mount Pleasant mail in two years? Wendy. Give me the bag." He's using his serious voice.

"How many fights is that? Ten? Twenty?"

"Give it."

"No!" I'm doubled over, protecting the bag like it's an infant, laughing harder as he comes up behind me, wraps his arms all the way around me, and hugs me. He doesn't even pretend to reach for the bag. I drop it anyway. I turn in his embrace until we're face to face. Well, he's a lot taller than me, so I'm looking up and he's looking down, when this happens.

Those brown eyes.

I have always wished for brown eyes.

Because if I had brown eyes, instead of these evil blue ones, I would not be the girl I am.

I would be more like him.

I would be sane, and rational, and maybe even normal.

He places both hands on my cheeks and smiles again. "I've fucking missed you."

"Me too."

"Why were we fighting again?"

"I have no idea."

He laughs as he kisses me. And that laugh fills me up so much that all the bad shit hiding inside is pushed out to the furthest edges of my limits. I love the way we kiss. It's like… paradise. That's what our kisses are.

He pulls back just enough so our lips separate. "Come on. Let's go inside. I'm making cookies."

"You are not."

"I swear to fucking God." He casually reaches for my mail bag on the ground and I don't move to stop him. He's not going to burn them or throw them away. We keep every letter like we're archiving some historical moment or something. We don't even erase voicemails. Each one of these things is a precious record of us and our weird, unorthodox relationship.

He pulls away for real, then walks over to my truck and opens the back cab door. My truck is full of bags and most of them are not presents. My truck is my home. I mean, I don't sleep in it. We don't sleep in our trucks, Nick and I. But this is just how we live, I guess.

Wanderers.

For as long as I can remember, Nick and I have been wanderers.

He's the only person on this earth who gets me anymore. Chek died before I truly turned into a drifter. And Chek never did the wandering like Nick and me. When I lived with Chek, we had this place, of course, which we came home to when we weren't working. But we worked a lot when I was a kid so we spent most of our time living in Company safehouses with other assassins.

Nick slings a duffle bag over his shoulder and then grabs the bag of presents.

"Here," I say. "Let me help you."

But I reach for the bag of mail and not the presents, so he moves out of reach and grins. "Nice try." Then he nods his head towards the cabin. "Come on, let's go inside. I made a big deal about this year."

"How did you know I would come? We haven't had Christmas in two years."

Our boots thud on the wooden steps of the porch as we climb them. "Two's your limit, Wendy. We've never gone more than two."

Huh. I hadn't actually noticed that, but he's right. Two is our limit. In more ways than one, though. We've never spent more than two in a row together, either.

Even though his hands are full and mine are empty, he pulls the door open for me and lets me go first. I really like Nick's manners. It's such a contradiction, but that's what makes it so appealing.

When I step inside, I stop so abruptly that he bumps into me. "Keep going," he laughs, pushing me forward.

I go all the way inside and get out of the way so he can close the door behind us. But I can't move after that. I'm too stunned by how the cabin looks.

"Wow," I sigh. "This is... wow. It looks like something out of a magazine."

"You like it?" Nick is already dropping my duffle in my bedroom.

"It's..." It's fucking gorgeous, is what it is. I mean, I don't even know how to process what I'm looking at. My little cabin has been transformed. And it smells like... *love.*

There is a Christmas tree in the corner. Not a big one. Maybe five feet tall. Real, but sparse and spindly.

Old-fashioned. Like maybe he cut it down from the forest in the backyard. But it's decorated like the ones you see in boutiques. And when I walk over there and touch one of the felt ornaments, I realize it has a theme.

Forest animals.

But not that overdone woodsy bear and moose thing that's so common. No red and black checkered patterns, either. It's all very muted. Very subtle shades of cream, and brown, and sage green, and pastel pink. Like a unicorn dropped by my cabin and sprinkled some magic.

Nick comes up behind me. His hands are free again, so he wraps them around my arms and presses his chest up against my back. "I was passing by this boutique in downtown Louisville on my way out here. There was a tree in the window that looked like it belonged in the living room of a sugarplum fairy. I bought all the decorations."

"I love it." This is not a lie. I love everything about this room right now. Not just the tree, which is perfect. The little wooden table that Chek and I sat at for eleven years has fresh flowers in the center, those red Christmas ones everyone puts out. But there are white roses too, and lots of dark greenery. It's situated in a large brass bowl that flickers with a dozen strings of Edison-bulb lights. And the table is set for two. Plates, and bowls, and champagne glasses. There are cloth napkins and placemats.

"I cut the tree down myself," Nick says.

I turn and face him. Study the way the lights flicker in his brown eyes. Memorize the happiness on his face.

"It's all so pretty, Nick. Did you hire a decorator? When did you get here?"

His smile falters a little. "I've been here since your birthday."

"What?"

"Yeah. I kinda knew you weren't coming last summer, but I stopped by anyway. Waited for you. Where were you?"

This last part isn't exactly an accusation, but there's a hint of annoyance in his tone.

"I've been working with Adam."

He barely reacts. "What do you do for Adam?"

"Little bit of this, little bit of that. Mostly, I just get information for him. Keep my eye out for things that might need our attention. He almost never listens to me, so I don't know why I even bother. But he pays me, so I guess that's why."

Nick does not believe me. Not the part about Adam. I'm sure he already knew I did odd jobs for Adam. No killing, or anything like that. It's been several years since I killed anyone. But he doesn't believe my answer as to why.

I don't need money. I have so much money stashed all over the world, I couldn't even begin to count it.

So Nick nods his head. Just once. It's not really a nod, it's a 'oh, I see' kind of gesture. One that says that question was more polite small talk than sit-rep. "I've left messages for you. So has Nathan."

"I haven't checked them, Nick. Not in a very long time."

He wants to be mad at me, I can tell. But he lets out a breath and his annoyance goes with it. "So you really did miss all my fuck-you messages."

I nod. And smile. "I did."

"Good." And now his good mood is back. "We're not gonna talk about work, Wendy. Not until after New Year's."

"That's fine with me."

"But on January second, you *will* still be here, and we *will* talk about things. Promise me."

"Nick—"

"No. Promise me. I'm serious. This is what I want for Christmas. Your promise that this year, you will not run."

"I mean... New Year's is a whole week away," I say. His smile grows. "How can I possibly put up with you for a whole week without wanting to slap you and walk out?"

He stares intently into my eyes. "You can do it, Wen. I have total faith in you."

Then he kisses me.

It's that same hello kiss we've been doing since I turned eighteen.

I have dreamed about this kiss over the years. I have yearned for it during some very dark nights. I have even tried to describe it with words in a letter once. And I never could find the right ones, so I gave up and did something else instead. I folded up the paper empty of words, and then I wrote on the front, 'Kisses with Nick,' and put it in my pocket. I have been carrying it around since birthday #18. And every so often a word will come to me, one worthy of how kisses with Nick make me feel, and I write it down.

That letter is in my pocket right now. The paper is worn and smooth and lots of the words are smudged because I wrote most of it in pencil.

Nick breaks the kiss and I take a moment to catch my breath. We look at each other. And I don't know what he's thinking, but I'm thinking, *This is my guy. He's my one.*

And even though I know, if I told him that, he would tell me the same thing back, I would never believe him.

I'm not his girl.

I'm just his stand-in.

I'm just his replacement for Lauren and Sasha, and maybe even Lauren's mother, who died long before I was lying awake at night thinking about Nick Tate. But she had to have meant something to him. He got her pregnant. And as far as I know, he's never let that happen again. There have been so many other girls before me. He is almost fourteen years older than me and I feel like he lived several lives apart from me before we settled in to what we have and who we are to each other.

These other girls, I can't compete with them. And in my small world, my life has only ever had two men in it. Just Chek and Nick.

And now he's the only one left.

So it's just him.

"What the hell are you thinking about?"

I let out a long sigh, then ease myself away from Nick and walk over to the kitchen, which is a mess of dishes and saucepans waiting to be washed in the sink. "Were you cooking?"

"Yes. I told you I baked cookies. But don't change the subject. What were you just thinking about?"

I turn to face him again, then lean against the butcher-block counter and fold my arms across my chest. "I was thinking that…" I consider lying.

"Don't lie," he cautions me.

Which makes me smile. "OK. Then… I will start with a question."

"I'm ready. Let's hear it."

"What do you do when we're not together?"

"What do I do? Like… work shit?"

"All of it. I want to know all of it."

"Ya know"—he pauses to grin at me—"you could always tag along one day. You could like… *not* walk out on me in a fit of hate and rage and instead get in my truck and see for yourself what I do all day."

"I could maybe do that. But I'm not asking what you *will* be doing, I'm asking what you *have* been doing."

"Wendy—"

"No. Let's hear it. Did you get any more?"

"Any more *what?*"

"You know what. And they're not a what. They are a who."

"So you're starting the fight early this time? Is that what you're doing? So you can what? Walk out before we even eat dinner?"

That *is* what I'm doing. And I don't even want to do this. I don't want to start a fight with him. I don't want to walk out. I want to stay with him forever. I want to marry this man. And I'm not the kind of girl who dreams about weddings, or anything stupid like that, but Nick is all I have left. And I'm so afraid of losing him, I want to kick him away before he figures out that I'm not worth saving.

I am exactly like those girls he kills.

I am an incurable disease.

He walks up to me, places both his hands on my cheeks just like he did a few minutes ago, and stares down into my evil blue eyes. "Everything you were just thinking, I want you to say it out loud."

I suck in a deep breath, shake my head, and look down at my feet.

Nick tips my chin back up, forcing me to see him. "Everything. Out loud. *Now.*"

But I can't say those things. Because I have this sneaky feeling that he's never thought of me that way. That he truly does love me. That I am his rock, the same way he is mine. And if I say these words out loud, he will change his mind about me. I will plant doubts inside him and those doubts will work their bad magic and turn our good thing into something rank and sour.

So instead, I pull out the smooth, worn, folded piece of paper with the words 'Kisses with Nick' written across the front, and I hand it to him.

He looks down at the paper, then back up at me. He takes these other words from my hand and then I do what I do best.

I walk away.

But I don't leave, that's the important part. I head towards the bathroom.

"Is this a fuck-you?" Nick calls after me.

"No." I stop in the doorway to the bathroom and then look over my shoulder. "I think it's... I think it's what you want to hear, Nick. But even if it isn't, it's how I feel. And that's all I'm gonna say about it."

Then I go inside the bathroom, close and lock the door, and start a bubble bath.

As I take off my clothes I think about the cure.

It always comes back to the cure.

PART TWO
the
wicked

"Wicked men obey from fear; good men, from love."

— Aristotle

CHAPTER EIGHT

TODAY

*"**Where are you, Nathan?** I've* been calling you for three days. Pick up the fucking phone! I had a call with Adam. *Adam*, Nathan. And do you know what he told me?" I pause. Because I'm shaking and it's starting to come out in my voice. "We need to talk. Now. Call. Me. *Back*!"

I press end on the screen and shove my phone into my pocket, then stare out over Dog River and sigh. I'm so wound up and tense, my neck and shoulders ache.

I'm in the backyard of the safehouse. Well, it used to be the safehouse. It's been abandoned for years now. I never sold it though. I never sell anything. You never know when you might need a place to crash in the South. Mississippi was never my first choice for this, but all of Florida is off limits at the moment. Louisiana too. Fucking Adam and his directives. Like I take orders from that asshole.

I don't.

But I don't want to fight with him over territory right now because no one is picking up my calls and this is not good. Not good.

I pull my phone back out, press Wendy's contact for the hundredth time, then... hope.

Pick up.

Pick up.

Pick up the fucking phone!

She doesn't pick up.

She hasn't picked up a call from me in eight months so this is nothing new, but everything is different right now. Donovan has changed the trajectory of my life and I don't like it. I need... assurances. I need to hear her voice.

How does she not understand this? Wendy Gale knows me better than anyone on this fucking planet. She is the only one who knows me. So, in times like this—in times of uncertainty—she should do me a fucking favor and pick up the damn phone.

This is not brain surgery, right? It's common fucking courtesy.

It's not like I'm asking her to check in or anything. Just pick up the phone. Two words. That's all I need from her, then she can hang up and not talk to me again until this is all over. But right now, I need to hear it. I need to hear her say, "I'm good."

That's it. That's all I want.

I run both hands down my face and continue to stare out across Dog River, my mind wandering back to the last time we used this house. Then I look over my shoulder at the trees that block the view of the house. Santos and I were collecting little girls in that house. Girls we should've killed, but didn't.

Instead, he pardoned them. And I sent them into what I now refer to as the Company foster care system.

This almost makes me smile. If it wasn't so fucking insane, I might give in to the urge. But it was a mistake. Letting them live was never gonna be the answer to this Company breeding program problem.

There were five of them that day. Angelica, the baby who is now called Hannah, Daphne, Avery, and Lily. Little killers. Well, only Angelica was an actual killer at that point. But the others were of the same breeding stock. It was all but inevitable.

Lauren was never on the kill list. She was always going to be placed with Sasha because I can't bring down evil and be a good father at the same time. I knew this since the day I picked her up when she was only a couple months old. And I guess my brother figured... if Lauren gets a second chance, why not these girls too?

What choice did I have? What the hell was I gonna do with five other girls? I couldn't give Sasha all of them.

So I doled them out. I gave Angelica to my sister, Harper, and James Fenici because James was the only one I trusted to keep that girl in line. I gave them baby Hannah, too. Because I wanted Harper to have a baby and I knew she would never get pregnant. She would never want to pass on the bloodline. And fuck it, right? Hannah was already born. The only way to stop it at that point was by killing her, and even I have a problem with killing babies. Even if one day she might lose her mind and turn into a maniac.

The only other guy I knew who could handle Company Zeroes was Merc. He was paranoid enough and scary enough to handle the three little sisters we took out of a breeding compound in Wyoming— Daphne, Avery, and Lily. All under the age of five. Plus, Sydney already knew the girls. She was part of that compound.

And it all worked out, right?

None of them have killed anyone. I think Angelica is even going to college somewhere in… well, I don't fucking know. Asia, maybe. But not a tightly regulated place. Some island, probably. If I wanted to find her, I probably could. But if I went looking, James would see me.

Overprotective doesn't even come close to how James feels about his adopted progeny.

And what would be the point of that? I have been pretending to be dead for a decade. There is no point in throwing all that away.

My phone buzzes in my pocket and my heart skips, hoping for Wendy.

It's not Wendy. It's Nathan.

I press accept and start walking back towards the woods. "Finally, you fucking asshole. What the hell, Nathan? I've been calling you for *three days*."

"Yeah, we've been a little busy here."

I stop walking. "Indie?"

"Good guess. Nathan's not gonna answer your calls. And I'm tired of you calling. It puts him in a bad mood."

"Do… you know who you're talking to?"

She scoffs. "What do I look like? A child? Of course I know who I'm talking to, *Nick*."

My heart skips again. Because even though I've known that everything I've been doing for the past fourteen years was a risk, and eventually it would all catch up with me, I never properly prepared myself for the actual moment and now that it's here, I don't know what to do.

"Hello? You still there?"

"I'm here."

"What did I say?"

"What?"

"That got you all tongue-tied? What did I say? Is it because I know who you are? Is it a big secret or something?"

"Yeah. Something like that."

"Well, what do you want? I can relay the message. I can't promise you he'll answer me, and he's not calling you back, but I'll let you know what I find out. Even if it's nothing."

"Why would you do that?"

"Because I like Wendy."

"How'd you know I was gonna ask him about Wendy?"

"Please." She huffs. "Unlike you, I didn't think I needed to *ask*. But. Do you know who *you're* talking to?"

"Trust me. I know way more about you than you do me."

"Probably true. Anyway. If you're worried about Wendy, then I'm worried about Wendy. And doesn't everyone worry about Wendy?"

I think about that for a moment. Because I always kinda felt that Wendy was well-liked, but it's weird to hear people talk about her. I've only been a part of her secret life and whatever friendship she has with Indie and Adam's crew is way outside of what she and I have together.

"But," Indie continues, "I don't think Nathan is in contact with her. Things have been kinda crazy here."

"Yeah. I've heard."

"Donovan is…" She lets out a long sigh. "In a bad way." Then she goes quiet. It's a weird quiet. And I'm trying to put my finger on what it means when she comes back. "I'm so upset over it, Nick. And I know you don't know me, but you just said you know me, right?"

I almost laugh. "Well. I know *of* you, Indie. And I thought Donovan was dead. That's what the grapevine is saying. So—"

"Cut the shit, OK? Adam told me you called. Well, Adam told McKay, then McKay told Nathan, and Nathan told me. I know you know he's still alive."

"So?"

"I love Donovan. He's like… well. It's hard to explain, but I need him, Nick. The way… the way Angelica needs James. You understand? I need him like that, Nick."

I don't know what she's expecting me to say to this, but I say nothing. Because she basically just admitted she's insane. That the only reason she still functions is because Donovan, or maybe Carter, has been holding her together. With tape, apparently. And not duct tape, either. That flimsy, cheap cellophane tape that barely holds anything together. Her grasp on reality has always been precarious but now it's in danger. And she knows this.

How does that feel? I wonder. To know you're about to unravel and there's nothing you can do about it? It's a mental death sentence.

"Do you understand what I mean?" Indie asks.

"Oh, I thoroughly get it."

"I need him to come through."

"He's fully awake then?"

"No. He woke up, but the doctor put him back into a coma. We can't take any chances that the... the... *personality* that survives is Carter."

"OK. So what do you want from me? This is what you're doing, right? Negotiating? I need Wendy, you need Donovan. You're gonna get me something but I have to do something for you, right?"

"Of course," she says airily. "That's how the world works."

"So what do you want?"

"It's not just me. It's all of us. And you already know. Adam already told you we're looking for Merc."

"Who?"

"Don't insult me, OK? I know you know him. What part of that aren't you getting? I have been filled in. Adam called Sasha and she agreed to make the call for us, but this isn't good enough for me. I don't know Sasha, but I know I don't *trust* her."

I don't want Indie to know Sasha. I don't want Indie to speak Sasha's name. I don't want Indie to even *think* about Sasha.

All of this is echoing in my head as my world narrows down into a black tunnel, but what I'm really thinking about—what's really lurking in the background as I live in this muted in-between existence of the phone call—is that this is the end. Every bit of the lie I've been living for the past decade is about to be over.

And when I imagine all of the millions of consequences that this conversation will lead to, every single one of them ends up with me and the girl I tricked coming eye to eye one last time.

I do not want this.

Regardless of all the daydreams I've had about seeing her again, I do *not* want to see Sasha Cherlin again.

It will be the unraveling of my lifetime and I'm not ready to fall apart.

Not yet.

Because I still owe Wendy that perfect present.

"—so do we have a deal?"

"What deal?"

"Do we have a bad connection? I just fucking spelled it out for you."

"Spell it out again."

"You get me this Merc guy and I'll find Wendy for you."

"How?"

"How do you find Merc? Or how do I find Wendy?"

"*Wendy*, Indie. Where the fuck is she?"

"Well, wouldn't you like to know?" She laughs a little. And again, her attitude is light and carefree. Must be nice to be an insane Zero. One who has been taken care of her entire life. One who still lives in the fantasy that she is safe. I wish her fear in this moment.

It's a shitty thing to wish for, and allowing that *meanness* inside me to take over, even subconsciously, is a bad move. It comes with all kinds of sad karmic moments in my future, even if I never utter this wish out loud.

But I want her to be afraid. Who does Indie Anna Accorsi think she is? She's no one special. She doesn't deserve this flippant existence.

Wendy does.

Wendy deserves to be that confident. That safe. That loved.

And I know that Indie has nothing to do with how Wendy's life has played out, but I want to blame her anyway.

I take a breath, ready to threaten Indie into submission and make her tell me where she is going to look, but she cuts me off. "I can find her. I promise you, I can. I know a little bit about her regular job."

"Regular job?"

"You know. What she does for a living."

"She... works? I mean, I know she works. She's... like... a..."

"She's a liaison, Nick."

"Right. *Liaison.* I knew that. I was just looking for the right word. I thought you meant she was like... settled in some normie job."

Indie guffaws. "Right. She's an executive assistant for a scumbag CEO. Good one, Nick."

"She works for me. Sometimes."

"She works for Adam too. Lots of the time. I know he only just got back a couple months ago, but they talk regularly."

"Regularly as in—"

"No. Not recently. I heard him calling her the other day. The day he talked to you, in fact. But she didn't pick up. Have you tried her home?"

139

"The cabin? I was there a couple weeks ago. She hasn't been home. Not since Christmas."

"How do you know?"

"I just do. She's not at home. She lives in her truck."

"What?"

"Not like homeless people live in their cars, or anything like that. She doesn't sleep in it. But she lives out of it. Like I do. Sometimes."

"Well, that's fucking weird. She can stay here if she needs a place. I could talk McKay into refurbishing the attic. It's not a bad room. It's a little hot in the summer, and we'd need to clean it out, but I think she would like it."

"Indie. Fuck. Focus, OK? She's not gonna stay with you. She could stay with me too. She has a home, for fuck's sake. She likes the road."

"Hmm. Well. I don't know what to say about that."

These fucking girls give me a headache. "So my question is, Indie, how the fuck are you gonna find her?"

"Get me Merc and I'll go look for Wendy."

"Get you *Merc*? I can't *get* Merc, Indie. I'm dead, remember? He and I were tight. He thinks I'm *dead*."

"Nick, I have a newsflash for you, OK? No one thinks you're dead. I mean, maybe last year people were still like, 'Yeah, Nick Tate. He's so dead.' But now…" I can almost see her wincing in my mind. "Nah. No one believes it anymore. And if this Merc guy is everything they say he is, he never bought into it either."

I let out a long, frustrated breath. "I can't, Indie."

140

"Because you can't look him in the eye?"

This girl. They say she's crazy, and she is, but she's not fucking stupid, that's for sure. She sees right through me. "Yeah. That's right. I can't face them. I'm not ready for it."

"Hmm. Well, I'm sure Wendy is fine then. But I gotta go now. I'm talking with a couple of other people who know Merc."

"Liar." I scoff. "If you had someone else, you wouldn't be bothering with me."

There is a pause here. I force myself to be silent with her. There is a technique to gaining the upper hand in a negotiation and it has a lot to do with what you *don't* say.

This silence goes on for thirty-seven seconds. I'm just about to hang up when she says, "Did you ever think that the reason Wendy isn't picking up is because she's not able to?"

"Of course. That's the whole fucking reason I'm calling Nathan."

"All right. In the spirit of goodwill and owed favors, I'm gonna tell you where she is."

"So you *do* know?"

"I have a pretty good idea. I mean, when I come up with a plot it typically works."

"What did you just say?"

"Ooops. Oh, well. I guess it's out now, isn't it?"

"What's out?"

"Come on. How you got your reputation, I'll never understand. You're kinda clueless, Nick. Do I have to spell it out for you?"

"If that will end this conversation sooner rather than later, please do."

She scoffs. And this is a scoff of contempt. She's disappointed in me. She thinks I'm stupid. Past my prime, probably. She might even feel sorry for me. "OK. Listen closely. Adam called Sasha asking for Merc's help. And unless Sasha lied and never contacted Merc, which I don't think happened, this means that Sasha told Merc that we were looking for him. So Merc is on a little mission right now trying to figure out who the fuck we are."

"So? What's that got to do with Wendy?"

"You ever heard of that association game Six Degrees of Kevin Bacon?"

"What the fuck are you talking about?"

"Well, turns out, inside the Company, our guys play one called Six Degrees of Adam Boucher. Everyone knows about Sasha Cherlin. She's the little maniac who planned the Santa Barbara massacre. She was the little gun-runner's daughter. The unsanctioned Zero girl. She knew everyone, right? So when you play this Six Degrees game, the quickest way to win is to find your way back to Sasha Cherlin. But here's the problem with that. Sasha retired a long time ago now. She's not current. And so many people are dead, sometimes you can't get to Sasha. But you know who you can get to? That's right. Your girl Wendy is the new Sasha. Her little part-time liaison job means she's a link to everyone. So if Adam reactivated Merc via Sasha, and Wendy is the most obvious sticky strand of web leading back to Adam, then... he's got her, Nick. Wendy is with Merc. That's why she's not picking up your calls. So whether you want to see him or not isn't the point anymore. You *need* to see him. Because from what I know about the guy, he's only good at two things. Killing and mindfucking. Either way, if he's got Wendy, she's not having much fun right now. But why am I telling you this? You already know how he is. Better than me, right? Since he's your old buddy."

"This is a threat. You're playing this card, hoping—"

"I'm not *playing*, Nick. I told you where she is and now you owe me. This is a real debt and you will pay it. You will bring Merc to us. Even if he doesn't agree, you bring him here to Old Home and let us take care of the rest."

My heart skips a beat, then thumps hard inside my chest as I waste two seconds wondering how long Indie might've been planning this move.

Wondering if I missed something.

Wondering if I'm being played.

"Nothing to say to that?" Indie asks.

My breathing slows and so does my heart rate. The building panic recedes and I pull myself totally together.

No. I'm not being played. Indie isn't acting. She's just being herself.

Everything is fine.

"OK."

"You agree?"

"I'll find Merc for you. But here's the catch. If he does have Wendy, and she's hurt, I will blow up this entire *fucking world* to make you pay for that, Indie. And I will do that by making sure Donovan dies."

She lets out a breath. Perhaps alarmed by my threat, perhaps not. "Call me back at this number when you're on your way. And Nick? Don't take too long.

Because I have many more ways to hurt you than you do me."

I don't care who you are, or how old you are, or how kicked-back you are—when someone you love shuns you for years at a time over something you can't really change, it hurts. And that time, as it passes, it feels like forever. It's an eternity of self-doubt and constant wondering... is this really how it ends?

That's how it starts. And if you're not totally in control of your world, this is the kind of shit that tears you up from the inside out.

I might not be totally sane, and for damn sure I'm nothing even close to normal, but I know how to lock out the doubt. I know how to plow ahead with blinders on.

This is kind of my thing.

So when Wendy walked out on me three Christmases ago, I plowed ahead. I put on those blinders. But I also showed up. I showed up for her birthday that year. She turned twenty-two. But Wendy wasn't there. Never showed up at all, and I stayed for a couple of weeks just to make sure.

At the time I was thinking, *Did she come? See my truck? Turn around and go the other way?*

But no. Because unless she was sneaking up on me through the woods or something weird like that, I would've heard her tires on the gravel driveway. Also, she didn't pick up the mail that first year. I know this because I broke into that fucking box of hers and there were birthday cards.

That distracted me for a day. It was nice, too. Reminded me of all those times—well, it really wasn't a lot of times. We're so hot and cold. So on and off. But the point is, opening the cards was nice. I even started matching them up with previous years. Wendy never threw any of the cards away. She had them all stuffed in garbage bags under her bed.

This cross-referencing didn't have a purpose, but it kept me busy. Kept my mind off of all the ways I was driving her away.

Anyway. That birthday she turned twenty-two.

I came by again for Christmas that year. Came early. Got a little tree. Bought some cookies from the nearby grocery-store bakery, I even found a Christmas carol playlist on my music stream.

No Wendy.

Fine, right? You wanna play hard to get? I can play hard to get.

So that next summer I did not show up for birthday twenty-three.

Well. I didn't show up early, anyway. But I was there on the day.

Did I stay two weeks, like last time, though?

No. I was strong. I was in control. I left the next morning and drove all the way back to my stupid farm in Nebraska.

Then I started calling her.

Well, first I posted on the board online. That's where we make plans. The board is an anonymous place. You don't get a name when you post. Well, I guess you could have a name—there's a place for one on the form when you make a reply. But if you use a name you are relentlessly ridiculed by every other anonymous person online. 'Oh, you're too good to be anonymous like the rest of us, you fucking loser?' Shit like that.

So I posted our code—this is something we've had in place since before we were even friends. It's how Chek and I used to communicate when Wendy was a teenager. We go to the board, we post a new message, and we wait. That message is only visible for about... oh, maybe... twelve hours. Then it falls off the front page, becomes archived and it's pretty much impossible to find after that. So you gotta post another one if you don't hear back.

I know it sounds like there isn't a chance in hell of communicating with people like this, but it actually works—*if* you're following the board. And Wendy and I have been chatty on that board for years. We're into it. Probably because we're losers. Trolling an image board on the chans is kind of a good time in our sad, pathetic world. So this method has worked well with us. If we're both on at the same time, we chat sometimes. Anonymously, of course. We have a little meme war, we shitpost about other anonymous losers, we sometimes even say things like 'good night' and 'see ya around.'

Anyway, I posted. I waited. She never showed. I posted next day, next day, next day... nothing. She never showed.

So I was thinking, *Is she mad at me? Like, that walkout was for real? Or is she somewhere remote with no internet access?*

This wasn't a true red flag for me a couple years ago because obviously we go long stretches of time with no communication at all. But right now, in the present day, the fact that Wendy is not on the boards is freaking me out because when she left me after our little New Year's date, we had a plan.

We don't usually have a plan. We wing it. We see where things go.

So this whole year has had me on edge because if we want the plan to work, we can't be together.

Which, *again*, is why we have *the board*. That's our number one way to contact each other. It's typically quick and easy because we're supposed to check the board once a day. It's like a little nighttime routine.

But we have two other ways. In our world, the backup plan always has a backup plan.

So then I called her.

But I wasn't actually calling *her*, I was calling a service. We change phones so often, we almost never have each other's numbers. So we set up a service. You push in your code, you get a beep, you leave a message. The person you're leaving that message for checks in, uses their code, and they get your message.

So I left a message. I said, "Are you really fucking mad at me over this Zero girl shit? Because that's fucking stupid." And I hung up.

Probably not the best way to defuse the situation we were in at the time, but I was starting to lose my patience with her. Plus, this was before I came up with the plan.

I checked the service every hour, on the hour, for like a week. And at the same time, I was also posting on the board every eight to twelve hours, trying to get her attention.

147

She did not check my message and she did not reply to my posts on the board.

Right. She was mad.

That was fine. We've got yet another way to make contact. The third, and least desirable, way is located in Mount Pleasant, Iowa. This little podunk town likes a good museum. They have like four of them. There is a country club, there is a Walmart, and there is even a tiny airport. It's so fucking American, you want to recite the Pledge of Allegiance and eat apple pie the moment you arrive.

It's a nice place, actually.

But we don't stop there because of the pie, or the history, or the whatever. It's pretty much just halfway between Wendy's little Kentucky cabin and my stupid Nebraska farm. And it's got a little roadside motel that consistently gets five-star ratings from travelers. So, ya know, if you and your long-distance soulmate are looking for a little hookup time, you can't go wrong with the Americana Inn in Mount Pleasant.

The guy who owns this place is called Wendell. His family has been running the Americana since nineteen fifty-three. And he likes us. He remembers faces. This is kind of a bad thing in our line of work, but what are ya gonna do? Kill the guy?

Nah. We embraced Wendell and his fam at the Americana. Made it our little hangout. And we set it up so that we can leave each other letters there at the front desk.

That's the third way Wendy and I stay in touch.

So once I realized she wasn't gonna post on the board and she wasn't gonna check my messages I got in my truck and drove to Mount Pleasant. And sure enough, Wendell told me that Wendy came by about a month back and she left me an envelope.

I know it's taking me forever to get to the fucking point, but all of this rambling has a fucking point and here it is:

Christmas #22. The card she left me in Mount Pleasant was a goodbye of sorts.

She didn't say she never wanted to see me again. She didn't say she hated me. She didn't really end things, but... I could tell this was an ending.

She was moving on.

It wasn't the good kind of moving on, either.

It was the self-destructive kind.

And it was a cry for help because she left me a phone number. A real fucking phone number.

I got a room and called her up and she and I talked for an entire night. I'm talking nine hours on the phone. She was obsessed with the idea that there was a cure for her out there.

And OK, this is not as far-fetched as it sounds. She's not really crazy because that's what the whole Purge was about when Chek was killed. But Megan Machette was working on a cure for what the Company had done to the kids, not a cure for Zero girls. And for whatever reason Wendy had gotten these two things mixed up. She was absolutely, one hundred percent positive that there was a cure out there that would fix her.

And if she could just find this cure, she would stop being Creepy Wendy and start being the person she was meant to be.

It killed me. That entire conversation broke my fucking heart. "Wendy," I said. "Just tell me where you are and I'll come get you, and we can do this together."

Because yeah, this idea that she needs to be cured is nuts. But it doesn't matter. If she believes it to be true, it's true. So I was on board. I came up with a plan. We were gonna hook up with Megan via Johnny Boston. I was gonna put everyone who owed me on this mission to find Wendy's cure.

But that wasn't what she wanted.

Oh, she made promises. She said we'd meet up but after we hung up that night, she disappeared for eighteen months.

Not exactly disappeared. She's not like Indie. She doesn't flip out, go insane, and then go rogue. No. Wendy Gale is far, far, *far* too professional for shit like that.

She just ignored me. Completely.

It wasn't until last Christmas, #24, that I finally convinced her to see me again.

This was when I made the real promise. The one she believed.

Because this plan would work, and she knew it.

It wasn't gonna be easy, and she was gonna take all the hits, but she didn't care.

Once I told her my plan, she was on board.

I had the cure.

Or, at least, I had access to it.

And even though, in my eyes, Wendy Gale is the most perfect woman I've ever known, I was gonna get that fucking cure and then we were gonna be together forever.

Right now I'm in the parking lot of the Mount Pleasant Americana Motel. My convo with Indie was yesterday and the moment she hung up on me, I drove here.

Wendell had a package waiting for me, a large padded yellow envelope. And inside was a phone. The phone had one programmed contact.

I press the screen and call the number.

A voice I recognize answers. "Very, *very* interesting life you're leading... *Nick*."

It's Merc.

And there is only one way he would know how to contact me at the Americana.

Indie was right.

He's the reason Wendy is missing.

CHAPTER NINE

FOUR DAYS AGO

Transcendent, everlasting, whole, perfect, beautiful, sweet.

I am on the hunt for Nick Tate.

He's not taking my calls. He's not picking up my messages, he's not on the board, and he didn't leave me an envelope in Mount Pleasant so I had no choice but to come all the way out here.

It's a nice summer day. Bright blue sky for as far as the eye can see. It's not even that hot today, even though it's August. There are wheat fields swaying in the wind, row after row of corn fields, and lots of other fields with short plants I can't identify. This is why they call it the breadbasket, I guess. Food just coming up out of the ground everywhere you look.

I am in Nebraska. Perkins County, to be specific.

This part of the state butts up against the very eastern edge of Colorado and just the mere fact that this is where Nick bought land is enough to trigger me.

Because he's not fooling anyone, is he? No one says 'I think I will buy a twelve-thousand-acre farm in Nebraska worth almost twenty million dollars' when they are twenty-eight years old and need to disappear.

You go to the Seychelles, the Maldives, or fucking Thailand like every other on-the-run rich asshole in the world. You do not buy a farm. He's not even a farmer. He's just an owner. And he doesn't even live in the main house—which is a mansion, by the way. No. He lives in one of the falling-down shitholes typically reserved for farmhands.

The only possible reason he could have for buying this massive working farm that produces like a billion pounds of food every year is its proximity to Colorado.

And we all know who lives in Colorado.

Sasha. Cherlin.

I can't even think her name in my head without the full stops. And when I picture her face, I want to give up my recently acquired Zen lifestyle and slip back into full-on assassin mode. I don't even understand why she makes me feel this way. I've never met this woman. I haven't even seen a picture of her since her face was in the fucking newspaper for shooting 'Nick' in the head nearly a decade ago.

Of course that wasn't Nick. It was his twin brother, Santos. But that's not the point. The point is, why do I care about her? Why? Why do I get so angry when I think about this stupid farm? It's not that close to where Sasha lives. She's in Fort Collins. It's a three-hour drive away.

But come on. Three hours? Are you kidding me? Three hours is nothing. Hell, I've been driving for thirteen right now.

Three hours. He practically moved next door. And yeah, I get it. His daughter lives there too. So I'm sure he does want to be close to Lauren. And Lauren lives with Sasha, but that's another thing. I practically raised Lauren until she was six. And fine, I was only nine when she was born, but by the time he shipped her off to Sasha, I was fifteen. She was like my baby sister one day, then the next—gone.

Living with Sasha. In Fort Collins. New life, new name. She even got a pony.

You know what I got? A front-row seat to a shadow government global war, that's what I got.

"Yeah," I mutter, taking a turn too fast so the tires of my truck skid sideways across the loose gravel. "I've got issues." I straighten out the wheel, barely avoiding a slip into the ditch, and then press my foot down on the accelerator. I'm not really sure where I'm at and the cell signal out here is spotty. So I sit up in my seat and peek around, trying to find a landmark.

Nick's house is between two fields. If this were winter the fields would not matter. They'd be empty and brown like all the others. But it's summer and that means the two fields on either side of Nick's shitty house are filled with sunflowers.

I scan the horizon for any sign of yellow, but there's mostly corn out here now and it's that super-tall genetically engineered kind, so I have to travel past two more fields before I find what passes for a hill in Nebraska. I stop at the top, which is like twelve feet above sea level, get out of the truck, climb into the bed, then onto the roof, and scan in every direction.

My lips creep up in a small smile when I spot it. A blanket of yellow off in the west.

But I don't get down right away. I stay there on top of the truck. Not a sign of life—other than grasshoppers and birds—for ten miles, at least. I guess it's nice out here. I can see the attraction of emptiness. It's a lot easier to live in your own skin when no one's looking at you all the time. And isn't that why Chek and I called Kentucky home? It's a different kind of emptiness, but it's all the same in the end.

Nick makes them plant the sunflowers for me. He told me that three years ago. That's the last time I was here. And every year, on my birthday he sends me a picture of them. And if he knows where I am, he sends a bouquet.

Nick Tate has been giving me sunflowers on my birthday since I was six years old. He graduated up to bouquets when I turned ten. I guess I was worth more than a single flower that year because Nick, Lauren, and I had been travelling the southeast coast of the USA like we were permanent tourists for almost eight months before that day.

Then Chek came and got me. I balked a little in the beginning, but once I was back I was back, ya know? I missed training and jobs. But I had already fallen in love with Nick Tate by that time. No, not *that* kind of love. I don't know if Nick and I will ever have *that* kind of love. Our love is something else. Something huge, and real, and even though we're almost never together, we're getting better at it.

We're tied together now, at least. And he's been helping me look for the cure.

You gotta love a man who helps you look for your cure. That's real love in my book.

I jump down into the bed, then hop out, land on the dirt road, get in my truck, and head towards the sunflowers. Twenty minutes later I stop at the end of his driveway, suddenly hesitant.

Nick and I are people who don't like to be found sometimes. And I've only been trying to get a hold of him for a couple days, so he's not exactly missing.

But something is going on and I can't put my finger on it.

So I'm here.

I look around, wondering if anyone is watching. This is just habit. But out here there is nowhere to hide. Unlike Kentucky with its thick woods and deep gullies, the Nebraska plains are... well, plain. I buzz my window down to listen. Birds, insects, somewhere off in the distance a tractor or some similar piece of machinery. This is the only house for miles and miles. All of this land—even the sections not owned by Nick's shell company—are just fields. They surround his house, and the sunflowers are tall, but I scan them for a good two minutes looking for any sort of movement and see nothing. The other two fields nearby are sugar beets, and that's not a tall plant. So I'm reasonably sure there's no one watching.

I could do a U-turn and leave now. No one would ever know the difference. Nick's dirt driveway is like a half a mile long. I can see the blue shack he calls home down at the end of it, but not any details. I look up, searching for drones. But it's unlikely that anyone cares about this place. The Company is... well, not gone. It's Adam, and McKay, and Donovan now. Well, maybe just Adam and McKay. But the point is, the Company isn't the Company anymore. I'm pretty sure Adam does his best to pretend Nick doesn't exist as much as possible. He would not be watching him. Especially now, with that whole Donovan situation looming large.

"I should leave." But my whispered words get caught up in the wind. And then I just turn into the driveway and crawl my way down it. The front lawn is mostly weeds, but it's been cut. Not recently. Maybe... two weeks ago? There are three outbuildings here. One is a legit outhouse that kinda tilts to the south. One is a chicken coop. I study it, looking for the filthy monsters. But he's never kept chickens in there and that hasn't changed. The third is a shop. There are lots of things going on inside the shop if you know where to look, but there are no cars or trucks in the driveway, so I don't think anyone's in the shop.

The house was blue once upon a time but now it's a funky shade of sun-bleached lavender gray. The wooden window frames are trimmed in white. There's not much else to say about it. It's a box with a pitched roof. The front door has a skinny... well, it doesn't even qualify as a porch. It's more of a five-step stoop with ugly metal railings on either side. And it's built into one of those mudroom additions that are so common in the Midwest. Every house out here has two doors, the one that leads to the mudroom and the one that leads to the house.

The AC is on. I can hear it humming as my truck crawls past the front steps. All the windows have curtains—most of them just pillowcases nailed to the wall, actually—and there is no way to see inside. So I shove the truck in park, turn it off, and then lean over to the glove box and get my gun. Another habit of mine.

But as soon as I step out of the truck, I remember why I have this habit.

The back door is wide open and the screen door bangs back and forth with the wind.

The AC is on. The door should not be open.

If someone is home, they know I'm out here. There is no way to stealthily make your way down a gravel road at a farmhouse this remote. The tires crunch. The motor of the truck hums. Everything about me is out of place and even dumbasses who didn't grow up assassinating people pay attention to that.

So I call out, "Hey, asshole!" and wait for an answer.

No response.

"Nick?"

Nothing.

"If anyone's in there, you'd better yell now. Because if I go inside and find you, there's a bullet coming your way."

No answer.

"OK. I'm coming in." I don't bother with caution. I can feel people at this point in my life and this place is empty.

The moment I step inside I get a chill. It's a weird kind of empty. Like… that feeling you get when you're being watched. This thought has me immediately looking for cameras. Surely Nick has cameras.

But he's Nick. So they aren't easy to find. I take a step outside, scan the back porch, and come up with two possible places where the camera could be hiding.

The doorknocker. Because doorknocker? On this piece-of-shit house? And the peephole.

I step back inside and check the peephole. Not a camera. So it must be the doorknocker.

I don't bother scanning the inside for cameras. They're here, but finding them without a camera hunter would be a waste of time. And anyway, if I really wanted details about his cameras, I'd just break in to his control room.

I'm not going to do that. He would be pissed. He'd say things like, "What the fuck, Wendy? If you want in, just tell me and I'll give you the code. Don't break my shit down!"

He's right, you know.

The house has four rooms. The front room, the bathroom, the bedroom, and the kitchen. I enter through the kitchen, so the first thing I notice is that it's very clean. No dishes in the sink. No random papers on the crappy Formica table. No food in the fridge.

"So," I mumble to myself. "You're not even living here."

I set my gun down, pull a wobbly chair out from the dining table and take a seat. Lean back a little. Think out loud. "If you're not here, then where?"

Maybe he's done with me?

Maybe last Christmas was a mistake?

Maybe he's thinking, *What the hell was I thinking*?

Alternatively, Wendy, perhaps the asshole really is in danger?

This is a problem.

I haven't a single clue of where else I might look, so instead my eyes track across the kitchen.

This is when I spy something. Something that may or may not be out of place.

It's a phone. An actual fucking wall phone. The kind with a cord.

I get up, cross the kitchen in three and a half steps, and pick up the receiver. Dial tone.

I press star sixty-nine. Ringing.

"Hello?"

"... Who's this?"

"You called me, sweetheart."

"Because you were the last person to call this number. I star-sixty-nined you."

"OK. So. What do you want?"

"I'm looking for the person who owns this phone."

"And?"

"And"—this rando stranger is starting to piss me off—"have you seen him?"

"Depends."

"OK. Well. Let's start here. Do you know who I'm talking about? Or does that depend on something too?"

"Wendy?... *Wendy?*"

"How do you know my name?"

"I'm God. No, really. Listen. You're wasting time here. Why are you talking to me? There are clues all around you. Look for them, for fuck's sake."

"What are you talking about?"

"You're looking for Nick? Well, I'm looking for him too. Look around, find some answers, and *then* you can call me back."

He hangs up.

I let out a long breath and replace the receiver. Well, he was an asshole. And all of that was weird.

Who the hell is that guy? He's not anyone I recognize. Not Adam, or McKay, and we all know it's not Donovan.

We, Wendy? You're the only one here.

Right. *Check the insanity, OK? Pull it together.*

I suck in a breath and blink my eyes a few times, trying to understand what's happening. Because this whole trip is weird. Why am I even here?

I look up and scan the room, then salute Nick's probable hidden cameras with my middle finger. "Fuck you. I'm leaving."

The phone rings before the last word is even out of my mouth.

I pick it up. "What?"

"You're not leaving. You're looking for clues. Find them and call. Me. Back." He hangs up.

So he's the one looking through the hidden cameras.

Got it.

I give him the one-finger salute again and then turn towards the door fully intending on getting the hell out of here, but then I see something else that's interesting.

An answering machine on the kitchen counter. And there's a blinking number four on the tiny digital screen.

I can't stop the chuckle. Only Nick Tate would keep a landline with an answering machine. This is probably a clue, and that bastard voice is probably dying for me to press play so he can hear what's on there, so this is usually where I do things just to piss

162

people off. Things like not pressing play on that machine. Not listening to whatever's on there. And not giving a single fuck about the consequences.

But I gotta know.

I can't help myself.

I walk over to it and press play.

"You have four new messages. Message one…"

"Don't forget to schedule the jobs in Florida. And maybe even Alabama."

Beeeeeeep.

"Next message…"

I press stop. That was definitely Nick. And that message was what? A to-do list? What jobs? Did I know about jobs in Florida and Alabama? He used to have a place on the Dog River, but that's Mississippi. And Adam does not like Nick doing anything that close to Louisiana. So what the fuck was this about?

I press play again.

"Don't forget to send Wendy sunflowers. Her birthday's coming up."

Beeeeeeep.

"Next message…"

I press stop again.

This machine is definitely a to-do list. But my birthday isn't coming up. It just passed two weeks ago. So this message is from what, three weeks ago? Maybe a month?

And the asshole did not send me flowers. First time in years that he didn't find me—wherever I was in the world—and get me those sunflowers.

"Duh, Wendy," I huff. "That's why you're here. He's *missing.*"

163

And some asshole is playing phone games with me.

Two more messages though. So I press play.

"So... Yeah. Sorry about that. I haven't been home in a while. I thought I would be, but I couldn't swing it. Don't be mad at me, OK? I'm fine. I'll see you soon."

Beeeeeeep.

"Next message..."

Wait. Who the hell is he talking to? Does he have a girlfriend? And did he tell *her* to send me flowers for my birthday? Oh. My heart will crack in half if he's been having some girl send my mandatory sunflowers every year.

Oh, my God, I'm losing my mind or something. Nick does not have a girlfriend. That's probably the dumbest accusation I've ever come up with.

And hold on. My birthday *is* coming up. It didn't just pass.

So... what the hell is wrong with me?

Holy fuck, I'm losing my mind. It's really happening. It's too late, there's no cure for me. I'm about to slip into some bizarre psychosis and...

I look around again. But this time, I *really* look around. Then I go to the bedroom and flip on the lights. The bed is made and nothing is out of place. And at this point, I should not be surprised. He just told me he hasn't been home in a while. So who was he leaving that message for?

I check the closet. Like the fridge, it's empty. No clothes, no shoes, no nothing. Then I check the tiny bathroom. Not even a toothbrush in the cabinet mirror. Not even a bottle of aspirin.

No one is living here.

So again. Who is he leaving that message for?

One more to hear, Wendy. Press play.

"You know how to find me. Stop playing around, Wendy."

Beeeeeeep.

"No more messages. Press one to delete. Press two to keep as new. Press—"

I press stop and lean against the counter.

I am perplexed. Because none of this makes sense. I don't even know why I'm here. In fact, I should leave. Now.

The phone rings.

I consider not answering it, but I'm like a fucking cat in this respect. Curiosity is going to get me killed one day. I pick up the receiver. "What?"

"What did you find out?"

"Who are you?"

"You'll know that soon enough." I'm about to protest, but he keeps going. "We have common friends. And by friends, I mean... you know, *friends*."

"Like who?"

"James Fenici for starters."

"Fuck you. You do not know James Fenici. Throwing his name around won't get you far with me. He and I? We're barely acquaintances. We're definitely not friends."

"Well, obviously, I know Nick."

"So you say. Just because you called his phone doesn't make you friends with him."

"I know he's supposed to be *dead*." There's a pause after that. Maybe he's thinking about these words the

165

same way I am. But then he whispers, "I know who he left behind too. And if she finds out he's still alive…"

Sasha. It always comes back to fucking Sasha. "If she finds out, what? Her little heart will break? She'll leave her husband for Nick? She'll ruin her whole family for some stupid promise that never really meant anything in the first place? Too late for all that, ha ha ha."

"Wow. You definitely have feelings about this, don't you?"

"Fuck you. I'm outta here. I don't even know why I came. I don't know who you are or what kind of game you're playing. And who cares where Nick is? He can take care of himself."

"That he can, Wendy. That he can. But consider this before you hang up and go back to your sad, lonely, pathetic existence out in those hillbilly woods you live in or rambling around on the open road. I'm someone you want on your side. Trust me."

I scoff loudly. "Do you think I'm afraid of you? Do you even know who I am?"

"I know exactly who you are. You're missing the point. You don't know who *I* am, Wendy. And your gun can't protect you from me. Because I can get in your *head*. And once I'm in, there's no way to get rid of me until I decide to leave."

"Big words. I'm shaking." I feign a yawn. But both the words and the yawn are just a well-practiced ruse. Because I understand what he's telling me.

I know exactly what he's telling me and a chill runs up my spine just as the word forms in my head.

PSYOPS.

Whoever this guy is, he is Company PSYOPS.

And there are only two living Company men who can do what this guy claims he can do.

One is Donovan Couture's second personality. And he's in a coma in Adam's mansion back in Louisiana.

The other guy… is *Merc*.

CHAPTER TEN

TODAY

"You better start talking, motherfucker."

Nick Tate sounds the same. It almost creeps me out how much he sounds the same. And it occurs to me that I would've recognized his voice anywhere. Even if I didn't suspect he was alive.

"Where's Wendy?"

I picture him the way he was the last time we were together. I didn't kill anyone that night. I wasn't an active shooter in the Santa Barbara massacre. I was the getaway driver. Well, captain, since our getaway car was a boat.

But even though I wasn't part of the attack, that whole thing—the mansion on fire up on the cliff, the way everyone's faces were lit up orange from the flames, the moon that night, Sasha crying and screaming when she realized Nick was staying behind with that worthless drug lord so that James could

169

escape with the files we needed—all of it is burned into my brain. It was branded on me.

It is one of those defining moments. That's what it was. Maybe even… *the* defining moment. The first moment in my life that truly mattered. The first time I started thinking about being part of something bigger than myself. Part of something good instead of evil.

It's a night I will never forget. Even if someone out there was capable of fucking with a person's mind the way I am, they wouldn't be able to erase that moment. It is inerasable. And, if I'm being honest, it's probably the only reason I didn't end up killing Sydney instead of saving her several years later.

Just thinking about that possible outcome hits me in the gut. What kind of life would I be living right now if Nick Tate hadn't shown me what a sacrifice looks like? If I hadn't stopped what I was doing with Sydney and used my powers to help her instead of steal memories from her mind so I could get my revenge?

Well. It wouldn't look anything like this one, that's for sure.

But my loyalties were to Sasha that night in Santa Barbara. She was the one I was protecting. I was on her team, not Nick's. And she was insane with anger and grief in the weeks and months after Nick's abandonment. Even after she was sent to live with Ford, she was sad.

She was never the same girl after Nick.

He changed her and I will never forgive him for that.

Then flash-forward ten years and he did it again. Only this time, he nearly destroyed her when he forced Sasha to shoot him in the head.

Only it wasn't him, was it?

It was someone else.

Someone who looked exactly like Nick Tate—*if* Nick Tate *hadn't* grown up the spoiled brat of a Company Untouchable living a life of pure luxury on a superyacht and instead grew up running drugs with the locals in the slums down in San Pedro Sula.

I always knew there was something wrong with how that whole thing ended.

I felt it.

And now I have the proof.

"Never mind Wendy," I finally answer. "What's happening right now has *nothing* to do with Wendy."

"If you hurt her—"

"You'll what?"

Nick Tate takes a moment to gather himself. But I can feel his anger and rage through the distance. I pause with him, wondering who he is these days. No one I recognize, that's for sure.

The Nick Tate I knew would never have done what he did to Sasha.

He used her. And for what?

"She's got nothing to do with this, Merc. This is between you and me."

"That's what I just said."

"Yeah, but you said it in a way that implies she has everything to do with me."

"Well, doesn't she?" These words come out low and threatening. I cannot even remember the last time I've been so angry. All I know is that it's been a very long time. Maybe... *maybe* since that day Sydney killed Garrett and saved Sasha and me up in the Montana woods.

171

My life since then has been pretty fucking good. Pretty fucking calm. It's been filled with my girls, pool parties, trips to Colorado for barbeque weekends, tropical vacations on the beach—and even though I've kept up a healthy dose of paranoia, that's just old habit.

No one came to attack us—no one even came looking.

I've been living as normal a life as a guy like me could possibly imagine and now this asshole shows back up and he is going to make my entire world implode.

The hate I have for Nicholas Tate right now would rival any of my old adversaries. This hate is at Defcon One. I am ready to take this motherfucker out by any means necessary and this attack is imminent.

"She has nothing to do with us, Merc."

"You're wrong there, Nick." My words almost come out like a sigh. Because I'm tired of this whole thing already and I've just barely gotten started. There is so much more to do.

"Let's just keep it between you and me."

"You and me? Sure. This sure is between you and me."

"So you're gonna let her go?"

I laugh. "No."

"Where the fuck is she?"

"Don't you worry about that. She's safe."

"I want to talk to her. *Now.*"

"I'm afraid that won't be possible. She's… indisposed at the moment."

He pauses. I am a precise person. An intentional person. If Nick remembers anything about me, he remembers that much. And that word, *indisposed*? Yeah, that's gonna trigger him bad.

"You'd better explain that."

"Let me tell you how this is gonna go, *Nick*. So we don't waste any more of Wendy Gale's precious moments. You're gonna stay right the fuck where you are and I'm gonna come to you. OK?"

"No. Either I talk to Wendy or this negotiation is over and what happens next is I hunt you down and take you out."

I laugh again. "We both know you're not up for that."

"Here's what we both know, *Merc*. I dropped three little girls off with you ten years ago and you've spent that entire time building pools, and fake beaches, and investing in things like strollers, and pony lessons, and family vacations. That's not how my life went. So I'll take my fucking chances."

"This isn't hardball. Not even close. I'm not quaking in my boots, boy. In fact, I find you rather amusing."

"You've got ten seconds. One."

"She can*not* come to the phone."

"Take the phone to her."

"I do not stutter, Nick. When I said she was indisposed, I meant it."

"If she has one fucking scratch—"

"You think I'm torturing her? Well..." I laugh for a third time. It's bad form and it's a wholly inappropriate moment, but I can't seem to stop it. "She's pretty fucked right now. But not the way you think. So this little I'm-OK-you're-OK chat you wanna have won't be possible. And if you argue with me, I'll

173

just hang up and proceed without your input, how's that?"

"What. The fuck. Have you done?"

"I need information. I need to know if you truly are a special kind of scumbag liar. I mean, I've seen the clues. You're on the board, right? You post on there? You and Wendy have a little code going, maybe? Yeah. I've seen it. So while I am fucking *astonished* that you would put Sasha through the kind of pain most people don't ever recover from, I am not entirely *surprised* that you really are that special kind of scumbag liar."

He stays quiet. Which means he's plotting something.

"Nothing to say to that?"

A *loooong* sigh from Nick Tate.

"So." I sigh too. "Wendy has been very helpful in figuring out what the actual fuck is going on here. And here's something that might surprise you, or perhaps make you a little sick—do you know who gave me her name?" Again, I laugh. *Stop it, Merc. It's just wrong at this point.*

"I'm gonna ask one more time. Where is she and what have you done to her?"

"Sasha," I whisper, ignoring his question. "Sasha gave me her name, Nick. Kinda karmic, right? I mean... you trick her into killing—who the fuck was that guy, anyway?"

"My brother."

"Your—wait, wait, *wait*. Hold the fuck up. You have a *twin* brother as well as a twin sister? You guys were triplets? Oh, fuck. You Company people are so... *gross*."

He pauses. Three whole seconds of pause from the legendary Nick Tate. Then he says, "You remember Vincent, right?"

"Vincent. What a pussy. I can't believe he ran on the beach that night."

"He didn't run, he swam. Right to the fucking superyacht, in fact. Right into the hands of Santos himself. That's the guy Sasha killed that day out in Kansas. Santos. The Saint. That's what they called him down in the slums of San Pedro Sula. Vincent didn't run away. Vincent got himself tangled up in a mess that hasn't even ended yet."

"What is your point? No one gives a single fuck about Vincent Fenici."

"My point is that he was James' twin, right? One of them was sent into the dark world of Company assassins, the other into the hands of the elite to be groomed for bigger and better things. You do realize that's how this world works, right? I mean, it's common knowledge in the Company, but you never were Company, were you, Merc?"

I scoff again. "What the hell is that? Are you trying to make me feel inferior because I don't have the blood of murderous assholes going back a thousand years running through my veins the way you do? Are you for real right now?"

"No. That's not what I'm doing. I'm explaining the ways of the world. You, as badass as you are, are no one in this world, Merc. And I do mean that literally and I do not mean it as an insult. I simply mean that you don't know what you don't know. Nothing you see around you is real. TV isn't real. And as much as people think they understand that they are watching actors, and sets, and it's all fake—they still don't get it. It just doesn't sink in that the whole world has been staged. It has a director, it has acting coaches, it has a script, and it has a little something called 'central casting.' I mean, come on. Almost no one on this planet has the resolve to bootstrap their way up in *any* kind of business—Hollywood, corporate America, global whatever... none of it is real. It's a setup, Merc. The entire world is nothing but a greenscreen playing in the background."

I kinda knew this. I mean, I've seen shit. I'm not Company. Not even a lowlife Company worker, let alone royalty the way Nick is. But I've been deep inside. I knew the whole world was fake. I knew the Company was pulling strings and that's why I keep my family well away from everything whenever I can.

But it was a general sense of fake. Like... OK. That fucking Bieber kid? Is this a joke? Where the hell did he come from, am I right? Sell-out concerts, screaming tweens, magazine covers and a world tour? What the hell is happening? And look at that asshole now. Fucking mess is what he is. There's a whole list of child stars like that.

But do I have to care about it?

I mean... not really. Whatever, right?

If the elites of this world want to fuck up their kids—well, I can't save them all.

But I get the feeling that Nick is saying something deeper here. So when he continues to talk, I begin to listen.

"We're part of central casting too, Merc. All of us inside the Company. We play our roles, and that's about all there is to life. And at first glance you might

176

think—well, Vincent didn't have it so bad. He grew up in… well, I don't really know where he grew up, but it was a nice place. Look at me, right? Harper and me, we grew up on that superyacht. Secluded, pampered, safe. So I imagine that's how Vincent's life went. So we all think that it was James who made the sacrifices. He was the one they trained to kill as a kid. He's the one who got captured down in Honduras. He was the one who—"

"You don't need to tell me this shit, Nick. I was fucking *there*, OK?"

"I get it. You're loyal to him. And that's fine. I love James. I do. I respect the fuck outta that man and he's been taking care of my sister for almost two decades now. I owe him. But if you've never been the one sent into the world of the elites to perform for them, then you can't even begin to understand what *that* life is like. I'm not looking for sympathy here—"

"Sure sounds like you are."

"I'm not. I'm just saying. Everyone plays their part. I played mine and Santos played his. I was destined to lead, he was destined to die. But he didn't *suffer* more than me, Merc. Because when they put him on that dark path the first thing they did was take away his humanity. By the end there, Santos just *wanted* to die. It was his last wish and Sasha granted it, that's all that happened that day in Kansas. It was one man's dying wish to sacrifice himself for something bigger."

I picture that guy with all those scars and tattoos. I only saw the pics in the online news. Never met the guy in person. But I felt sorry for Nick Tate when I thought that was him. I imagined that his life was pretty shitty since he gave it up to save the rest of us that night

177

in Santa Barbara. Up until this moment I had almost imagined Nick as some kind of martyr. Someone willing to go down on principle because he knew in the end it would save the people he loved. Now, all I feel is disgust and betrayal. "Whose idea was it, Nick? To make Sasha deliver the kill shot?"

He goes quiet.

"Aw, no. You're not shuttin' down now, partner. I'm just getting started. I want to know right the fuck now, whose idea was it to make Sasha kill you?"

He lets out a breath. "Mine. Santos didn't know Sasha, remember? It was my idea. And it worked, didn't it? She got out, she got married, she got kids— my kid, Merc. She got *my* kid. She got a real life and she got to leave all this dark shit behind. All because she did her job that day. She played her part that day."

Did her job. Played her part. I let those words roll around in my head for a second or two. I even allow myself to picture ten or twenty different ways I might make Nick Tate pay for his professional expectations of a heartbroken girl who had already lost everything.

"Whatever you're doing with Wendy, it's over now."

"Is it?" I laugh a little. Everything's so goddamn ironic today.

"If you want to make me pay, don't take it out on her."

"Trust me, Nick. I absolutely *do* want to make you pay. But I won't need to hurt Wendy Gale because you're gonna do exactly what I say."

"And what would that be?"

"You're gonna stay right where you are. And I'm gonna come to you. Hear me?"

"What about Wendy?"

"What about her?"

"Are you bringing her with you?"

"Nah, she'll keep. Go back into the hotel office and tell Wendell you want a room. Then text me the room number."

"Then what?"

"You'll find out."

CHAPTER ELEVEN

FOUR DAYS AGO

Merc.

The word echoes in my mind as I let him wait on the other end of the phone.

"Nothing to say?"

I take a deep breath. "OK. I know who you are. What do you want?"

"Well, can I make a list?"

I can't tell how serious he is. And I don't know this guy. I've heard a lot about him, but I never bothered getting too close because whenever any of the other Company assassins would bring up Merc's name, it always came with a warning.

When you're one of two men on the planet who can run a PSYOP right inside the mind of a target, you're in demand. And lots of new guys over the years have tossed around the idea of hiring Merc for his services when they had a particularly smart target who had pertinent information. Torture is so... old-school, right? Only a truly sick fuck wants to torture a person for intel before they kill him. Torture takes time. It requires a place where your target can scream loudly for hours on end. It's not quick and easy and believe it or not, the Company assassins I know are all relatively well-adjusted men who just want to get the job done as efficiently as possible.

Whenever that happened—whenever some new guy thought bringing Merc in for a job was a good idea—the more worldly assassins would set him straight. It went a little something like this:

You want to know how to find Merc? We all know where he lives, but if you get within five miles of that place and you're not passing by on the highway going eighty-five miles an hour, you will be followed by an armed drone until you leave the area.

If you try to ambush him into a conversation at the local coffee shop or grocery store—especially if he's got his family with him—he will shoot you in your sleep that same night.

If, by some miracle, you actually get on his property his daughters will shoot you between the eyes and then feed you to their personal face-eating German shepherds.

When the oldkills, which is what we call the seasoned professionals, said all this, at first the newkill guy would laugh. Smile about it. *Oh, this is so funny.* What a good joke.

I mean, why wouldn't he think that? He's a fucking Company assassin. And there aren't that many of them. Maybe fifty, total. So he's one of the top fifty most dangerous men on the earth. Why should he be afraid of anyone, let alone some old, washed-up asshole who is so paranoid he has armed drones flying a pattern over his house twenty-four seven?

But about a minute later he would recognize the silence for what it was and realize no one was joking and that smile would drop. Thirty seconds after that he'd say something like, "Fuck that guy anyway. I don't need to run no fucking PSYOP to get what I need."

And everyone would let the newkill have his moment. No one would joke around or embarrass him for backing out of his great idea. Because every single one of them was afraid of Merc too.

It's kinda weird how that happened. Because not a single one of them has ever *seen* Merc actually work. He's been retired for more than a decade.

But that's why they're so scared of him.

Retired, you say? How does one go about *retiring* from the Company?

One doesn't.

I mean, Adam's not a bad leader, all things considered. But if you try to just pack up and leave your job... yeah. He's gonna send in one of your oldkill friends to change your mind. And by change your mind, I mean he's gonna make you dead.

So they all wonder, what kind of magic power does this Merc guy possess that he just gets to walk away?

Then you gotta tell them the whole stupid story. Merc isn't actually Company.

What? It comes out incredulous. *Bullshit.*

It's not bullshit.

Back in Merc's working days the Company still had subcontractors. They found Merc at an MIT recruitment weekend. And the moment you say 'MIT' to these wide-eyed newkills, their mouths drop open. *Ohhhhhhh.* They start nodding, getting it. Now it kinda makes sense. He's not an assassin. He's a brain who just knows how to fuck with your head and kill you a hundred and twenty-five different ways.

"You still with me, Wendy?"

"Yeah. I'm here."

"Do you still want to know what I want?"

"Sure. Why not? I mean, since I've got you on the phone and all. It's kind of a big deal, talking to you. If the newkills could see me now…"

"I don't know what that means. Don't even care what that means. I'm interested in what you know about Nick Tate."

"Well, obviously, we're close. I'm standing in his house talking on his phone."

"Close… how?"

"All the ways, really. He's family to me."

And for some reason this provokes an uneasy silence from the infamous killer on the other end of the landline.

"Merc? Are you still with me?"

"So you've known him… how long?"

"Well." I pause to count. "Pretty much my entire life. You remember the Santa Barbara massacre?"

"I was *there*."

"Right. That's right. I think I knew that. I was there too. But I was only five, so I wasn't partaking in the killing that night. Obviously. I was on the superyacht. Nick ended up on the yacht too, and… we met. Few years later I was babysitting for him. He didn't take to single fatherhood immediately and he needed a backup. So I was backup. And then, of course, we've done lots of jobs together, so I've been his real backup on about… mmmm… lemme think.

Maybe… thirty jobs? Lots. I mean, maybe thirty jobs isn't a lot to someone like you, but I think thirty is kind of a big deal."

"Anything else?"

"If you want to know if we're fucking, eh. Sometimes we do that. But I'm not his girlfriend, if that's what you're wondering. He's not my boyfriend. That's not how we work. We are something much more than that."

"How do you two work? How important are you to him?"

A chill runs through my body. It's got to be ninety-five degrees outside and even though the AC is on, the front door is still open, so it's hot in here.

The chill is a warning.

Something is *wrong*.

Something is very, very wrong.

CHAPTER TWELVE

TODAY

"If you hurt her—"

But the call has dropped. There is nothing on the other end but empty silence.

"Fuck," I mutter. I'm outside the motel in the parking lot. There are a few people packing up cars, but other than that, there's no one around.

Where is he?

Somewhere close?

Somewhere far?

In this hotel right now?

If he's not here in the hotel, and he's coming here to meet me, will he bring Wendy with him? Or will he really leave her where she is? Does he have help? Will there be someone watching her?

I'm worried about this development.

Even back when I was technically 'alive,' I didn't really know Merc all that well. He was some random guy who ran in my circle. And, of course, he was part

187

of all that craziness that happened. But when I gifted him those three little Zero girls I didn't do it because I thought he'd be some kind of great father. I did it because I knew for a fact that he could control them and those girls were already connected to Sydney and Sydney was connected to him. I didn't really give a fuck about Merc's people skills that day, let alone his parental instincts.

But I give a lot of fucks about that shit right now.

Because I don't know what he's capable of these days. If he really does have Wendy under some kind of mind control, he could easily damage her.

But will he?

That's the question.

It's pretty clear that Merc has a big problem with me being alive. He has chosen sides. Sasha's side. And as far as he's concerned, I hurt her.

And I get it. I did hurt her. I take full responsibility for that. But I saved her too. Twice.

Actually, more than twice. I mean, I'm not counting or anything, but I had Sasha's back when we were kids. I always put her first. And what the fuck, ya know? I gave her my daughter.

This line of thinking will lead to daydreams about Lauren and I can't afford to lose focus now—not when we're deep inside the middle of things. So I push all thoughts of my girl away and just concentrate on what comes next.

Wendell and a room key.

I go back inside, get a room and text the number to Merc, and then I lock myself in there. I pull the blackout curtains closed and figure whatever plan Merc has for me, he's put a lot of thought in to it. Because the first time I broke Sasha's heart—and trust—I left her in a hotel room a lot like this one.

I woke her up that morning. "What do you want?" That's what I said. And even though her mouth replied, "Pancakes," that wasn't what her heart said.

Her heart said, *You, Nick. I want you. I'm your promise, you're my promise, and we're going to do this together.*

I know that's what she was thinking because that's basically what she told me like ten seconds before I asked her if she was hungry.

And then I got cruel. For the first time I felt compelled to set her straight. Nothing like the meanness that came later. It was just a little sneak peek. And, in my defense, leaving her in that Wyoming motel room was my way of saying goodbye. *Here, kid. Have four hundred dollars and a stack of pancakes. See ya in another life.*

But I knew what her next move would be.

And when Sasha Cherlin—being that she is Sasha Cherlin—caught up to me in Santa Barbara, she brought an army with her.

Not that kind of army.

A very violent cartel kind of army.

A shiver runs up my spine when I picture it in my head. Because the ones who lived through that night— well, we didn't exactly become friends. I would not call what they did to me friendly. But those men were all I had for a while.

I look around the room, logging all the things one finds in a cheap motel room like this. The king-sized bed, the long dresser with a mirror, the TV on the dresser, the tiny microwave, the little fridge, the single-serving coffeemaker. There are the two mandatory nightstands with the two mandatory lamps and the mandatory phone on one and the mandatory alarm clock on the other.

Then my eyes swing over to the table and chairs in front of the window. It's like motel owners have some kind of industry floor plan for where they put the furniture because I have never seen the table and chairs on the side of the room where the bathroom is. I have never seen the bed under the window, either.

Maybe that's something cool about motel rooms. They are comfy because they are predictable.

I pause here to think about that.

Maybe that's why Wendy won't give in to me?

Am I not predictable enough?

Is she not able to be comfy with me?

All this rumination about the room is not even the point. Because I'm not worried about the table, or the phone, or the single-serving coffeemaker. I'm looking at the pen and little pad of paper sitting in the middle of the table.

I walk over there, take a seat, and then reach out and drag the little pad over to me.

It's a familiar pad. It's white and there is a vintage truck with the word 'Americana' printed in retro letters across the top. Underneath that is all the business details. Address, phone, web, etc.

I pick up the pen and have another flashback of that day with Sasha in the Wyoming motel.

I wrote her a letter. I like writing letters. So I left her a note with the pancakes and four hundred dollars. It said,

Dear Sash, I'm so sorry. But you and Harper—you two are the only reason I'm doing this. And if I took you with me, I'd be just as bad as my father. I'd be just as bad as James. I'm coming back, don't worry. I paid the room up for two weeks and I'll be back. I'll find you a home, Sasha. I swear. You're gonna have that life I told you about. Just stay here. Don't call anyone. Don't leave. Just please, stay here so I know you're safe. I can't be your promise, it's wrong. But you're the only girl I've ever wanted. I hope you know that. Nick.

The only way I could've handled that worse was if I had written the note on a napkin.

Is it any wonder that Wendy doesn't trust me with her heart? Can I blame her when something like this is out there floating in the wind? And OK, I know, what are the chances that Wendy knows anything about this note I left for Sasha? Zero, right?

Wrong.

Wendy is like a bloodhound. She can sniff out information like a fucking dog on track. She doesn't even have to try hard. When Wendy Gale has a question, answers quake in their boots. This is why people hire her. This is why everyone knows her. Indie was right. About that, at least. Wendy is *connected*.

I look at the pen in my hand. 'Americana' is splashed along the white plastic barrel in candy-apple red. Another piece of cheap promo material.

And now I have everything I need.

So I begin.

Dear Wendy,

I am so sorry for not understanding what you really needed from me all these years. But I get it now. You know that, right? I proved it last Christmas? And I know that you can take care of yourself, but I would like to put it on record that if Merc hurts you—he's done. I don't give a fuck how many kids—

I pause, then rip that piece of paper off, crumple it up, and throw it at the little trashcan, always next to the microwave.

Then I take a deep breath, let it out, and start again…

Dear Wendy,

Do you remember what it felt like when you came home last Christmas?

I pause again. But this time I do it so I can smile and conjure up the memory for myself.

There was snow on the ground, a chill in the air, and a queasiness in my stomach I almost mistook for the flu—until I realized it was nerves.

I was nervous.

This was the make-or-break moment for Wendy and me. I was putting shit out there. I had the whole grand gesture planned. By the time we left the cabin we'd know two things for certain.

One. Whether or not we'd ever see each other again.

And two. Whether or not we could forgive each other again.

Funny, though. Right now I don't actually know the answer to number one even though I know the answer to number two. Because she stayed all week. We got over things. We started new things. We forgave each other.

But this whole 'little girl shoots Donovan Couture in the head with a dart gun and sends him into a psychotic coma' kinda put a kink in things. Wendy and I aren't even supposed to meet up again until her birthday, which is a little less than two weeks away.

It's also kinda curious that I even know she's missing. Because I have gone years without seeing or talking to Wendy Gale and never thought she needed help. I never looked for her. I always gave her space.

But this time, everything is different.

She's not avoiding me, she's trapped.

And I felt it.

I knew it.

Even before I called Adam. Even before I heard about Donovan. Even before I knew he wasn't dead.

I *knew* we'd end up here.

I rip the piece of paper off the pad and try for a third time.

Dear Wendy,

Can you blame him for snatching you up and taking you prisoner? If this summer didn't work out, trust me, babe—I was gonna kidnap your ass myself.

Because you're just that kind of girl, Wen. You are the kind of girl I want to tie up. You are the kind of girl I want to collar, and leash, and handcuff.

I want to own you. Because I want to hold on to you. Because life without you isn't worth the fucking hassle.

See ya on the other side,

Nick

I fold the note up into fours, then again until it's a stubby square between my fingers. Then I unfold it, straighten it out on the table, then fold it again, this time in half. I don't like pristine paper. A note like this deserves a proper history.

Then I leave the room, go to the lobby, hit Wendell up for an envelope, stuff the note inside, seal it up, and then place it in Wendell's open palm. "You know what to do," I tell him.

And he winks. Because he does.

I go back to my room and prepare for Merc.

Because now this shit is real.

We are *all* part of Central Casting.

And if I want the happily ever after, I need to play my part.

CHAPTER THIRTEEN

TODAY

I end the call and stare at the phone in my hand, taking a moment to appreciate what just happened. Nick Tate is alive. I just talked to him and in a couple of hours, I'm going to be face to face with this guy.

I'm not sure how I feel about that.

But there's no time to work it out. I push through the door, cross the yard, and watch Harrison tuck his phone away into a pocket on the thigh of his cargo pants.

He's an old guy now but for some reason, he still looks the same to me. Same neatly trimmed white beard, same athletic build, same tanned and weathered face. He's been living in the Keys running a private jet service for rich assholes almost this whole time. And he's come a long way from that little plane he used to cart us around in. He's got a whole fleet of them now. And some are big enough to fly all the way to Australia.

But this little jet sitting in the middle of the lonely dirt road today was chosen for speed. I can't be away long. Only a few hours. Mount Pleasant is about a thirty-minute flight from where we're at right now. Then I imagine it'll take about an hour to work things out with Nick, and I can be back here in three hours, tops.

It'll be OK.

My phone buzzes an incoming text. *Room 17.*

Perfect timing. "You ready?" Harrison asks as I approach.

I nod. "Let's go."

"You're gonna fill me in on the way? Because this whole thing is starting to look a little too much like the old days for my comfort level, Merc."

"I'll fill you in. But I want you to go in without this explanation, Harrison. I just want your honest take on it when it's over."

"Don't want me to overthink it, huh?"

"Right."

We get in the jet, he does his pilot shit, and ten minutes later we're in the air.

Harrison doesn't ever talk much when he's flying, and this little jet is kinda loud, which discourages conversation, so I spend the entire flight just staring out the window. Nothing but farms and the occasional town. But Mount Pleasant has a proper small airport, so when we land, it's not on a dirt road, it's a real runway.

It takes longer than I remember to get shit situated with the plane and I realize I didn't factor this in when I calculated how long I'd be gone. Typically, I don't wait around for the details of landing. That's Harrison's job. But I want him with me when we meet up with Nick. I need his take on things. I need to know if I'm doing this right, because I'm not sure I am.

He knows Sasha. He's been on her side for a long time now. So he's gonna see things from that perspective. I need that because right now I'm being pulled in a couple different directions.

On the one hand, I have my family. My girls.

On the other, Sasha.

And then, of course, there's Adam and his little request. Which I was pretty sure I wanted nothing to do with just a couple of days ago, but now... it's starting to feel inevitable.

And that's a little bit... maybe exciting is the wrong word. But then again, maybe it's not.

It's been a long time since I did a job. I'm not worried about my skills. I'm good. If anyone can unfuck this Donovan guy, it's me. I'm not worried about performance. But I am a little bit worried about how this all *feels*.

I didn't realize I was gonna feel this way until I found Wendy and things started falling into place. But I do. I miss this life. My girls are growing up. Daphne is almost sixteen. She's thinking about college and boys. She wants to move to Fort Collins for her senior year of high school. Kinda slide into a more normal life before she leaves us for adulthood.

And I'm OK with that. She's worked hard to be the girl she is today. She earned her chance at a more normal-looking life.

But then Avery isn't far behind. Just a couple years and she's gone too. Then my baby, Lily. It just went by so fast and I don't know what life without the girls looks like. Will Sydney want a job? Will we move into town? Buy a timeshare somewhere?

Will we be normal?

That's my question. Because I don't want to be normal. I've never been normal and I'm not just OK with this, I love it. I like living on the edge of society. Because I miss it. And maybe it doesn't feel good, exactly. But this sense of anticipation I feel is a little bit intoxicating. We've been safe for so long. No one tried to kill us. It feels a little bit like no one even cared.

I can try to convince myself that it's a one-off. A little spice in my life, so to speak. Then back to civil domestication. Except this kind of spice comes with serious consequences and I know I should be worried about that but... yeah. I have issues.

The best way to handle this—I figure, anyway—is for me to go unfuck this Donavan character and get it out of my system.

So I guess my internal dilemma is—will this Donovan job be an epilogue to a life that's over? Or the beginning of a whole new story?

I sigh to myself as I wait for Harrison to sign some papers in the airport office, then turn away from him and shove my hands into my pants pockets.

I've spent this whole week lying to myself. I need all the intel so I can keep everyone safe.

But that's a lie. We're not in any danger. Whatever is happening with this Adam guy and his friend Donovan, it's got nothing to do with me. I am a service provider. When it's over, and Donovan is fixed, if that's the right word, I will go home and my perfect life with Sydney and the girls will resume.

So. I'm doing this because I like it. One last job before retirement.

Wasn't that what I said last time?

Harrison finishes up and points to the little terminal as he approaches. "There's a taxi line over there."

I nod and join him as we walk. And sure enough, out front, there is a taxi line. No taxis, but there's a sign that says 'line starts here' and a Ford truck sitting at the curb which ends up being our ride.

It's a two-minute drive to the Americana. We could've walked. But that would've taken twenty minutes and I'm already starting to get nervous about being away so long.

It was a mistake. I knew it when I made the decision. But I need to look Nick Tate in the eyes before I give him what he wants. I need to hear the whole story. I want the entire ten years spelled out for me and I don't want him to feel too comfortable while he's doing that.

We get dropped off at the front of the motel and I pay the driver cash. When the old truck pulls away, Harrison and I just look at each other for a moment.

"What?" he asks. "What's going on, Merc? Why are we here?"

I let out a long breath as I scan the line of doors, stopping to stare when I get to seventeen. "There's someone in room seventeen I need to meet up with."

"OK. You want me to hang here?"

"No. You gotta see this." I direct my gaze back to Harrison. "I'm gonna ask you for some advice tomorrow."

"Tomorrow?" He kinda laughs.

"Yeah."

"Why not today?"

"Because I think we'll feel different about it tomorrow."

He palms his neatly trimmed beard as he thinks. An old habit, one I rather like. "OK. I guess whatever is waiting for us in room seventeen requires processing time?"

"Exactly."

"Got it. Do we need guns?"

I pat my thigh pocket. "I got a little .380, but no. I don't think we need guns."

"All right. Let's do this."

I nod, thinking I'm ready. But then I get a sick feeling in my stomach. Like this is one of those defining moments.

"Merc?"

"I'm fine," I say. "Let's go." And then, before I can change my mind, I head towards room seventeen. I knock once. It takes four seconds for Nick to open the door. And those seconds go by way too fast. Because there he is. Right in front of me. The dead man himself.

"What the—" That's Harrison. He doesn't finish his sentence.

Nick glances at Harrison, kinda looks him up and down, then focuses on me. "Merc." He opens the door wide and steps aside.

I move forward, but Harrison has my arm. "Wait. Am I seeing—"

"Yes," I say, cutting him off. "You're seeing this right. Nick Tate, meet Harrison. I'm sure you've seen him around."

Nick extends his hand, like Harrison might actually shake it.

Harrison does not shake it. He says, "What the actual—"

But I cut him off again. "Inside, Harrison. That discussion will happen behind a closed door."

Harrison looks over his shoulder and lets out a breath. Then he looks me in the eyes and gets it. Part of it, anyway. Not all of it. But enough.

We go in, Nick closes the door, and then he turns to me. "Nice to see you again, Merc. I wish it were under better circumstances. Where's Wendy?"

"If things go well, you and Wendy will be reunited in about an hour and a half."

He glances at a clock on the bedside table then scrubs his hands down his face. "What do you want?"

"What do I *want*?" I look at Harrison and almost laugh. Harrison isn't looking at me. He's staring at the ghost in front of us.

"What the fuck is this?" Harrison asks, finally getting to finish a sentence. "You're dead. I saw your dead fucking body in that FBI safehouse."

"That was his twin," I explain. "So he says."

"Your twin? Your fucking—" Harrison turns to me. "What is going on?"

But when I answer him, I'm looking at Nick. "That's what we're here to find out. I want the whole story, Nick. From that moment we left you on the beach to this one right here—"

Nick scoffs. "That's like a whole novel of shit."

But I put a hand up. "Make it a short story. You've got twenty minutes. Then we're back in the air. Wendy won't keep forever."

Nick's face goes hard. "What the fuck does that mean?" He looks the same and utterly different all at once. He's still got that golden-boy persona, but it's not the first thing you see anymore. It's hidden now. His hair is a little too long and it's not surfer blond the way it was when he was a teenager.

His brown eyes seem a little darker than before, but that's probably just the shadows in the dimly lit room. Because the way I remember them, they were golden too. He's tan, well-muscled, and tall. Nearly as tall as I am, which is a change. The last time I saw him, he was eighteen and not nearly this big. He's wearing a black t-shirt, a pair of black tactical pants, boots, also black, and a watch. Not the smart kind because it's got hands.

His whole I'm-a-mercenary look aside, he comes off pretty normal.

I wasn't in Kansas when Sasha shot his twin. I didn't see any of that. I was only brought in after it was all over and that was just to pick up my girls. So for me, there is no disconnect with the way he looks. But Harrison is having problems.

"You're not him," Harrison says.

Nick smiles indulgently. "I'm Nick. Trust me. That guy you saw in Kansas was my twin."

Harrison squints his eyes, trying to decide if he's telling the truth.

"He's telling the truth," I say. Then I look back at Nick. It *is* Nick. There is no doubt. I mean, I didn't really have any doubts about his identity coming here—there were all those clues—but it's good to know definitively that this is the same kid I knew all those years ago. "We don't have much time—"

"Why? Why don't we have much time?" Nick is agitated. "Where the fuck is Wendy?"

"The sooner you start talking, the sooner you'll be reunited with her."

Nick turns his back to me.

It's a mistake. Not that I have any plans to attack him, I don't. But he should know better.

He turns back around quickly, like he's reading my mind and this thought just occurred to him as well. "Where do you want me to start? And don't say the beginning. This is not a twenty-minute story. It's thirty-eight years, Merc. The beginning starts with the day I was born. The Company isn't an organization, it's a *plan*. And what I'll tell you is just my role in the plan. The whole thing? That's a thousand years old, at least."

Harrison huffs and Nick turns on him. Fast. His reflexes are no joke. He's not a kid anymore, but he's a lot younger than both me and Harrison.

"You think that's fuckin' funny?" Nick snarls. And finally, the man I was expecting shows up. "I don't really know who you are—" Nick puts up a hand when Harrison begins to fill him in. "Oh, I know what you *do* for them." He nods his chin at me, indicating I'm part of 'them'. "You're the pilot. You've been around a long time. I get that, Harrison. But you don't know shit about how this world works." Nick's gaze rotates over to me now. "And neither do you. You saw a lot, Merc. Hell, you *did* a lot. Much more than any other outsider in the history of the Company, that's for sure. But you don't know why you were doing it. You have no clue."

"So fill me in," I say. "That's why we're all here, Nick. Tell us why you had to break Sasha's heart. Tell us how that pain benefits the Company. Because you're still in, aren't you? It didn't go away, did it? And sure, I'll admit that I'm out of the fucking loop. By choice," I growl. "But that just means you're *in* the loop by choice as well."

Nick's laugh is loud. "Judge me? Really? That's what you're gonna do here? I talked to Indie, Merc. I know what this is about. Donovan, right? Or should I say *Carter*? You're trying to decide if Adam Boucher is gonna kill you and your family if you don't help him out with his little problem. That's why you're here. That's why you have Wendy. But you should know, Wendy is loved. Adam might hate me, but not Wendy. She is our Sasha."

It takes all my learned self-control not to hit him when those words come out of his mouth. I rage inside for almost five full seconds. But when I finally speak, I am calm. "Our Sasha? Is Wendy the new pet, Nick? You got big plans for her, huh? Is that why you're so mad? You need her to kill you—"

He hits me and then there's no going back.

We fight.

CHAPTER FOURTEEN

I've had enough of Merc and we've only been face to face for about sixty seconds. But I've been watching him this whole time. I've seen him. I know him far better than he knows me, that's for sure. And somewhere along the line in these past nine and a half years since I've been officially dead, I decided that I don't like Merc.

He's not one of us.

He cannot be trusted.

And now he wants my secrets if I want Wendy back?

My fist hits his jaw hard. Merc's head spins a little and I'm just about to gloat about that when his knuckles deliver an uppercut under my chin. My teeth crash together, the vibration hard enough to shake my brain. Then... fuck if I know what happens. It all goes way too quick to do a blow-by-blow.

We wind up on the floor between the bed and the little table.

Harrison kicks us apart. "OK, OK! That's enough. Get up. This isn't getting anything accomplished."

He's wearing pointy-toe cowboy boots, so it's effective. Besides, the pressure between Merc and me has been released. Not eradicated, but we needed this little tussle in order to get past the anger and feelings of betrayal.

I get to my feet wiping blood away from my lip. "You think I'm not pissed?" I snarl at him. "You think I wanted any of this? Is that what you think, Merc?"

He's back on his feet too. There's a cut along his left brow where my ring caught him just the right way, so he's busy wiping blood out of his eye. "You wanted it enough to keep it going, right? Because it is still going, right?"

"Do you really think the Company is ever going away? No. Dude. It's a thousand years old. It's not going anywhere. Do you have any idea how many people are involved? Easily two hundred thousand. And I'm not talking before we killed most of them off a few years back. I'm talking right fucking now, Merc. They are cockroaches. They breed. There are whole towns, villages, hell, even cities that are nothing but Company. They don't even *know* they're Company. That's how fucked up it all is."

"How do they not know? That's fucking stupid. They know. They get money——"

"They get money from *jobs*, Merc. Think about it. Put yourself in their place for a moment. You are born into a small town. You grow up there. Maybe you leave for college, but more than likely you don't. You were not bred with that kind of desire. So you stay where you are. You marry your high school girlfriend. You get a job at the bank, or the real estate office, or maybe you even own a dealership. And let's get this straight, that's best-case scenario, most of them end up on drugs because their minds can't comprehend what's happening around them."

"What do you mean what's happening around them?" Harrison says. "Because what you're describing sounds an awful lot like the place I grew up."

"Harrison," I sneer. "You're a fucking pilot. People in these towns, they work dead-end jobs. They get drunk at night. They wake up, they do it again. They don't learn to *fly planes*. Towns like this have three classes of Company people. The ones who own Company businesses and *know* they own Company businesses. Dealerships. Banks. Real estate offices. Places where large sums of money get exchanged on the daily. Then you have the middle class. Business owners who think they're in charge, but aren't. Restaurant and bar owners. Corner stores. Garages. They exist to keep the third class happy. And the third class is everyone else. And I do mean that literally. People who know they have no power at all, they just follow orders. Cops. Mayors. City Council members. Teachers. Secretaries. Mechanics. Plumbers. Retail. Working class, get it?"

Merc doesn't look impressed with my revelations. "What's your fucking point?"

"I'm trying to explain how big this shit is. How pervasive they really are. An entire town can be owned, Merc. And ninety percent of them never even know about it. Because the Company is careful. They only take what they need. They breed those kids—"

"What the fuck are you talking about? I own a fleet of planes in a town just like the one you're describing. And I'm not on any Company payroll." Harrison is getting pissed. And I don't blame him. It's a lot for this guy. He's not Company. He's not Merc, either. Sure, he's seen some shit, but that was a long time ago.

"Congratulations. You *don't* live in a Company town. But just because you're not part of it doesn't mean it's fake."

Merc snaps his fingers to get my attention. "Get to the fucking point. I don't need a history lesson."

"History lesson? Is that what you think this is? You think, what, Adam is some… stupid leftover? He's not. He's not doing any of the shit I'm talking about here because he's not evil. Not like that, anyway. But he knows about it. They breed them, Merc. There is no way to stop it. They need them. All of them. All ages, all races, both sexes."

"Need them for what?" Harrison says.

I actually laugh. "Organs."

"Oh, fuck you," Harrison says. "That's all bullshit. There is no underground organ trade. There are no Russians drugging people in Vegas and removing their kidneys while they sleep."

"You're right," I say. "That's not how it's done. I just *told* you how it's done. Small towns in the USA and Europe for the premium stock. But there are thousands of villages all over the world where the same thing is happening, minus the secrecy."

Harrison huffs and looks over at Merc. "Are you falling for this shit? I mean, I don't know where he's going with it, but—"

Merc's low, solemn voice cuts him off. "It's not bullshit."

"What?" Harrison is in complete denial. "Come on—"

"I've seen it."

"Where?"

Merc looks at me and something inside him deflates. "Do you know what I was doing? Before the girls, I mean. Before Sydney?"

"PSYOPS," I say.

"Sure. Yeah. But it was more than that." He looks over at Harrison. "I was on a team. We hunted…" His eyes dart over and meet mine. "The runaways. They weren't… for harvest."

"*Harvest?*" Harrison is gonna lose his shit. We might need to knock him out if he wigs.

"Harrison," I say. "Shut up. Listen to what we're telling you." I look over at Merc. "You shouldn't have brought him here."

Harrison takes a step towards me and then with two flat hands to my chest he pushes me back. "Don't talk like I'm not here. Just because I need a minute to grasp the idea that an entire population of people exist for something called a *harvest* doesn't mean I'm a dumbass."

"Fine." I put up my hands in surrender. "Then I'll stop fucking around and get to the point." I look at Merc. "You have no idea what's really going on in this world. Adam keeps the whole thing manageable. He hunts them down now."

Merc's eyebrow shoots up. "Them?"

"Not you. Well, if *were* still working for those assholes, he would kill you. But you're not important, Merc. Not in his mind. He's looking for stragglers. He's looking for those dealership owners. Those small-town bankers. That's who he's after. The ones who didn't get the 'cure.'" I do air quotes for that word because it was never meant to be a cure at all. And that's why I'm fucking here in the first place. That's why Wendy is in Merc's clutches right now. And I'm so tired of that goddamn word, I wish I never had to speak it out loud again.

"The cure?" Harrison asks. "The cure for what?"

"It's not important," I say. "It wasn't a cure."

Merc sighs. "I'm still failing to see any points here."

"Wrong," I say. "You had a point. You said they weren't for harvest. The people you were hunting. Who were they?"

Merc takes a moment to wipe a fresh trail of blood away from his left eye. "The mothers. The ones who ran." He looks at Harrison. "People like Sasha's mom. Harper's mom. The upper elite women who thought they'd be able to make that choice—"

"The promise or death," I say for him.

"Yeah. Most of them," Merc continues, "they just gave up. The way you describe the lower class in the Company towns."

"The druggies," I say. "The drunks and the criminals."

"Right," Merc agrees. "Most of the mothers were like that too. They gave up long before they started having babies." He looks back to Harrison. "When these elite women give birth, and they have a girl, they either send them right back into the Company as assassins, like Sydney, who are used, and abused, and sent on missions—"

"Like Sasha?" Harrison asks.

"No," Merc and I say at the same time.

"Not like her," I say. "Her mother took the other choice. Which is self-sacrifice. Her mother died minutes after she gave birth so that Sasha could be free—like Harper. So she could grow up to be someone's *promise*."

Merc's voice goes low. "Married off to another elite. Most of the time a very old man who wants one more chance at a boy."

"What the fuck?" Harrison says. "Why do the mothers have to die? I don't get it."

"So they can harvest them," I say.

"For what? Hearts and shit?"

"Whatever is needed. Skin. Eyes. Organs. Fucking toes. All of it. But more importantly, they have to die so they can keep the masses in check with fear. The Company controls people with fear."

Merc sighs. "And it works."

"Like a fucking charm," I agree.

Harrison makes a face. "That's sick."

Whatever. "This is the world we live in, Harrison."

"The world *you* live in. Not me."

"Newsflash, buddy. We *run* the world you live in. We *let* you exist here. But make no mistake. I don't care how many jets you own, you step one inch over that line, Harrison, they will kill you without even blinking."

"This Adam guy, you mean?"

"No, Merc. Fuck's sake, man. Aren't you listening to me? Not Adam. He's cleaning up, remember?"

"Then who are you talking about?" Merc is annoyed. And I don't blame him. If he was selling *me* this line of shit, I'd be annoyed too.

But I don't answer him right away. I have to be really careful what I say here. Everything depends on how I handle the next couple minutes. One wrong move and everything goes sideways.

Merc gets impatient. "Who? Tell me now."

"Well, this answer is gonna complicate things a bit."

"Why's that?" Harrison asks.

"Because." I look straight at Merc. "That guy— Donovan? Rather, his dominant personality, Carter?"

"Oh, fuck this." Merc's not dumb. He doesn't need this shit spelled out for him. "Fuck this. I'm not doing it." He grabs Harrison's arm and tugs him towards the door. "Let's go home."

"Listen," I say loudly. Merc and Harrison both pause in front of the door. But neither of them looks back at me. "You can walk out. That's fine. But Donovan is worth saving. He is, Merc."

Merc looks over his shoulder at me. "Why's that?"

"Because he's…" I pause, having trouble forcing the words out.

"He's what?" Merc does turn now. "Spit it out, Nick. Or I'm leaving."

I put up my hand in surrender. "OK. But do not kill the messenger."

He sucks in a breath and his eyes narrow down. "Tell me."

"Carter Couture, he's the father."

"The father of who?"

"Come on, Merc. Who do you think?" He knows what I'm saying, he just doesn't want to believe it. Cognitive dissonance, man. It fucks with you hard. "Daphne," I say. "Avery. Lily."

I expect an outburst from Merc, but he goes pale and silent. Then, a couple seconds later, his one-word response is a whisper. "What?"

"You heard me. Turns out Carter Couture kind of... kinda made himself... I mean, what's the right word for it? Patriarch? He bred them, Merc. All those upper-class Company women. He took that whole 'spread your seed' thing literally. He's got about..." I pause to mentally calculate how many kids are in his bloodline now. "Maybe... fifty or sixty little Zero kids running around out there right now. And by Zero kids, I don't mean girls. He never culled the boys, either, Merc. They're out there too."

"This is who Adam's cleaning up?"

"Yeah... no. Me, actually. I'm the one cleaning up that fucking mess. Adam doesn't even know about it yet. He's still mucking about with the small-town bankers. This is what I've been doing since Sasha killed Santos. This is what *I've* been up to, friend. Sasha gets to live, Lauren gets to live, and I get to clean up the fucking mess. That was the deal. So you can hate me all you want, I'm just doing the best I can."

"OK. Hold on." Harrison is back in action. I knew he would be. "Who cares?" He looks up at Merc, grabs him by the shirt, tugs. "Who gives a fuck? Let that asshole die, right?"

"Just let him die," I agree. "That's an option." Merc drags his gaze away from Harrison and looks at me, real fear in his eyes now, because he knows I'm holding something back. I wouldn't be telling him this if there wasn't a catch. And there is. There is always a catch. Always a wors*er*-case scenario peeking around the corner in the life of a Company man. "You can let

213

him die, but your girls were part of the program, Merc. You *know* that."

He shakes his head. "They're just fine." And these words come out confident and with authority. "They're better than fine. They're great. Well-adjusted girls. There has been—"

"Hey." I cut him off. "I'm not here to evaluate your girls. That's your problem. They're not on my list. What I'm here to tell you is—and you already know this—they're *not* fine, Merc. They're not fine because they are part Untouchable. They are me, Merc. They are Harper, they are James, they are Vincent, they are Santos, they are Adam. They are *us*. Well, half us. Who knows who the mothers were. The point is, Donovan—I mean, Carter. Fuck. Even I get confused about that shit. Carter, he's got a crew, Merc. He's been breeding little girls for his own personal Zero program for fifteen years now. They're everywhere. But that's not the point, either. The point is… the point is, Merc… girls like them, they don't live long lives."

Merc goes silent but Harrison is still with me. "But Sasha," he says. "And Lauren."

"And Harper." Merc is nothing but predictable right now. I got him off his game because he falls right into the trap.

"Sasha isn't from the Zero bloodline. Lauren isn't either, because I'm not actually from the Zero bloodline either." I point to my eyes. "Brown. They're brown, not blue. My father wasn't my father." Merc looks completely confused. "I'm not the Admiral's real son. None of us are the Admiral's real children. He did this on purpose. Everyone knew this."

"Not everyone," Harrison says.

"He doesn't count," I tell Harrison, nodding my head to Merc. "What Merc knows never mattered. He was hired help. You think you know things, Merc, because you've got three little Company girls living in your house and tamed a Company girl once upon a time? But you don't know shit about how my world works."

Now he's back. Pissed. "So fill me in. You're what? Some kind of lesser evil because you've got brown eyes instead of blue?"

The laugh comes out of my mouth before I can stop it. "Not exactly."

"Not exactly what? Spell it out for me, Nick. I'm tired of this game you're playing. And what does eye color have to do with anything, anyway?"

"Eye color has everything to do with it. Because those blue eyes, they come with a certain gene that helps control them. The girls?" I say. Because Merc already looks confused.

"Right. I get that part. But what about James? He doesn't have blue eyes either."

I point at Merc. "Good observation. No. James and Vincent do not have blue eyes. Same way I don't. Or Harper and Santos. They did experiments on this in the Seventies. I don't understand the science, so don't ask me how they know this shit, but certain behaviors can be tied to the gene that expresses eye color. They did all the combinations. Blue, green, brown and… hazel."

Merc shrugs. "OK. So? What happened?"

"Not much, actually. The blue eyes were desirable, obviously. Because in girls, at least, it toned down the insanity. Didn't work that way for the men, that's why the Company stopped breeding boys for the Zero program. What we have now, with these blue-eyed Zero girls, that's as controllable as they come. With either careful or sloppy breeding they come out like Sasha. See, Sasha wasn't a real Zero. She was a mix. Sloppy breeding saved Sasha. She and Lauren, they're the only sloppy examples that I know of though."

Merc doesn't say anything, but I can hear all the questions in his mind. *What about my girls? Were they carefully bred?*

It's Harrison who asks the question. "What's this got to do with Daphne, Avery, and Lily?"

"Don't forget baby Hannah," I add. Because I need Merc to understand that he's not alone in this. We're *on the same side.*

Merc isn't looking at me. He's staring blankly at the curtains covering the hotel window. "Hannah, huh." He looks at me. "What about Angelica?"

"She's a real Zero. That's why we were hunting her that year. She was *very* carefully bred. Like this Indie girl that Adam has. Like Wendy too."

Merc's eyes narrow down into slits. "Spit it out, Nick. What are you not saying?"

"I already told you. Your girls came from Carter Couture's program. They were carefully bred, but not in the same way. Carter was looking for a more... pliable... version, I guess you'd call it."

"Pliable, as in—"

"Easily manipulated."

Merc lets out a breath. "OK. So that's good, right? They've got the blue eyes and they've conformed. They don't act out, Nick. They're not like that. They're good kids."

I put up my hands again. "I'm not hunting your girls, Merc."

"Then why are you telling me all this?"

"Because I think you and Carter Couture need to have a conversation about it. Or one day you might wake up to something very unexpected. You and I both know you're gonna help Adam save Donovan. But just in case you get cold feet, I want you to know you've got something to lose if he dies as well. Now." I pause to suck in a deep breath. "Where the fuck is Wendy?"

CHAPTER FIFTEEN

NOT SURE WHAT DAY IT IS
NOT SURE ABOUT ANYTHING RIGHT
NOW BECAUSE...

Something is wrong.

Wrong? No. That's not the right word. The sick feeling in my stomach is familiar. I know it well. It's the signal that I missed a very important detail and now I'm about to pay the price for this fuckup.

"Wendy."

I feel like time has somehow... skipped. But I'm still on the phone with Merc and his voice is stern now. Commanding.

"Answer my question."

I don't even remember the question. I feel like an eternity has gone by since we last spoke. But it doesn't matter. I wouldn't be answering it, even if I did. I slam the phone back into the cradle and spin around. And then take a good, long look at Nick's house.

It looks the same. I mean… I recognize the dishes in the sink. The curtains. The old table in the middle of the kitchen. The view outside. That all looks right.

I turn and go into the living room, scanning it with a critical eye. Couch, coffee table, more curtains. The wood floors, the rugs, even pillows. It's all… *right*.

But nothing about this is right.

The phone rings, but I do not pick it up. Instead I walk into Nick's bedroom and flip on the lights. Everything looks the way I remember. When he left here, whenever that was, he didn't make his bed. That's typical. So I feel good about the mess of sheets. When I open the closet, I find a familiar laundry basket filled with dirty clothes beneath t-shirts hanging from a rod and jeans and tactical pants stacked on shelves to my right. There are boots on the floor.

This is Nick. Everything about this closet says Nick.

But something is *wrong* here.

Didn't I just check this room before the phone call? And wasn't it empty? And there were no dishes in the sink. Just a few minutes ago—was it a few minutes ago?—no one was living here. And now…

Yeah. Something is definitely wrong with this place.

I leave the room, flipping the lights off as I pass through the door, and I go to the second room. The one I refer to in my head as the control room. The locked room. The room I've never been in.

I don't think about it, I just kick in the door. The door jamb splits easily and this isn't my first clue, but this is the one where my situation starts to become real.

The phone stops ringing.

I enter the room and find it empty.

Of course it's empty.

I have no idea what's in this room. I've never been in this room. But I do know that I should not be able to kick it open with almost no effort because Nick keeps important things in this room.

Maybe guns. Maybe computers. Maybe files and cabinets to hold them.

These are all good guesses and just as they enter my mind, they appear in the room with me.

Fuck, fuck, fuck. Do not panic, Wendy. You don't know anything yet. Do not jump to conclusions.

I'm good at what I do. Damn fucking good at what I do. But I can't stop the instincts that kick in when the reality of my situation starts to hit me. So I force myself to pause. I plant my hands on my hips, look down at my brown boots, and start talking myself out of a fucking heart attack.

They trained you for this, Wendy.

You're trained. He's good, but he's not as good as you.

The silent pep talk in my brain isn't working because suddenly there is a sharp pain in my chest and I'm gasping for breath.

The phone rings again.

I do not answer it but the machine comes on and Merc's voice is loud. It booms through the house. "You're OK. Take deep breaths, Wendy. You're *juuuuust* fine. Nothing's gonna happen as long you keep your shit together, do you understand me?"

I'm still gasping, but keeping my shit together is an instinct at this point. So I close my eyes tight, block out his voice, and just breathe and count.

"Good. Now I want you to lie down on the couch—"

Fuck that. I make a break for the kitchen. I cross it, pull open the door, and I'm already bounding down the steps before he gets to the end of his sentence. I head straight for my truck—and then skid to a stop. Falling on my ass as my boots slide in the gravel.

"What the fuck? What the *FUCK!*"

"Wendy." Merc's voice is still loud and booming even though I'm outside and there is no way I should be able to hear the fucking answering machine from outside.

That doesn't even make sense, Wendy. It's an answering machine! It's not supposed to be a real-time two-way conversation!

OK. OK, calm down.

But I can't calm down and who cares about how the fucking answering machine works? I don't have time to think about that bullshit, because my truck is gone.

But it's not just my truck—it's everything. Everything is gone! The road is gone, the yard gone, the half-dead trees, the fields, the sunflowers, the sky *is gone!*

And in place of all that is… nothing.

"Wendy." Merc's voice is calm now. Low. Steady. "Can you hear me?"

No. This isn't happening. This isn't real. I did not fall into this trap. No. I would've seen it coming. I'm not the kind of girl you trap!

"Answer me. Now."

"Yes," I say. Even though I don't want to talk to this asshole, I feel compelled to do so. "I can hear you."

"Good. You're OK. Now close your eyes—"

"Where the fuck am I?"

"You're somewhere safe—"

"No! Where. The fuck. Am I? What the fuck is this place?"

"Close your eyes and I'll tell you."

My heart is pounding. And somewhere, like in some far-off place, some other reality, some other dimension, some other Wendy—I hear... beeping. Like a heart rate monitor.

"Close your eyes."

I close them.

"Good." His voice is soft now. Almost soothing. "I'm in your head, Wendy. But there's nothing to worry about because you're OK. I injected you with some drugs to knock you out two days ago. Where you are isn't as important as what I'm doing."

Holy fucking shit.

I am being mind-fucked by a psychopath Company PSYOPS agent. He picked me up *two days ago*? I'm asleep? Clearly, I am not asleep. I'm thinking. I'm walking around. I'm talking.

Aren't I?

I try to open my eyes but they feel like they are glued shut, or they are so damn heavy, it's not possible to open them.

I start gasping for breath again.

"Calm down. Everything is fine. You're gonna be fine. But you need to talk to me, Wendy. You need to answer my questions and give me what I want."

"What *do* you want?" But I already know. Before I'm even done talking, I know what he wants.

Nick. He wants Nick.

"That's right. You know what I want."

And now the whole mental delusion disappears. The shitty farmhouse is gone and everything around me is just black. "Wake me up. Wake me up now!"

"I don't think so. I like you… *still*. I watched you for about a week, Wendy. You're kinda dangerous."

"Says the asshole who's inside my mind."

"It's pretty good, right? I guess that's why this Adam guy wants me. Do you know Donovan?"

I don't answer him. Instead my mind flips back through time to training sessions with Chek when I was a kid. He told me about what these Company PSYOPS men could do, but it was all theoretical. There were no more PSYOPS agents in the Company to do defensive training with when I was growing up. Nonetheless, Chek was pretty thorough with his lessons. At least I thought he was. But this mental prison Merc has locked me in? Yeah. No one told me about this shit. I don't know what to do.

"All you have to do is answer me, Wendy. Don't bother fighting it. You're talking, sweetheart. None of your thoughts are private right now. You just said all of that out loud. You've been saying everything out loud. I heard your whole story. All those touching moments with Nick and Lauren. Christmases and birthdays—

Fuck. He's good.

"I'm very good. The best there is. And not just because I'm the last one left, either. Why do you think I'm still alive and the rest of them are dead?"

Well. If I were in charge of defunding the Company PSYOPS program, I'd have taken this asshole out first.

Merc laughs. "You're kinda fun, Wendy. It's been a long time since I fucked with someone like this. *Looooong* time. But I'm in a serious mood at the moment. People are popping back up in my life and I'm quite pissed off about that. I had a deal when I left. Kinda. I mean, no one really knew about this deal except for me, but there was an understanding, you see. They leave me the fuck alone, I leave them the fuck alone. But then I'm just kicking back at the pool last week and all of a sudden, names start spillin' out a friend's mouth. I don't know any of these names, but you do, right? You know who Adam is, right? So we're gonna start with him, because I give no fucks about that guy. He wants to get a hold of me, fine. I've got nothing against introductions. Who is Adam, Wendy?"

I don't wanna answer.

"I know you don't, sweetie. But you're *already* answering. And I'm not interested in hearing your complete internal monologue. We've been stuck on your relationship issues for two days now. Let's get past that shall we? Focus, please. Who is Adam?"

"He runs the Company."

"OK. But how did this happen? Last I heard, the Company fell almost a decade ago."

I snort-laugh.

"That's funny?"

"That's very funny."

"Explain."

"Well, I don't know you, but I've heard of you. So I know you were an ancillary part to that whole FBI black ops takedown in Kansas. I wasn't in Kansas, I was part of the Florida operation with Johnny Boston."

"OK. What's this all about?"

225

"The Bostons? They handled the Company money-laundering."

"Not the Bostons. I know who the Bostons are. What's that got to do with *Kansas*, Wendy?"

"It all went down at the same time. When Sasha was killing…"

"You can say it. I already know he's alive. We really are at his house right now."

"What?"

"Focus. While Sasha was killing whoever the fuck that guy was out in Kansas, you were…?"

"I was hooking up hidden cameras inside an estate crawling with Company elite so we could keep an eye on the kids we had to leave behind."

He pauses here, maybe thinking about that. What I just said isn't a lot of information and if he has no context, it doesn't make much sense to him.

"You're right. I don't know what you're talking about. Do I need to understand this part of the story?"

"Depends, I guess."

"On *what*?"

"Whether or not those girls of yours need a cure."

CHAPTER SIXTEEN

"You've got her at my house?"

I am a little bit impressed at this revelation. Also, Indie. That girl is either in on this—and I don't think she is because there is no point in that—or she's got a scary sense of intuition.

I need to keep her in mind should there be any backlash about what's happening right now.

Merc raises his hand. "Back up a minute. You said Carter Couture and I need to have a conversation or one day I might wake up to something very unexpected. What the fuck does that mean?"

I scrub my hands down my face and think about shaving when I get home. Then I think about home and how Wendy is already there. I'm slightly concerned about her condition right now, but it's no longer a nagging urgency like it was before Merc showed up. Also, I like that she's at my house. It's familiar. And it's not just my house anymore, is it? It's our house. Same way that her cabin is ours now too. This is kind of a best-case scenario in my opinion.

"Nick." Merc's voice is tense. He might even be a little scared. He should be scared. He thinks he got out. But it's really hard to get out. And if you've got skills the way he has skills, you're never really out, are you? And don't even get me started about those girls.

Merc is just about to walk over and grab me by the throat when I finally answer him. "Have you ever heard of something called the cure? And when I say 'cure,' imagine quotes around that word."

"Cure for what?" Harrison asks.

I need to be careful here. I don't want to say too much, but I can't afford to say too little, either.

Merc is clearly running out of patience because his next words are forced out through clenched teeth. "You heard him. Cure for *what?*"

"Have you heard of it?" I ask.

"Maybe."

"OK. I'm gonna take that as a yes. Did you drag it out of Wendy? Or did it pop up before you took her?"

"It came from her."

I nod. "All right. What did she say?"

"Never mind what she said. What do you have to say about it?"

"Ya know, I'm not gonna take it personal that you're getting all edgy with me, because I get it. When you hear the word 'cure' you think 'disease' and then 'death,' right? So I get it. I'd feel the same way if someone were talking about my daughter in conjunction with that word too."

"Nick. I swear to fucking God, I am not playing games here. Tell me what the fucking cure is."

"What it is? Well, that's a hard one. Let's start with the disease. Because we're all familiar with the disease. It's called the Zero Program, right? Babies are born, they grow into kids, and these kids turn into little killers. Now, do you remember, way back in the day when we were planning Santa Barbara, there was a discussion or two about Sasha and triggers?"

I think Merc actually forgot about this, because it takes him a couple moments. And then it's not even him who speaks. It's Harrison.

"Yeah," Harrison says. "I do remember that. But it was bullshit. Sasha never had a trigger."

"Nope. She never did. I'm like ninety-nine point nine-nine percent sure no one ever really fucked with Sasha's mind the way they might've—and I'm just using this as a 'for instance'—Angelica."

Merc lets out a breath. "Does James know about this?"

"Yeah. He does. He was part of some dark shit— as we are all aware—in his formative years. So even though I've never had any conversations with James about a trigger for Angelica, I'm sure he's kept it in mind."

"He never said anything to me. And maybe I don't see him regularly, but we've met up at least a dozen times over the years."

"I'm sure Angelica is fine," I say. And I mean this. "She's what, eighteen now? I hear she's got plans for college this fall. I think if it were a problem, it would've shown up by now."

"Wait," Harrison says. "This trigger. It's like... innate? Something genetic? Or it's outside stimulus?"

"No one knows, Harrison. Let's forget about Angelica and your girls for a moment. Let's talk about Indie Anna Accorsi."

Merc squints. "This is Adam's girl?"

"Correct. She *was* triggered."

"What?" That comes from Merc. Harrison actually gasps.

"One hundred percent. She's gone off script so many times, it's kind of a miracle she's still alive. She tried to kill Adam when she was sixteen. That same day everything was going down in Kansas he was talking to my brother Santos. And Santos warned him to get rid of her. Same day, Merc. He goes home, catches her with a boy, was gonna kick the boy's ass—as is his right—and she lost her mind for about two minutes. She *fucked* him up. I'm talking Adam was in the hospital for three months. Brain surgery and everything. He could barely walk when he woke up. Almost an entire year of PT to get back up to speed."

"What the fuck?" That's Harrison. Merc is silent.

"Then," I continue, "she tried to kill them *all* a few years later. Even McKay. And I get that you don't know her, but Adam didn't raise her alone. He brought her up as responsibly as he could. Better than you did your girls, that's for sure. And I'm not being disparaging here, Merc, because Adam did a helluva lot better than James too. He has a guy called McKay. A bonafide Company Zero trainer. He did all Indie's care and feeding through the years. And Adam had Donovan too. AKA Carter. Which, OK, fine. It was probably Donovan-slash-Carter who triggered Indie in the first place. But there's no way to know that for sure unless—"

"Unless I go in and pick apart his mind."

I point at him. "That's the logical conclusion, right? But that's not what Adam wants you for. No one really cares about Indie's trigger anymore. They think it's over. She bounced back. Kind of. She's stable now. No. Adam wants you to *kill* Carter, Merc. Kill Carter and save Donovan."

"But if we kill Carter," Harrison says, "then we lose the guy who has all the information."

I point at him. "I never thought you were a stupid man, Harrison. But I have seriously underestimated you over the years."

"Thanks?" He smiles at me. And I figure this is going way better than I could've hoped. I mean, I was kinda worried about explaining all this to people who, for all intents and purposes, have no real clue about what the Company actually is.

But they are following along quite well.

Harrison, obviously. Since he likes to play fill-in-the-blanks. But Merc's silence says way more than his words ever could.

He gets what I'm saying here. And I haven't even said it yet.

"So." Merc paces across the room, then turns on his heel to face us. His next words come out as a sigh. "What's this shit about the cure?"

"Well, this is where those Boston people come in. You see, Johnny Boston's woman—her name is Megan—she's a Company scientist. Kind of. Her father ran some genetic program out in the Caribbean and she was part of this crazy plan to make people immortal."

Harrison's laugh comes out like a bark. "What?"

"At the very least, they were working on longevity. Life extension. And they had some success with rats. Don't laugh." I point at Harrison. "Because it was a true breakthrough. It was never gonna work on humans, don't get me wrong. The whole thing is stupid as stupid comes. But Megan's father was fed up with his role in all this Company bullshit and he turned this success into something real. An injection. Which didn't prolong life, it actually fucked up a lot of shit inside the Company elites who were taking it."

"Whoa." Merc puts up both hands in a full-stop motion. "Back up. What the hell?"

"It's complicated. But basically, the doc set them up with an injection they took on the regular. Like monthly or something. I'm not real clear on the protocol, it doesn't even matter. The injection made them sick *but* as long as they kept taking the injection, no one even knew they were sick."

"Ohhhhhhh," Harrison says. Yeah, he's way smarter than I ever gave him credit for. "They stop taking the injection, *then* they get sick."

"Exactly."

"So they had them by the balls," Harrison adds.

"Good and fucking tight."

Merc is nodding like he's beginning to understand. "Is this what happened to the elites then? When all those people suddenly died a couple years back."

"No. Not exactly. See, the elites aren't as stupid as we think they are. Or maybe they are? But they are super fucking suspicious of everything and everyone because they are such lowlife pieces of shit, they assume everyone around them is a lowlife piece of shit too. So they gave these injections to all their kids as

232

well. An insurance policy, I guess. Because they made sure that Johnny Boston's niece had that same injection. It's kinda hard to kill your brother's kid, even if it is for the greater good."

"Oh, fuck," Harrison says.

Merc actually grabs his stomach. Like he's gonna get sick.

"Don't worry, Merc. Trust me, if your kids had those injections, they'd have died years ago like the others."

His relatively calm expression turns into panic. "The others?" It's not a good look for him.

"I'm not being callous here, but the whole let's-kill-the-Company-for-good take-three operation, AKA the estate massacre that went down a few years back, actually *worked*. For the most part. But there was a *lot* of collateral damage."

There is a sudden heaviness in the room with us as Merc and Harrison try to picture what this might've looked like. I'm sure they are seeing Santa Barbara in their minds. Or Kansas. But neither of those two attempts even come close to what happened during the estate incident.

I look down at my feet. I don't need to try to picture it. I was there.

And so was Wendy.

Seventeen days before Gwendolyn Gale turned seventeen, something horrific happened. Something none of us thought she'd come back from.

But I pulled her through.

She's still here.

And she's gonna stay here.

233

I don't care what I have to do to make that happen, I will never stop looking for Wendy's cure.

When I look back up, both Merc and Harrison are sitting at the little table in front of the window. Heads in hands.

Reality, man. It bites.

Merc looks up. "So what's this have to do with me?" I don't answer him right away. I wait until his panic is juuust about to turn into anger.

Then I say, "I'm not sure, Merc. But you know who is sure?"

"Carter," Harrison says.

"Carter," I agree. "What you need to be concerned about, Merc, is the trigger. Daphne is coming up on that age, right? You need to find out how the trigger works and you need to save Donovan so you can get that information out of Carter. You need to save that fucking dumbass if only so you can get peace of mind."

Merc sighs and resumes holding his head in his hands. "What do I have to do?"

"You know better than I do, brother. Whatever it is you do when you're inside their heads." I don't want to say the next part. I want to play it cool. But I can't help myself. "Is that what you're doing to Wendy right now?"

He nods.

"And you left her alone?" Again, I don't want to say this. And I *really* do not want that edge creeping into my voice. This entire situation is precarious and this man right here is the key to everything. But I'm angry about what he's done to Wendy. And worried, too.

Even though I know Wendy is capable of handling just about anything, and she's nothing like Indie Anna, she's been teetering on the edge of a complete breakdown since Chek died. That's why she works so hard. That's why we don't see each other too much. I'm not just a reminder of what happened that day, I'm a trigger too. I don't think Donovan or Carter did that to her. How could they know she and I would grow close like this? So I don't think it's personal. But the risk is still there.

Even though I like the fact that whatever Merc is doing he's doing it at my house, that place is a beartrap of past memories for Wendy. And I want to *see* her. I need to hold her in my arms very soon or I'm gonna be the one losing my mind.

Finally Merc looks up again. "She's OK. I have her on a very safe maintenance cocktail. And we've only been gone"—he checks his phone—"an hour and fifty minutes."

"Well, I did my part. Don't you agree?" Merc doesn't answer me, so I assume he does. "Take me to her. *Now.*"

Harrison is the one who actually gets up, not Merc. "I'm ready. He's right, Merc. We need to get back. Come on." He grabs Merc's shoulder and squeezes. This is when I realize that Harrison isn't just some pilot who flies Sasha and Merc around when they need to get somewhere fast. He's a friend. He's been there since—well, fuck. Since I was eighteen years old. He's been there for all of it.

Merc gets to his feet, but he's not the same guy who walked in the door. Before this little conversation Merc was a man who was sure of himself and his place in this world. He was in control. He was handling shit. And he's been doing a damn good job. So I hate that I'm the reason he feels defeated right now.

I've been there. I have felt that way about Lauren more times than I can count and even though I haven't even seen my daughter since she was six, that sense of defeat—no, *failure*—it doesn't go away. 'Out of sight, out of mind' doesn't apply to this situation at all.

I push all thoughts of Lauren away out of instinct. It's a protection mechanism. If I start thinking about her, I'll never stop. And then one day I'll find myself standing on a quiet street in Fort Collins, in front of a rambling one-story brick house, and I'll fuck it all up.

That cannot happen.

That will not happen.

So I push Lauren away and concentrate on Wendy. Wendy is the one who needs saving, not Lauren. Lauren is just fine.

Merc and I follow Harrison outside. It's sunny still. Not even dinnertime. Which surprises me for no good reason because I knew I was in that room for less than an hour, but it feels like several lifetimes of confessions just took place.

Harrison secures us a ride, and then, just fifteen minutes later, I'm climbing aboard his little Cessna jet. It only seats four, plus the pilot and co-pilot. But it's nice. Luxurious. Nothing at all like the little plane he was flying two decades ago when he first got a front-row seat to the end of the world as we know it.

I take a seat in the back, of course. But Merc sits up front with Harrison. He's probably sick of me. I'm a bad reminder of just about everything evil that's ever happened to that guy, so I can't say I blame him. But sometimes being Nick Tate really sucks. And what sucks more is that no one sees it that way. Just about everyone thinks I'm dead, so all the people I care about stopped caring about me a decade back. And the ones who never did care about me give no fucks at all about what kind of life I've been living since Kansas.

The flight proceeds without incident and thirty minutes later Harrison lands on my private dirt road and taxis right up to my shitty front yard.

A few minutes later, we're walking around to the back of my house. I push Merc out of the way when he tries to enter first, then go in, not sure if Wendy is in my bedroom or on the couch.

It's the couch. She's hooked up to an IV and she's sleeping. Deeply. Because when I sit down next to her and try to shake her awake, she doesn't even moan. I bend down and whisper in her ear. "Wendy."

"She can't hear you. I have her in a cloud."

I hold in my anger. *It does you no good to fuck things up now, Nick. You've come this far. Hold it together.* So when I say, "Wake her up. Now," I am almost able to hide the snarl.

Merc is focused on Wendy now, so he's not paying much attention to my mood as he messes with a tackle box filled with ampules of drugs and lots of syringes. He fills a syringe and pushes the drug into her IV. Moments later, Wendy begins to cough.

"That's normal. It's just a reflex."

I know this. And I tell myself that I know this. It's just a side effect of the drugs he's using. Wendy is OK. She's gonna be fine. But it hurts me to see her like this. I actually have a pain in my chest as I watch Merc check her vitals. I have an urge to do it myself, but luckily the inner voice calms me down and reminds me to step back.

There is no logical reason to be emotional right now. It's all gonna work out.

But giving yourself the pep talk and actually buying into the pep talk are two very different things.

"You OK there, partner?"

I turn and find Harrison looking at me intently. He comes across as worried—which is understandable, since I'm having a silent freakout. And he probably is concerned, but he's not *just* concerned.

He's suspicious.

Yeah. Harrison is a wild card and I need to be careful around him. I didn't realize he was as tuned in as the rest of us and that was a mistake. Not a fatal one, but it's serious enough that I need to make sure he doesn't become the reason I fail.

"I'm fine," I say. Merc is ignoring us. Wendy is trying to sit up now and he's focused on removing her IV before she rips it out. I want to pay all the attention to her recovery, but Harrison is still looking at me, so I feel the need to keep going with him. "I'm pissed, actually. I mean, what the actual fuck? You knew who she was, you knew this was a bad idea—"

"I'm OK." I turn and find Wendy trying to smile at me. "It's OK, Nick. I'm OK."

I walk over to her, kneel down, and smile as we lock eyes. It's a real smile. "You sure?"

She nods. Then she narrows her eyes and directs a scowl to Merc. "You're an asshole. Stay the fuck away from me. And I mean that. If you—"

"OK," I say, cutting her off. "He gets it." I send Merc the compulsory warning look, which just makes him narrow his eyes at me, daring me to threaten him. But I don't. We're done with Merc for the moment. I want Wendy all to myself. "Come on." I brace her against my shoulder and help her to her feet.

"Whoa. Slow down there. She needs to sit for a while or she'll just pass out."

"I got this," I tell Merc. "I'm taking her to the bedroom."

Merc looks like he wants to object, but Harrison cuts in. "Let him go. We need to talk, anyway." And then he's also narrowing his eyes at me.

Lots of suspicion being thrown around this room at the moment. And I should probably hang back and wait for Harrison to voice his concerns to Merc, just so I'm up to speed. But fuck them. I need to get Wendy somewhere private, and that needs to happen now.

I pick Wendy up, cradling her in my arms, and then I take her into the bedroom and kick the door closed with my foot. I set her down on the bed, then turn, lock the door, and let out a long breath. "Are you *sure* you're OK?"

Wendy coughs again and sits up, like she needs to catch her breath. I'm instantly hot with anger over how this played out. "Wendy." My voice is stern now. Because if she ignores me, then she won't have to answer. And if she doesn't answer, then she doesn't have to lie either.

She takes a couple more breaths. "I'm OK. I promise. It was—"

"Never mind that. We'll talk about that later." Her speckled blue eyes meet mine and she coughs again. "In private," I whisper. This makes her look up and around for surveillance. I don't know if Merc broke into my control room and took over my cameras and microphones in the house, but if I were running his side of this little operation, that's what I would've done.

Wendy nods, getting it.

"Now tell me the truth. Are you really OK?" I'm not so worried about the coughing. I know this is a side effect of the drugs Merc used. They tighten up the alveoli in the lungs and this is what triggers that reflex. It's not going to kill her. The symptoms will wear off over the course of the evening

What I'm worried about is her *mind*.

He was inside her.

It feels every bit the violation it sounds like.

He was in her head. He had control of her. He manipulated her.

And I. Am. Pissed.

"I'm fine." She whispers this. Then pats the bed. "Come on. Here. Come lie down with me."

I want to. I haven't seen her since last New Year's and I just want to fucking hug this girl and never let her go. But I can hear Merc and Harrison talking out in my kitchen. So I hold up one finger, letting her know I'm listening.

Then there's a sharp knock at the door. "What?" I say. It's loud and sharp too. But I don't open the door.

"Harrison has to get home. I'm going to the store to get food. You don't have much here."

That's because I don't actually live here full-time, you dick. That's what I want to say. But instead I just say, "Town's about twenty-four miles north of here. Pick Wendy up a cookie-dough Blizzard from DQ, will ya?"

She snickers softly in the bed.

"Anything else?" his snide scoff is clear, even from the other side of the door.

"Tacos." Wendy smiles at me. "From Roberto's on the corner of Main and Sunflower."

There's a long silence on the other side of the door. And I imagine Merc and Harrison shooting each other looks, coming to a conclusion on what to say next. I'm pretty sure Merc is mad about letting me take Wendy into the bedroom now that he's stuck on the other side of a locked door. But he's truly not here to hurt us. He just wants info. And I know he just wants info, so I'm taking advantage of his desire to keep this whole operation as clean as possible. And he's already fucked up. I don't know if he meant to steal Wendy's mind—was that part of his plan? Or was Wendy about to get the best of him when they met up and the mind-fucking just turned into a last resort kinda solution?

I won't know that until she and I can talk freely.

Finally, Merc has something to say. "Are you gonna be here when I get back?"

I look over my shoulder at Wendy. It's her call. She's in charge, and she nods. "We'll be here," I tell him.

There are a few more minutes of whispers and shuffling from the kitchen, but then the back door smacks closed. I walk over to the window, peek through the pillowcase curtains, and watch Merc and Harrison having a final conversation. They walk down the driveway towards the jet, which is parked in the middle of the lonely dirt road, and seem to come to some kind of conclusion. Then Merc walks back this way and gets into Wendy's truck as Harrison gets into his jet.

Two minutes later, they're both gone.

I turn back to Wendy and smile. "Hello, Mrs. Tate."

She smiles back. "Hello yourself, Mr. Tate."

There is no way to stop my wide grin. She bites her lip as I study her. She's been through some shit over the past several days, but she's here and she's OK.

I walk over to her and collapse down onto the bed. She immediately grabs a hold of me and fits her body next to mine, her head on my shoulder, her fingers grabbing my t-shirt, one leg thrown possessively over my thigh. She lets out a long sigh. "We gotta stop meeting this way."

It's not really funny, but it really is funny. So I laugh. "That's a sick joke."

"Sick? How do you figure?"

"You know how."

She chuckles a little. "Did you miss me?"

"Fucking missed the hell out of you." I sigh and run my fingers through my hair. "I was really worried."

"I swear, I'm OK."

"We'll talk about that later. Outside." I look down at her and find her looking up at me. I'm not smiling now, even though I'm happy, because I'm still a little bit pissed about how this turned out. Wendy is smirking up at me like she's got a secret. I can't help it. I break and grin back at her. "What's that look for?"

"I missed you too. We really gotta get together more often."

I almost guffaw. "Yeah. That would be an alternative way to run this marriage."

She chuckles in that cute way I love. "There's nothing wrong with our marriage. It's working, right?"

I shake my head and look down at her again. "You're nuts. When you asked me to marry you last New Year's Eve, this wasn't what I was picturing."

"Hold on." She holds up a finger and resituates herself so she can look me in the eyes. "I didn't actually ask you to marry me."

I laugh again. "You literally said—"

"I said *prove it.* And you said, 'How?' And I said, 'Marry me.'"

"And then I said, 'Let's do it.'"

"No. You said, 'Right fuckin' now, Wendy. I'll marry you *right fuckin' now.* How do we do this?' And your voice was all growly and shit."

I roll my eyes. "And then you said *Branson, Missouri.*"

She snorts. "What? What's wrong with Branson? It's a halfway mark between your farm and my cabin. I thought it was a stroke of genius. We can meet up there every anniversary."

"Beautiful, Wendy." I stroke her cheek with the back of my hand. "Once this Donovan bullshit is over, we won't be meeting up anywhere because we're never gonna be apart again. And for the record, we're done with Mount Pleasant too. No more Mount Pleasant."

"No. Wendell will miss the fuck out of us if we stop meeting there. Our crazy love story is like the highlight of his life."

"You know we're gonna have to kill Wendell if he really does write that tell-all book about us."

Wendy snorts again and I hug her tighter. God, I love her happy. There have been so many bad years,

243

but this one—this year right here—this has been the best year of my life. Even though we haven't seen or talked to each other since the end of our six-hour honeymoon in Branson, just knowing she's mine now, mine for good, is enough.

"You are not the kind of man you marry, Nick Tate. You are not even the kind of man you date."

I smirk. Because she's remembering it too. Standing in that little chapel, empty except for us and the reverend, as we said our vows.

"You're not best-friend material. You're not boyfriend material, that's for sure. And regardless of what you think, you're never going to be husband material."

I shake my head and laugh. "The look on that reverend's face when you started talking—I died."

She laughs too. "He was like… 'What the fuck is going on here?'"

"But we did the whole thing with a straight face. I fucking loved that we did that.

Wendy reaches up and places a hand on my cheek and when I look down at her, the expression on her face is one of adoration. "We are like…" She pauses to think. "We're like the world's greatest liars. In fact, from now on this should be our title. Like our noble title. May I present to you, the World's Greatest Liars, Nicholas and Gwendolyn Tate. It's catchy, don't you think?"

"Without a fucking doubt." I point my finger at her, serious now. "But we never lie to each other."

"Not if we can help it."

I can't stop the smile. Because, of course, if you're married you should not lie to your partner. But everything has a caveat and we both know that. Sometime I worry about the lies she's telling me, but then again, I'm not really worried. Because I only lie to her for her own good and she only lies to me for my own good. And we've accepted the fact that she knows what's best for me and I know what's best for her—so... in our sick Company assassin minds... this works. But I feel the need to remind her of the caveat. "Not if it's for the *greater good*, you mean."

"Yeah, whatever." Then her smile drops. "Oh, shit. Cameras?"

I shrug. "Meh. I would love to see Merc's face if he's recording this. Let him try to figure us out, Wendy. He'll never understand us."

"No one understands us."

"Just us," I say.

She nods and snuggles up against me. Then she sighs. "I really am OK."

I sigh too. Because I'm trying not to think about Merc's fucked-up trip into her mind and this reassurance is a signal that while she isn't OK yet, she will be. So I redirect her thoughts back to our crazy, impromptu, desperate clinging-to-each-other-before-we-had-to-separate wedding.

"Wendy Gale, you're not the kind of girl you marry. You're not even the kind of girl you date. You're not a friend with benefits, you're not a one-night-stand, and regardless of what you think, you have never been a rebound. You are the kind of girl I want to kidnap. You are the kind of girl I want to lock in a basement so you can't ever escape. You're the kind of girl I want to tie up. I want to put a collar on you. A leash. Handcuffs. I want to gag your mouth. A blindfold isn't

245

a bad idea either. Because Wendy Gale, you are the kind of girl I grab on to—any way I can—and I never let go. You are that special to me."

Her eyes search mine for a moment. I love those speckles. She knows this little speech by heart. I've been saying this to her for years now, long before we ended up standing in front of an altar in Missouri. She knows what comes next. She is as sure of it now as I was back then.

"Wendy, you only need to know one thing about me, babe. Just one. No matter what happens, I will *never* let go."

And I won't.

Last Christmas was a tipping point for us. We had been playing the old how-do-we-move-on-after-that-shit-happened game for almost seven years. And you know what they say about the definition of insanity. You can't do the same thing over and over again and expect different results.

So why were we still playing the insanity game?

It was time to end it.

And by end it I mean begin it.

It was time for drastic measures.

It was time I gave her that perfect present.

It was time I told her about the cure.

I don't care what happens next.

We're seeing this through to the end.

PART THREE
the wise

"Knowing yourself is the beginning of all wisdom."

— Aristotle

CHAPTER SEVENTEEN

"OK," Harrison says once we're outside. "What are we doing?"

"You're going back to Fort Collins."

"Why?"

"Pick up Sasha. Bring her here."

Harrison stops walking. "Are you sure that's the right move? I mean... it's been nearly ten years, Merc. She doesn't need this."

I agree with him. Up to a point. And I know Sasha doesn't *want* this, but something is happening here and Nick is at the center of it. "Doesn't she?" I ask Harrison. "It's one thing to pretend we don't know the truth, it's quite another to turn a blind eye."

"You think she knows Nick is alive?"

"She knows. She doesn't want to admit it, but she knows. It's better to get it over with. Confront it. Because I need her help here."

"For what?"

"Keep walking," I say, looking over my shoulder. "I don't want to talk too close to the house."

We go up the driveway and stop in front of the jet. "OK," Harrison says. "Now explain. What's really going on here?"

"That's what I'm trying to figure out."

"You think Nick is up to something?"

"I *know* he is. Everything about this is off."

Harrison shrugs with his hands. "Off how?"

"I'm not sure. But it's all connected. Wendy, Adam, Nick, Donovan or Carter or whoever the fuck that guy is. They're up to something."

"You're worried about your girls?"

"Well. A little," I admit. "It's disturbing. But I don't think they've got a trigger. Nick said that Indie girl went off script all the time."

"Well, from what I understand, she was living with the puppetmaster. So..."

"Yeah, I get it. He had lots of opportunities. But Nick made it sound like this was just her natural personality. My girls aren't like that, Harrison. You know they're not. They're like Sasha. Good kids who just know too much."

Harrison nods. "OK. I agree with you. So maybe we just go home and forget about all of it?"

"We *can't*."

Harrison makes a face at me. It is a look that says, *Bullshit.* "No. We absolutely can. You just don't want to. After ten years of fatherhood and domestic problems you've finally found yourself in the middle of something big and bad. You're the one who can't walk away, Merc. Because if it were up to me, I'd get in my plane, go home, and never think about these fucking people again. I sure as hell would not go back to Fort

Collins and rip Sasha's life apart by bringing her in on it."

"She's the one who brought *me* in. Don't you get it? Adam called *her* looking for *me*. And she knew this was where it was gonna end up. She has suspicions about Nick's death too. She's far more connected than I am. She knew I'd find him. She's not a little girl anymore, Harrison. She can handle the truth."

"And she knows things. That's why you want her here."

"I want her here because something about all of this is off, OK? And yeah, I'm paranoid and suspicious, but that's not what this is. Can't you *feel* it?"

Harrison lets out a long breath, then runs his fingers through his thick silver mane of hair when he looks back towards the house. "Yeah. I feel it. And that's why I think we should leave and never come back."

"That's not gonna happen."

Harrison laughs. "Well, if this was some kind of plot, they got you, right? Dangle a mystery and a Company PSYOPS agent in front of Merrick Case and he jumps like a fucking frog."

"Are you gonna go get her or not?"

"Hey, it's your dime, I guess. I'll go wherever, but whether or not she gets on the plane with me, that's not my call. And I'm not gonna talk her into it."

"Trust me, Harrison. You won't need to."

CHAPTER EIGHTEEN

Everything about last Christmas was spontaneous.

Well, maybe not everything. I planned our holiday. But after Christmas was over, so were my plans. A couple days. That's about all I get with grown-up Wendy.

Here's something no one but me knows about Wendy Gale—she's really shy and she hates to be the center of attention. I love that about her. But there's a problem with us. An unavoidable, elephant-in-the-room problem with us.

She doesn't trust herself to be alone with me for too long. Not even after the wedding.

And it's funny, ya know? Because I'm sure if I were to ask any of the people she works with, like Adam, if they would describe Wendy Gale as someone who second-guesses herself constantly, they would say no fuckin' way. Wendy is the girl you go to when you need something done properly. And not the same way, for instance, that Indie might do something 'properly'. Wendy handles shit delicately. She always has. But ever since her seventeenth birthday she has been fragile. She has been straddling the edge. Always on the cusp of something. And not in a good way.

I am desperate to change this.

That's why I agreed to the wedding. It really was her idea, not mine. And I figured it took a lot for her to make marriage the proof she was looking for and even more to actually follow through with the ceremony once we got to Branson. I thought it was a good sign.

I might still think that if Merc hadn't gotten inside her head.

Now I have to evaluate things again. I need to tread carefully. Every move from this point on needs to be executed perfectly. There is no room for a mistake.

And now I have wild cards.

Not Merc. I can handle him. I know what that guy holds close.

But Harrison. Yeah. I definitely underestimated Harrison.

And Indie. No. There was no contingency plan for an encounter with Indie Anna Accorsi. I was counting on Nathan St. James to play her part and now he's suddenly unavailable.

What's that about?

I don't know her well, but my one conversation with Indie pretty much gave me the highlights. Indie is a car crash. She's a bull in a china shop. She's a get-it-done kind of girl too, but in a let's-blow-it-all-up kind of way. She is not subtle. And maybe that's not fair because I don't know her the way I do Wendy. But

Wendy is so, so, *so* fuckin' different in the way she handles things.

When Indie walks into a room, she brings a Metallica soundtrack with her. It's very much a *Kill 'Em All* kind of beat going on. She is powerful, distinct, and unmistakable.

Wendy is a Brahms's Lullaby. She slips into your life with soft silence. She's in the background. Elevator Muzak. You don't notice her until it's too late.

And you'd think that this would make her arrogant. That she'd have an ego a mile high. And sure, she comes off that way at times. If she feels cornered, she's not above making boastful threats. It's not her skills that she second-guesses, anyway.

It's everything else.

Her hair, her make-up—if she wears it—her clothes, the tone of her voice, the way she walks, how she dances—she won't dance, ever—all that shit that teenage girls worry about when they're thirteen. But here's the difference: those teenage girls figure it out. And by the time they're twenty-four, they have some kind of system going. They have a hairstyle, they know what kind of clothes look good on them, they have perfected the art of eyeliner and understand lipstick.

Wendy never did that shit when she was thirteen. When she was thirteen, she was in her prime assassin days. She was an accomplished professional. None of that girly shit mattered when she was thirteen. She was way too busy being Creepy Wendy to give a single fuck about boys, or dates, or best friends.

But everything changed when she turned seventeen.

That day. What a fucking day.

She went… backwards that day. I don't really have another word to explain it. And I'm not saying she reverted back to some stupid little girl—Wendy Gale has never, *ever* been a stupid little girl. But something… snapped.

I really thought I was doing the right thing. I really did. And I want to tell her this, but she wouldn't even know what I was talking about.

Hell, I wouldn't even know where to start explaining.

"Hello? Nick? What are you thinking so hard about?"

I smile at her, but don't say anything.

Because I'm thinking… I have regrets.

And I don't want her to know that.

CHAPTER NINETEEN

Nick is worried about me and I hate it when he worries about me.

"Just thinking about you, Wen." He sighs. "I want to ask you all the questions right now. But I can't. Just..."

"Just tell you I'm fine?"

"No." He actually laughs out loud. "I mean, yeah. But only if it's true."

I laugh too. "It's true. I'm fine. We're good."

He picks up my hand and brings it to his lips, kisses my knuckles as he smiles at me. "Mrs. Tate."

"Mmm. I've been thinking about that. Do I have to be a Mrs. Can't I just be Wendy Tate?"

"Pretty sure that's the tradition. Title comes with the marriage."

"Yeah, but it's us. Right? Are we traditional?"

"Maybe the better question is do we want to be traditional?"

It takes about two seconds of thought for both of us to laugh and shake our heads. "Nah."

He pulls me closer to him and I've missed this. I always miss him when we're apart, but this time it really does feel different. Not just because we're married now and this is the first time we've been together since all that happened, but also because... everything feels so *on track*.

"Now I wanna know what *you're* thinking."

Hmmm. Here's something no one knows about Nick Tate except me—he's a *really* nice guy. I'm talking open-doors-for-you nice. Hold-your-hand kind of nice. He will grocery-shop *and* put everything away when he gets home. He will come when you call, be there regardless if you don't, and if you ever need a new heart, he'll either find you a replacement or give you his own.

I know this.

Because Nicholas Tate gave me his heart seven years ago when I needed a new one.

And he never asked for it back.

I sigh as I stare up into those brown eyes. Fucking eyeballs. Who knew they could hide so many secrets? These brown eyes are why I trust him. He's not like me. Not at all like me. I don't trust anyone like me. Not even Adam, and I like Adam. He's a nice guy too, but he's got those blue eyes. He's one of *them* and Nick isn't.

Nick taps my forehead with the tip of his finger. "Come on. What the hell is going through that head of yours?"

When he asks me this I always lie. But he knows I'm lying, so it's fine. This is how we keep the even keel when all the waters around us are stormy. And it's not really lies, anyway. It's more like a daydream. "I was thinking about our wedding. It was pretty fun."

He swipes a piece of hair away from my eyes and smiles. "It's almost time for the real honeymoon. Are you ready?"

It's a serious question designed to be hidden inside innocent words. "I'm so ready."

He pauses, letting out a small, silent breath before he responds. "Good. Because we're almost there, kid. We're almost there."

I let out a long, tired breath myself. And the stress of being under Merc's capable, yet very frightening, hands goes with it. I'm here. I'm fine. He didn't hurt me and he didn't get any secrets, either. It's like... best-case scenario, right?

"Go to sleep now. You need to rest."

"I think I've been sleeping for days. I am super in need of the bathroom right now."

"Oh, shit. Let me help you." And he does. Nick is out of the bed before the last word even leaves his mouth. Then he's carefully pulling me up and walking me to the bathroom. I'm still a little wobbly. I know I'm not making a big deal about this whole Merc thing—big deals are never good in the long run—but it's kind of a big deal that the most dangerous mindfucker in the history of the Company just had a grip on my brain.

Still, I don't want Nick to think too hard about that, so when he says, "Do you need me to help you?" even though I kinda do, I say, "No. I'm fine. I'll be right out."

He closes the door and I listen for his creaky footsteps as he makes his way into the kitchen. Probably to mix me up a powdered electrolyte drink. And I spend the next thirty seconds or so clinging to the edge of the sink, staring into the drain, as I wait for my head to stop spinning from the walk.

When my brain is mostly settled, I pee, then stand back up and try not to look at myself as I wash my hands.

My mouth feels like cotton. But I'm at Nick Tate's house. And this is never a bad thing when you're teetering on the edge of insanity and need something real and normal to pull you back.

When I swing open the mirror vanity and find a little plastic box with a piece of black electrical tape across the front with the name 'Wendy' written on it in silver Sharpie, I say a prayer of thanks for my Nick.

Here's something else no one knows about Nick except me. He has beautiful handwriting. Once, when I was like eleven, we were in the bookstore, and you know those bargain shelves? They have all kinds of pretty colorful coffee table books in that section. And kits of things. Like... learn origami kits. Or bullet journal kits. Shit like that. On that day I wanted a calligraphy kit. Lauren was only like two and a half when this happened, so she didn't care one way or the other. But Nick bought that kit for me and we spent an entire week at Hilton Head resort, sitting at the beach or the outdoor restaurants, and he learned calligraphy with me.

So my silver Sharpie name written on that random piece of black electrical tape is an example of some of the most beautiful letters ever imagined. And I wasn't the one who wrote it. I wasn't the one who put a new-in-the-package toothbrush in the little plastic container, either.

That was Nick.

Because I'm telling you, he might kill little blonde girls for a living, but he's a *really* nice guy.

When I come out of the bathroom Nick is sitting in one of two chairs at his crappy kitchen table. There are two electrolyte drinks, one in front of him and one in front of my chair.

Told ya he was making me a drink.

He's grinning too. "Sit. Drink. Tell me everything."

Not everything, because we still don't know if it's safe to talk. But that's not what Nick means. When he says 'tell me everything' he means I should catch him up on what's been happening in my life since we saw each other last. Nothing serious. Stupid things.

So I take a seat, drink, and then I start talking.

I tell him random things about the last eight months. I keep a journal so I don't forget these things, but the journal is kept hidden in the backseat armrest of my truck and I don't have any idea where my truck is right now, so I just wing it.

There is a short story about a donut shop in Peoria, Illinois, a hotel I stayed at in Mississippi, and a roadside stand in Ohio where I bought some deer jerky that was to die for.

Nick smiles through all of it. "Welp. I'll put it all on the list for the honeymoon."

That's right. Our honeymoon is a road trip. We're gonna road-trip the fuck out of this planet. Like, I'm

261

talking six continents of road trips. We're gonna ride bikes, and drive cars, and ride wild horses in Mongolia for our road trip. The Arctic comes with dog sleds. I'm really fucking excited about the dog sleds. We'd do Antarctica too, but the Company running shit down there is a whole other story and they shoot you if you get too close. Not even Adam could road-trip across Antarctica. So whatever.

"Now it's your turn," I say.

He leans back in his chair, making it squeak. Nick Tate is a very handsome man. I get it. He's a lot older than me, but he only got better with age. And even though he's way up in his thirties now, I still see him as that frantic twenty-two-year-old with the new baby at the airstrip.

His hair was very blond back then but it's gotten darker over the years. His eyes are still the same, that warm brown color that glows amber in the sunlight. He's always had an athletic body—lean, but muscular. That's just his genetics. And he's always tan, because even though he owns this giant farm in Nebraska, he's almost always near a beach. I have a feeling that he'd rather live on the ocean than land. And if it weren't for me, and his desire to remain close to Sasha and Lauren, he'd just buy a yacht and sail off, never to be seen again.

Nick Tate has the most amazing smile too. His teeth are so perfect. Like he had braces as a kid. And they are white. He shows them off a lot because unlike a lot of other Company men, he likes to smile. He finds reasons to smile.

The bright side.

Nick Tate is my bright side.

He tells me random things too. Mostly he's been preparing for the honeymoon, he says. And thinking about me. He's written it all down, he says. But that's for later. I nod, understanding. Same, same, right?

And then we're all caught up, the sun is setting, Merc isn't back, and we're settled now. We can stop thinking about risks, and plans, and how everything might blow up in our faces and just concentrate on us.

That means sex, by the way.

We get up from the table. No words. He takes my hand, gently. Then he leads me back into the bedroom and closes the door.

It's dark in the bedroom since the curtains are pulled shut. But that's OK. There's enough light to see vague outlines.

He leads me over to the bed and I climb in. He never takes my clothes off before we get in bed because he thinks that would be presumptuous. And Nick Tate is a really nice guy, remember?

One day though, after I'm cured and we're on the honeymoon, he's gonna do it different.

He will stop being careful, he will stop wondering if he will hurt me or I will hurt him, and he will start being presumptuous. That's what he says when I complain about all this special consideration.

One day, I will be cured and he will ravish me properly. But for now, he must be considerate.

I almost laugh out loud thinking about that particular conversation. But then we're both in bed and Nick's gentle fingertips are slipping under my t-shirt and sliding around on my stomach. He touches me so softly. So carefully. It sends chills through my whole body.

263

I stop thinking at this point. I just sigh and give in. Because having Nick Tate's undivided attention is pretty much the best feeling in the world and even though we're married now, we don't spend a lot of time together. We *can't* spend a lot of time together. So these moments are precious.

He always goes slow, too.

One day, he says, he'll throw me down on the bed or fuck my brains out against a wall, but not yet.

We have to do things a certain way until I'm cured.

CHAPTER TWENTY

I caress her stomach with the tips of my fingers and her skin prickles up almost immediately with a chill. I love this part about being with Wendy. I love the intimacy. Because she is the only person in this world I can be intimate with. She is the only one who understands me.

I go slow with her for two reasons. One, she needs it to be slow. Her mind is always going so fast, slowing down is always good. But two is for me. Because time has a way of slipping through the cracks if you don't pay attention to it. You gotta control it. You gotta be the boss of time and tell it to slow the fuck down. And the way you do that is by being careful. So every minute I spend with Wendy is careful. It's deliberate and intentional. Because I don't want to miss a single fucking thing. I've given away too much already. No one is gonna steal time from me, not even time itself.

After a few minutes of slow caresses, she is relaxed. Her eyes are closed, her breathing is even and easy, and her fingertips are beginning to find their way underneath my shirt. We angle into each other and then her eyes open and she smiles.

This is her signal.

I'm not sure if she knows she does this, but this is how she tells me she's ready. That sad, sad smile I know to be real. It contains all of her. All her days gone by. Not just sad things, either. It's happy things. Lots of them, really. Her life could've been so much worse. And I know that sounds like I'm trying to justify how it all went, but it's true. She was born who she is the same way I was and it could've all gone so much worse.

I ease her shirt up her body and place my lips on the hard, taut muscles of her stomach. Her free hand finds its way to the top of my head and then she slips her fingers into my hair.

I kiss my way up her stomach, carefully pushing her t-shirt out of my way. I stop to open the front clasp of her bra and then take a moment to appreciate her full, round breasts as they spill out.

She puts both hands on my head now. To encourage me. And I take one nipple into my mouth and suck on it, nipping at the tender skin once or twice to make her gasp. I squeeze the other one and then her back bucks up a little and I smile.

She grabs my shirt and pulls it up my back. I pause my attention to her breasts and lift my shirt over my head, tossing it into the corner of the bedroom. Then I resume as she fumbles with the button on my tactical pants. She gets it open, pulls the zipper down, and then she makes a fist around my cock.

I was already getting hard, but the moment her palm squeezes me, it's done. I'm ready.

But she's not, so I forget about my desires, and my dick, and stay focused on her.

Being this close to Wendy Gale—well, let's just say I'm the only one who gets this close to Wendy Gale. She has instincts. Chek did this to her. And whatever—he did what he thought was best, but still, he did this to her.

It's dangerous to be this close to Wendy.

Everything about intimacy is a trigger for her.

But I'm careful. I know how to keep her calm.

And she wants this, or trust me, I wouldn't have gotten this far.

Wendy Gale has tried to kill me five times since I met her nineteen years ago and three of those happened during sex even though we started out just like this—easy, slow, and nice. She was angry. Not about the sex. Our fights have nothing to do with sex. Or feelings, really. She just gets angry about things. And I don't blame her. My job is to kill people like her. Why would she ever trust me?

She shouldn't, and she knows she shouldn't.

But she does anyway.

She hasn't killed me though. That's the important part. And not just because I didn't let her. She doesn't want to kill me. She wants to love me.

"Keep going." She senses my hesitation and I fucking hate myself for that. "Please don't stop."

I grab her breasts again, kissing and sucking on one nipple while I caress the other one into a tight little peak. She bucks again. Her hand is pumping my cock now. Her breathing is picking up and when I glance up to look at her face, her eyes are closed and her mouth is open.

I lean up and kiss her. I can't help it. Her tongue crashes into mine and then she's grabbing my hair and I'm mostly on top of her, and I know this is pushing things, but when we get here, to this place, every single time I lose interest in living. I just want more.

We writhe on the bed, her hands on my face as we kiss. I slip my fingers down her shorts, right between her legs, and she gasps into my mouth. "Keep going. Keep going," she begs.

I have no intention of stopping, but I take a breath and ease us down again using soft, slow fingertips over her clit. She hisses, arches her back and draws up her knees to give me better access.

I push a finger inside her and she holds her breath. It's enough to make her come. Wendy is easily pleased in the sex department. She gushes over everything I do to her. But even so, I want to do more. I want to make it all special each time.

"Oh, God, Nick. Don't stop. Please, don't stop."

She has nothing to worry about. I push her knees together, then slip her shorts and panties down and over her legs, tossing them into the corner with my shirt. Then I open her up again. I spread her knees wide and position myself between her legs and watch her face as I lower mine down to the smooth, soft skin on the inside of her thigh. Every time I find myself in this position, I have an overwhelming urge to bite her. Not hard, or anything. I just want to nip that skin and make her yelp a little.

But I don't. It would ruin everything if I did.

Instead I kiss and suck my way up her inner thigh as my fingers part the lips of her pussy so that when

I'm out of leg my mouth can cover her and my tongue can slip inside.

She's moaning, "Oh, shit. Oh, shit."

She likes being licked, so I take my time here. She comes, maybe even twice, but she never gets tired of sex. We don't have enough sex to get tired of it, but even if we were getting it on the regular, I don't think we'll ever get tired of sex.

I know I won't. I want to possess Wendy every minute of every day.

Her hands grip my hair, urging me to keep licking. Like she's reading my mind and this is a gentle hint that I'm thinking too much. I twirl my tongue around in a slow circle, then nip her, just a little, with my teeth.

She hisses, then laughs, her hips squirming. I slowly push two fingers inside her, easing them deeper and deeper as I watch her face. Her breathing is ragged now, her back still arched, her neck stretched taut. I pump my fingers in and out and then her muscles contract around them as she lets go. A small gush of warm liquid spills out past my fingers and drips down into the palm of my hand.

"Now you." She says it again. Insisting. "Now you."

I would stay here between her legs for hours if she'd let me. But she's come several times already and she won't settle until I'm inside her and get my release too. So I crawl my way up her body, pausing to suck on her breasts and kiss her neck. Then I knee open her legs as she takes my cock in her hand and guides me to her entrance.

When my cock slips into her pussy we both moan.

She feels so good, I want to spend the rest of my life inside her.

She urges me to go fast. To fuck her hard. But we've tried that a couple times and it's too much for her to handle, so I don't do that. I go slow. I push deep instead. I make her gasp as I fill her up and then I pull back and do it again.

She drags her nails up and down my back because she knows me, same way I know her, and this drives me crazy. She likes to drive me crazy.

I kiss her a little bit harder and she bites me. A moment later, I taste blood, but I don't stop and I don't go faster.

One day maybe I will fuck her hard.

But then again, maybe I won't.

It doesn't matter to me.

I will take Wendy Gale any way I can get her.

She lifts her legs up and begins fucking me back. I let her, but only for a few moments. I kiss her as I pull out and then she's squirming around on the bed, trying to put my cock in her mouth so she can suck me off as I come.

I want to come inside her, but I don't. Won't.

There are no kids in our future.

Not genetic ones anyway.

She can't take birth control. The hormones are very bad for Zero girls. And yeah, I could use protection, but the condom might break and we can't even take that small chance that she gets pregnant.

There are no abortions in Wendy's future either— her mind would not recover from something like that—so if it happens, it happens.

And it *can't* happen.

270

We settle next to each other on the bed when we're done. She snuggles herself up to me, assuming the position, her head on my shoulder, her hands on my chest, one leg possessively over my hip.

I know she's sad. She's always sad after we have sex.

But I also know what to do to make her feel better.

"Dear Wendy…"

She huffs. "You don't have to do that. I'm fine."

"Dear Wendy," I say again. "It has been eight months, four days, seven hours, and eight minutes since I last saw you and I miss you terribly."

"Dear Nick. I'm gonna start writing Dear Nick letters."

"Bitch, do not tease me like that."

She giggles.

"I would kill for a Dear Nick letter."

"Well. I'll write some then. You need to make a little drop box outside your house."

"Our house," I correct her.

"Whatever. That way I can drop them off when I'm passing by."

We're both silent as we think about this. How our lives have been for the past seven years. Well, we were always two ships passing in the night while she was growing up too, but it was different. I didn't write her any Dear Wendy letters until her eighteenth birthday. Because that was the year I thought there would be no Dear Wendy letters in her mailbox when she came home for her birthday and that could not happen.

But of course, there were letters that year.

I don't understand the letters. I'm just glad she had them.

Wendy and I were a little team when she was a kid. She helped me, I helped her, but trust me when I say this, we were not in love. There were no secret looks between her and me when she was fifteen. She didn't flirt with me and I certainly didn't flirt with her. She started hating me at thirteen, I guess. It's a typical girl thing. I looked it up. I was a little hurt when she started throwing me attitude but that was nothing compared to how she felt about me when I sent Lauren away. She wanted to kill me and it took almost three years for her to forgive me for that.

Even on her seventeenth birthday, right after Chek died and she was at her most vulnerable, she still didn't really *like* me. She was still mad about the change in our previous routine. Because she didn't know that I was gonna send Lauren to live with Sasha. I couldn't tell her. She had a job to do when that was going down.

This is what pissed her off.

I did not lie to her. But I did leave out information. And she didn't see the difference.

But there *is* a difference.

At any rate, she was angry. So when she gave me the chance to make it up to her after Chek was gone, I took it.

She wanted that cure so bad. Once the letter-opening was over, the cure was the only thing she talked about. And maybe it was a way to justify what happened to Chek. That's possible. But I knew better. She didn't want to justify Chek's death that day. I know this because Wendy Gale has no idea what she did that day that Chek died.

But I do.

I saw the whole thing.

And then I did what I had to do.

"Dear Wendy," I whisper again.

She huffs a little breath.

"You are sweet, beautiful, perfect, and whole. You are everlasting, transcendent, exceptional, and extraordinary. You are remarkable, exquisite, priceless, and sublime. You are flawless, marvelous, divine, and sensational. You are heavenly, powerful, glorious, and delightful.

"You are lovely.

"You are majestic.

"You are gorgeous.

"And I will never let you go."

CHAPTER TWENTY-ONE

My phone rings in the grocery store. I know who it is before I even look at the screen. I press accept. "Sasha."

"Merc."

"What's up?"

"What's *up*?" She scoffs. "Harrison is standing in my kitchen right now telling me that you're requesting my presence in Nebraska. That's what's up. Why do you need me in Nebraska?"

"He didn't tell you."

"No. He said, 'Merc needs to see you in Nebraska. Do you wanna come with me?' And I'm like... I dunno. Do I wanna go with him, Merc?"

I let out a long, tired sigh.

"What's this about?"

"I'll tell you when you get here."

I expect a fight over this. Sasha hasn't been a bossy little brat for a long time now, but I expect her to put a foot down. I expect a little bit of resistance. An argument, at least. So when her silence goes on for almost twenty whole seconds, I know *she knows*.

She knows this is about Nick. She might even understand that I'm bringing her to see him, but she's not going to argue with me.

"Sasha?"

"I'm here." He voice is small now. Low and soft. That's the woman she turned into. Someone soft. And I don't mean that in a disparaging way, even though if I ever told her this, she would be insulted. I mean that... she got *out*. She let it go. Somehow, some way she put all that Santa Barbara and Kansas shit behind her and moved on.

It's a sign of strength. And I would say this to her, if we ever had this conversation for real. I would tell her, *Don't regret the soft, or the easy, or the good. Because you, of all the girls they used up and threw away, you are the one who made it. And that is strength.*

But she wouldn't want to hear it, so I just concentrate on the present. "So you'll come," I say.

"Is this gonna ruin my life?"

I have to pause. In the old days, and for people who are not Sasha or anyone I seriously care about, I'd just lie about this and say, *Nope.* But I can't lie to this girl. She'll know, first of all. And second, I don't want to ruin the trust we have. When you're surrounded by lies truth is more valuable than gold. Because truth, even if it's bad news, breeds trust. And trust is worth even more than truth.

Plus, something is happening right now and for whatever reason, these Company people have decided to place me on their chessboard. I'm a game piece at the moment. I can feel it. And I need help. And maybe it's not fair to expect this help to come from Sasha, but she truly is the only one I can turn to. I can't call

Sydney. She's not that kind of Company girl. And I'm sure, by now, Syd knows something is up. But she trusts me to take care of it and get back to our family in one piece.

So I'm phoning a friend, as they say on that TV game show. I'm placing my own chess piece onto the gameboard. A twist, if you will.

"Merc?"

"Look," I sigh. "I can't answer that. Not yet, anyway. But I'm calling you because I need you. That's all I want to say over the phone. I need you."

"It's..." And I swear, Nick Tate's name is on the tip of her tongue. I don't know why she doesn't finish her thought or say it out loud, but I can take a good guess. If she says it out loud, it becomes real. So instead she says, "OK. Should I pack an overnight bag? Find a babysitter and bring Jax? Pull the kids out of school and clean out my bank accounts? How deep is this going?"

"It's not that deep. At least, I don't think it is. You know I wouldn't put you in danger, right?"

"I do know that."

"So I would leave Jax at home with the kids. And one night—you don't even have to stay the night, actually. I really just need your opinion on something and I need to get that opinion in person."

There is another long pause. Then she blows out a breath. "OK. I guess we're leaving now. See you in an hour or so."

She ends the call without saying goodbye, but I don't think it's because she's mad. I think she's just a little off balance.

Because she knows.

And she's coming anyway.

I put my phone away, pay for the groceries in my cart, grab the tacos and ice cream from down the street, and head back south to the farm.

Nick is sitting at the picnic table behind his house when I pull to the end of the gravel driveway. He doesn't get up, or greet me, when I get out. He doesn't say anything at all, actually.

"I'm kinda surprised you're still here," I call, grabbing grocery bags. "Where's Wendy?"

He nods his head towards the house. "Taking a shower."

There's something different about him now. I can't put my finger on it because I don't know this guy. He's not shootin' me a look or anything. His answer didn't come out snide or resentful. But something *is* different. "You gonna help me out here?"

He gets up, walks over to the truck, and grabs several bags, then turns and takes them in to the house without another word.

And this is when I get that feeling in my gut.

It's hard to articulate. But it's kind of a sick feeling and it means I missed something.

I don't miss a lot of things. This is not customary for me, so this feeling and my reactions to it aren't well honed. But I've had it enough times to recognize it for what it is.

A mistake.

Somewhere along the line I have made a mistake with Nick Tate. I have missed something.

And the funny thing is—well, it's not funny at all, actually. The *ironic* thing is that the most prominent memory I have of this feeling is from that day out in the Montana woods. The day when Sydney Channing almost killed Sasha and me because she was triggered and under Garrett's orders.

Garrett was my mistake that time. I underestimated him. Not his skills, per se. But his *hatred* of me, I guess. He wanted me dead and he used Sydney to finish me off.

I'm still standing by the truck when Nick comes back out.

What I'm doing is not normal. I mean, I don't know how long I've been standing here, but obviously something is on my mind and that's why I haven't gone back into the house with the groceries. But Nick says nothing. Just grabs the remaining bags, and dinner, and walks away. The screen door slams behind him.

I take my groceries into the house. Nick is already putting things away and the fridge door is wide open as he haphazardly shoves milk and eggs inside.

"You got a lot of fresh food." He narrows his eyes at me from over his shoulder. "You plan on staying here a while?"

I study him, trying to figure out the mistake. Trying to retrace my steps to where it went wrong. It can't be that far back. I mean, we've only been together a couple of hours. So I guess the hotel room.

But it doesn't feel right.

That wasn't when. I was careful then. A mistake happens when you're not being careful.

I decide to be direct the way Sasha was. "I don't know what you're doing, Nick. But I know you're doing something."

He turns away from the fridge, shuts the door. Stares at me as he leans against the kitchen counter and crosses his arms. For as long as I have known him, I have had trouble meeting his gaze. And looking back, I wonder why that was. Those eyes, they're brown, not blue. They're not piercing or overly dark. They're kinda amber, actually. But it's like this man can see through me. Even when he was a kid, he saw things I never did because he's had access to information I never will.

But right now, he's not glaring at me. His eyes come off as rather lazy. He is comfortable, at ease, and unconcerned about what I might think he's doing.

"So walk out." He shrugs his shoulders.

It's a casual dare. So casual, it comes off like a threat only people like us can decipher.

He knows I'm not walking out. I'm in. No matter what happens, I'm playing his game until it's over. So when I don't say anything back, he pushes off the counter, walks past me, and goes back outside.

I stand there for a moment, still holding my grocery bags.

"You know you owe me now, right?"

I glance over at the hallway and find Wendy. She's dressed in Nick's clothes—a pair of denim shorts that look like she just cut the legs off five minutes ago and a white Shrike Bikes t-shirt, which takes me aback a little. That fucker has a Shrike Bikes t-shirt? He has no fucking shame.

Wendy's hair is still wet. It makes her look different for a moment because even though I can still see streaks of blonde, it's dark. And she's in the shadows of a dying sun, so her eyes come off dark too.

Illusions.

These girls are like that.

They trick you without even trying.

I set my bags down on the counter and start putting things away. She waits me out. So I finally say, "I'm good for it, Wendy." Because I did take her mind without permission and if she were just some random nobody, it wouldn't be that big of a deal. But she's not a random nobody. Something tells me that Wendy Gale is now a permanent fixture in my life. So she's right. I owe her.

"Where's Nick?"

I nod my head to the backyard. "Out there, I guess. You saw our conversation?"

She laughs a little. And this is when I notice it's kind of a sweet laugh. Wendy is a dangerous girl and she's not even close to being sane. But she's not a mean girl. And she's not nasty, either. She's a lot like Sasha in this respect.

"What's funny?" I ask.

"Just that you *know* him."

"What?"

"You know. You said '*saw* our conversation.' And that's Nick for ya, right? When you have a conversation with Nick, half of it always takes place inside his head. But you heard all the things he wasn't saying, didn't you?"

I turn and look out the back window. Nick is just coming out of one of the outbuildings twisting a cap off a beer bottle. He must keep a fridge out there filled with it, because there's no beer in this fridge. But I checked that building when I got here and there was nothing in it but a couple old trucks and a tractor.

"I guess you're the same way." Wendy laughs. "But I speak that language, Merc. Just so you know. I hear all the words you're not saying too." Then she nods her head at the window where I'm looking. "Yes. He has a little man cave out there in his shop. There are slot machines, and pinball, and a card table, and a pool table, and a fridge filled with beer. But no one comes here. No one but me, anyway. So I've always thought it was kinda sad, ya know? That he built a secret man cave but he has no family and friends to share it with. So I make a point of always asking to go out there when I'm here. Which is almost never, so. Yeah." She sighs. "I didn't know him before Santa Barbara but I do know that he's not that kid. That he hasn't been that kid since that day I met him on a superyacht. And whoever you think he is right now, that's not who he is."

"Who is he?" My response surprises even me. I didn't mean to ask.

But Wendy answers anyway. "He's mine. That's who he is. And I know you think you got the best of me, but you didn't. So if you even think about hurting him—"

Her threat is cut off by the sound of a low-flying small aircraft.

Both of us look up at the ceiling. Why do people do that? A reflex, I guess.

"Your friend is back."

"Yeah." I let out a long breath. Because I'm suddenly having second thoughts about the play I set in motion.

Wendy and I both walk to the front of the house and drag the cheap blackout curtains open just in time to see Harrison's jet coming to a stop at the end of the driveway.

Neither of us moves and I'm holding my breath until the door opens and the stairs swing down, then it comes out in a long, low rush.

"What's going on?" She feels it. Something is definitely going on.

Just as I think that, Nick appears to our left, his boots crunching on the gravel driveway as he walks towards the plane, beer in hand.

Wendy breaks for the front door. She's got good instincts.

But I reach over and grab her arm before she gets more than two paces away. "Don't," I say. And I mean it.

"What have you done?"

I don't need to answer her question because movement down the driveway draws her attention back to the window and that answer becomes obvious when Sasha Cherlin appears in the open doorway of the jet.

She stands there for a moment, shielding her eyes from a blaring sunset, and then she comes down the stairs and the sun moves behind a cloud.

She stops short when she sees him.

And Nick Tate drops his beer bottle onto the gravel driveway like he's the one who just saw a ghost and not her.

CHAPTER TWENTY-TWO

When Sasha Cherlin appears in the jet hatch my first thought is... *Fuckin' Merc. He got me.* Because I have been so busy trying to keep things straight with Wendy, I really didn't see this one coming.

But then I snap back to the moment and reality catches up. So the next thing I think is... *Welp. It's over now, I guess.* Which is just as inappropriate as my first thought. But twenty full seconds later, when Sasha still hasn't moved from the bottom of the stairs, I'm really not feeling so bad about this.

She's not happy to see me.

She's not relieved that I'm alive.

There will be no hug, no kiss, no tears.

Because even a decade later, I can still read this girl like nobody's business and she is *pissed*.

I want to look back at the house to see if Wendy is watching, but I don't dare. Hopefully, she's still in the shower.

Hopefully, Nick? I almost laugh out loud.

Merc didn't get me once, he got me twice. Because the last thing I need fucking up what I'm doing with

Wendy is Sasha. The one girl on this entire planet who makes Wendy feel like second best.

"*Fuck*," I mutter.

Harrison appears in the doorway and when our eyes meet, he shrugs. This shrug says, *Wasn't my idea.*

No. This little play has Merc written all over it and I did not see it coming. I figured he'd... well. He'd *lie*. At least for a little while. Then maybe a phone call. Feel her out. Maybe Sasha wouldn't even want to see me. Hell, maybe she prefers me dead?

At this point the awkward silence has gone on for over a minute and someone has to make a move, so I decide it will be me. I walk forward, but then stop when Sasha takes a step back.

I shrug with my hands. "What are you doing?" I don't say it loud but the fields surrounding my shitty farm house have gone silent so my voice carries across the distance between us.

She doesn't move or say anything, so I continue my little stroll down the driveway until I'm close enough to see her properly.

Sasha shakes her head. Her eyes are narrowed down into slits. Her hair is pulled back into a pony tail. She's wearing a pair of worn-thin cotton army pants with strategic frayed rips that tell me they come from a catalog and not a surplus store. On top she's wearing a black tank top, but it's frilly. It's got cotton ruffles for straps and a screen-printed rose in white across the front. She's wearing a pair of well-worn sneakers on her feet and there's a little hole in the left one near the toe.

I've been watching Sasha this whole time. Nothing about how she looks right now is a surprise. But everything about her takes me back in time to that hotel room in Rock Springs.

I ruined her life that day.

Or is that just my ego talking? Because her life is far from ruined right now. She has been forced to live it a little too close to the edge, but she hasn't fallen off yet.

If I could do it over again, would I make a different choice?

I mean, by the time we got to the beach at the foot of that Santa Barbara mansion there was no turning back. Things had been set in motion and James was the one who needed to get away, not me.

But I could've made a million different choices leading up to that night. I could've been Sasha's promise.

The four-carat diamond on her finger catches the fading sun and sparkles, flashing me in the face and snapping me back to the present.

I blink and she speaks. "Nothing to say to me?"

Oh, Sasha Cherlin, I have an entire eternity of things to say to you. But not when Wendy Gale is a hundred feet behind me.

"Well? You guys brought me here, what the fuck do you want?"

When I don't answer her, she starts walking towards me and my heart begins to beat like crazy. I'm talking it's practically fluttering inside my chest.

When she's about six feet away from me, she stops and her eyes find mine. They are filled with... what? Is that hate? Sadness?

No. Worse. It's disappointment.

"OK. Fine. I think I get it. You didn't know I was coming, did you?"

I barely manage to shake my head no.

"Merc brought me here. He said he needed my opinion on something, and I'm going to assume that's you, I guess."

I don't think it's me. I think it's Adam's offer. Because Merc needs someone to tell him it's OK to be that guy again. The one he's been hiding away. That person inside him who is capable of kidnapping a girl, pumping her full of drugs, and taking over her mind until he gets the answers he wants.

Once a Company man, always a Company man.

I don't care that Merc doesn't have Company blood flowing through his veins, you don't do the things he's done and keep your distance.

Bringing Sasha here was a cold, calculating move on his part. One that might set me on edge and possibly make me sloppy. That is a fantasy. I am one hundred percent in control here.

But he also brought her here to point him in the right direction. Should he go meet up with Adam Boucher and save Donovan, or shouldn't he?

And now, thanks to me, he's got another choice.

Should he kill Carter Couture or save him for a rainy day?

This makes me feel a little better because it means Merc is still in the dark about what's really going on. If Merc knows anything else about what I'm up to, he hasn't shown his hand. And right now would be the time to play that card. We're just about there. We're so close to getting back inside Harrison's jet and taking it down to the Old Pearl River in Louisiana, I almost itch from all the mosquito bites in my future.

But I don't say any of that out loud.

I do, however, look over my shoulder at the house. Because Merc should be outside by now and he's not. And then, when I look back up at the plane, Harrison isn't there anymore. He went back inside.

So. Maybe this confrontation wasn't Merc's main purpose, but he's gonna let it play out.

I prepare for what comes next by drawing in a long, deep breath and exhaling very slowly.

Sasha notices my calm-down technique and nods her head. "OK. We're in assassin mode now? Or what?"

"What?" I barely manage this word.

"Do I scare you or something? Because I'm not that girl anymore. Haven't been her since that day out in Kansas when I *killed you.*"

"No."

"Tell me, Nick. That's who you are, right? Because that's who you look like. Tell me which part I got wrong."

"I'm him, yeah. But no, we're not assassins. This isn't... *that.*"

"Then what is it?"

I look over my shoulder.

"Why do you keep doing that?"

"Because, Sasha, I didn't bring you here. Merc did."

"You don't want me here?"

"No. I mean..." But I can't change that reply, so I just sigh.

I haven't been fantasizing about this moment. I was never going to see them face to face again. Her or Lauren. It was done. It was over. And yeah, I like to look at her life from a distance. I live a little vicariously through Sasha Cherlin's suburban mom life. So kill me. But I was never going to see her again and I sure as fuck was never going to bring her out *here*. To this shitty, run-down fucking farmhouse that—

OK. Maybe that sounds bad because I bring Wendy here. But Wendy shows up here. And the only reason that happens is because I own this place and sometimes, I'm actually home. I have never thought of this house in the middle of my massive farm as anything other than a waystation.

But now that it's been invaded by my past… I am starting to resent the intrusion.

"OK." Sasha chuckles, but it's not a fun chuckle. "You had better say every single thought that just ran through your head out loud or I'm getting on that plane and I'm leaving."

"I don't want you here. So if you leave—" I stop. Take a breath.

"You don't *want* me here? You… you… *you* go on a fucking killing spree ten years ago, show up at *my* house—my fucking home, Nick!—to tell me to *do my job,* and then you make me kill you—"

"No."

"*Kill you.* Shoot you in the fucking head. And I find out today it was a *lie.* And you want me to know you don't *want me here?*"

"Fuck. You." I growl. "I did not lie to you. I *never* lied to you."

"Wait." She holds up a hand. "You never *lied* to me?" She guffaws. "You left me in a fucking hotel room in Wyoming. Stranded me there, Nick. I was thirteen years old."

"Funny. I recall you showing up in Santa Barbara just a few weeks later."

"You left me a couple hundred dollars, a Styrofoam take-out container filled with soggy pancakes, and a note that said—"

"What's your point?"

"What's my *point*?" She guffaws again. "What's *your* fucking point?"

"You want to hear my point? Here it is. I love you and I only want what's best for you."

This is a dick fucking move and her face crumples. She is thirteen again. She is thirteen and I'm about to break her heart with my fucking practiced speech. I didn't have to do it then. I could've just done the whole thing with her. Hell, she showed up and played her part anyway, didn't she? What was the point of abandoning her the way I did?

I am ashamed to say that I don't even remember. That's how far away that day is for me.

But this look on her face right now, as those words came out of my mouth—she is not far away from that hotel room in Rock Springs.

She's still there.

I could stop. Right now. I could stop, and apologize, and own up to what I did, but I'm not going to. She needs to hear this today just as much as she did two decades ago. Because I did not fucking lie to her.

"I want you to go to school, Sasha."

"Stop." She puts up a hand. "I don't want to hear it."

"And live in a house," I continue. "And never pick up a gun again. I want you to wear dresses and go to dances. And have dates with boys who take you to eat hamburgers. I want you to study dinosaurs"—she lets out a sob, but I keep going—"and travel the fucking world looking for stupid clues about the past that no one else cares about. And once you've done all that *without me*—" She is full-on crying now. Tears are streaming down her face. "Once you've done all that *without me*, Sasha, you're gonna realize that you can love more than once in a lifetime."

"You're an asshole. You're a dick. I hate you, Nick Tate. I fucking hate your guts. I will never forgive you for leaving me in that hotel room. *Ever*."

"Now who's the liar?"

She just stares at me. "You think." It comes out as a whsper, "that I *forgave* you?"

"You *begged* me that night."

"I was thirteen. We were a promise."

"We didn't make that promise, Sasha. It was a filthy fucking blood bond between two men who trade and sell children like they're animals."

"It was different for us." Her words are low. Tears are still pouring out of her eyes, but her sobbing is over.

"It sure was," I agree. "It was very different for us because we got to *choose* who we made our promises with. Are you unhappy?"

"No."

"No," I agree. My voice is low now too. "You went to school, Sash. You lived in an amazing house across the street from City Park. You have two

292

brothers, two sisters, real parents, and a pack of dogs, for fuck's sake. You got a kitten for Christmas the day James dropped you off. You got straight A's, went to private high school, dug up dinosaur bones in Peru, and then you met the love of your life. None of this *sucked*. James, and Ford, and Merc, and Jax—they gave you a helluva lot more than I ever could've."

She looks down and wipes her face. Then she sucks in a long breath and meets my gaze again. "You lied to me. You made me think that I killed you."

"It was my brother."

"It was *sick*."

"It had to be done. He needed to die. Hell, he told you himself, Sasha. He wanted to die."

"And he needed *me* to do that?" Her words come out as a sob again.

"Of course he needed you to do it. The FBI was all over you back then. And when I say FBI, you and I both know that I don't mean FBI. Those guys were Company. And when you killed Santos, you brought that whole fucking corrupt system down and you. Became. The good guy."

"The good guy?" She shakes her head as she sniffles like crazy. "That's hilarious. I had nightmares. I cried for months."

"Months," I say, "are nothing. Your life is a fucking fairy tale right now. You have the house, the kids, the husband. And tell me, Sash—tell me you hate it, tell me you would give it all up to go on the fucking run with me for the next twenty years, and I'll apologize."

She hesitates.

"Tell me. Tell me you'd give them all up for me. That's the only way I'll feel sorry for what I did." I pause, giving her a moment to actually say that, knowing she won't. And then I continue. "I did what was best for you, Sasha. Because I owed your dad that much."

Her face crumples again. And it occurs to me that maybe she hasn't thought about this in a very long time. Maybe she pushed it all away, the same way I did, and just moved forward out of instinct.

So I walk towards her, tip her chin up and look her in the eyes. "I owed him, ya know. He helped me a lot when I was a kid. You know he never wanted us to be together. And can you blame him? He did everything in his power to save you. He never wanted you to be my promise. He died protecting you from them. No fucking way was I gonna steal your life. And yeah, it sucks. What happened to you at thirteen sucks, but you saw romance and that's not what it was. That's not what we had."

She shakes her head and steps around me, putting distance between us. I turn too, and that's when I notice that Wendy is standing on my front stoop, watching us.

I walk past Sasha, leaving her at the end of the driveway, and when I'm twenty feet away I extend my hand to Wendy. "Hey. Come here. I wanna introduce you to someone."

Wendy's eyes dart over my shoulder to Sasha, who has followed me down the driveway. "I know who she is. I'll leave you two alone."

I grab Wendy's hand before she can leave. She attempts to pull her hand from mine, but I hold tight and step forward until there is almost no distance between us. "Nothing. Has changed. Understand me?"

I pull back and look her in the eyes. She nods. But she's uncomfortable now and I hate that. Still, I force myself to smile as I turn back to Sasha. "Sash, this is Wendy. Wendy, Sasha."

They stare at each other, but neither of them says hello.

Merc appears on the other side of my screen door. Fucking coward. He clears his throat. "Sash. So glad you could come."

"Is this what you wanted my opinion on?" She flutters a hand in my direction.

"Yes." Merc nods. "But there's more to it than that." His eyes dart to mine. "A lot more, actually."

Harrison comes up behind us. Another coward. Not that I blame them. If the situation were reversed, I'd have hidden during that confrontation too.

"Fine," Sasha says. "I'm here. So fuck it. Tell me everything."

CHAPTER TWENTY-THREE

The sight of Sasha Cherlin at the top of the air stairs triggers things inside me. Not an urge to kill her, thank God. But in my mind, it's almost as bad. My breathing becomes erratic and quick. My heart thumps so hard, my ears begin pounding out this rhythm. My eyesight focuses, like it does when I'm on mission and I spot the target for the first time. This reaction has always felt a little... technical to me. Like I'm not really human at all. Like I'm some kind of machine. Of course, that's not it. Just a fantasy. This focus is not instinct, either. Not entirely. It's a well-practiced technique taught to me by Chek himself.

The focus comes with tunnel vision. For a split-second I lose all peripheral vision and instead I see only a single spot in front of me.

In my other life, this spot was my target.

But Sasha is not a target so I blink, then blink again, then again, until the focusing stops, and my heart settles, and my breathing is no longer ragged.

This takes about.... two seconds.

"Nice."

When I look at Merc, he's not smiling. He appears a little uneasy. "What?" I snap.

"That... reaction." He nods his head towards the driveway. "To Sasha?" He doesn't seem too sure, but he continues anyway. "I've seen Sydney do it, but she was not... well. Not on your level. Not even close."

"Sydney," I mutter. "Channing, right? Daughter of some senator."

"Yeah. That's her."

"She and I are nothing alike."

"No." And maybe I don't really hear it, but I hear it. In his head he's thinking... *Thank God*. "She wasn't nearly as well-trained as you. She's not blonde, either. No blue eyes."

"In other words, she's not crazy and evil."

"Oh. No." He kinda chuckles. "That's not what I meant. She totally has her crazy and evil moments. She was brought up... she would kill me—not literally—if she knew I was talking about her like this. She's real private. But you get it, right? You get what she is, even if she's not exactly like you? They did things to her. Terrible things to her. She lost her shit."

I think about this for a moment. "But you married her, right? You're still together, right?"

"Oh, fuck yeah. I love her."

"She doesn't frighten you?"

"Nah." Merc says this with a long sigh. "I mean, when she gets pissed at me over normal shit, I kinda like it." He smiles. "And she's not like..."

"Go ahead. You can say it. She's not like me."

"I mean that in a good way for you. You're one of those super-soldiers, right? They invested time, and money, and training into you, Wendy. Sydney was an afterthought. So when I say she's not like you, what I mean is that she's a lot more vulnerable."

I ponder this for a moment as I watch Sasha Cherlin make her way down the air steps towards my Nick and he waits for her.

I have imagined this moment ever since I learned what Nick really did that first day we met. I was too young and too new to understand what was happening offshore in Santa Barbara that night. And to be honest, I didn't really like Nick before I went to live with him and Lauren. When I looked at him back then all I saw were secrets and lies. Of course, I didn't know anything about his secrets and lies the way I do now, so it always put me off.

Normally I hate liars, but Nick's lies were never really lies. He always tells the truth, he just almost never tells the *whole* truth.

I'm OK with it. Because sometimes I need these almost-lies. Other times I don't, and then I pick my way past what he's saying and hear what he's not saying. I feel like he gives me a choice. Do I want to be ignorant? If so, take him at his word. If not, dig deeper.

I like the choice. I like that he gives me the choice. It's how he protects me. And even though I don't want to know what he's protecting me from—I prefer the almost-lie in that regard—I love the fuck out of him for doing it.

Nick makes a move, stepping forward towards Sasha. I inhale sharply, unsure how I feel about this. But then Sasha takes a step back—like she doesn't want him to get too close—and I let that breath out.

I can't see Nick's lips. He knows better and has his back to me. I've never told him that I can read lips, but at this point in our relationship, he knows. He's a careful man.

Sasha's clothes are... I dunno. Predictable ex-assassin, I guess. Her look says, *Yep. I'm a mom and I live in the suburbs, but don't fuck with me.* At least, that's what I see.

Her lips move just as her diamond wedding ring sparkles in the sun. *Nothing to say to me?* So apparently Nick isn't talking. *Well? You guys brought me here, what the fuck do you want?*

"Maybe we should give them privacy?" Merc says.

"Knock yourself out," I snap. His comment made me miss something because now Sasha is walking towards Nick. And he's just letting her!

My heart is beating fast again, the tunnel vision starting. I close my eyes, missing even more, as I pull myself together.

I am in charge of me.

Sweet, beautiful, perfect, whole.

I am in charge of me.

Everlasting, transcendent, exceptional, extraordinary.

I control me, no one else.

Remarkable, exquisite, priceless, sublime.

When I open my eyes again, my heart is back to normal and Nick is looking over his shoulder at the house. But it's just a quick look and I don't think he spots Merc and me in the window.

Do I scare you or something? Sasha laughs. *Because I'm not that girl anymore. Haven't been her since that day out in Kansas when I killed you.*

Well. She's not subtle, is she? Goes right for the kill shot.

I miss what happens next because Nick looks over his shoulder again and I lock in on his face for that brief moment and memorize it. Then analyze it.

What is he thinking right now?

He loves her?

He wants her?

I miss more, because Sasha's now demanding to know Nick's thoughts. And then... it's like the dam breaks and there is a flurry of words coming out of Sasha's mouth. But they come with hand gestures, and movement, and *feelings*.

So many, *many* fucking feelings.

I lose track again.

And then... then her whole face changes. She's not angry, she's sad now. She *cries*. And I know this affects Nick. Maybe she planned it that way? Because he takes steps and steps towards her, and she does not back up this time.

Then they are so close I can't see her face anymore. I break for the door. Merc makes a grab at my arm, but I pull out of his reach, throw the door open and stand on the front stoop. Just... watching them.

Sasha sidesteps away, and Nick turns and see me watching them.

Everything changes.

Sasha stops crying.

Nick turns away from her, walks down the driveway to me, and as he gets closer, he extends his hand.

I don't want to meet him halfway, and I don't. But I do come down the steps. I can't help myself.

"Hey. Come here. I wanna introduce you to someone." When he reaches me, he takes my hand. But I'm focused on Sasha now, because she followed him.

Of course she followed him. I know the stories of these two. They were promised. Her dad was forced to make a deal with his dad and that was gonna be it for them. Marriage, Company kids, whatever.

Nick was the one who walked out.

Sasha was always the one who couldn't let go.

"I know who she is," I say. "I'll leave you two alone."

Nick has a hold of my hand when I try to pull away, but he tugs me towards him until we bump together. "Nothing. Has changed." His voice is low, but clear. "Understand me?" Then he pulls back a little so he can look me in the eyes and wait for my answer.

I nod.

He turns and smiles. "Sash, this is Wendy. Wendy, Sasha."

Sasha Cherlin and I stare at each other. We could be twins, maybe. If I were older or she were younger. Same blonde hair, same evil blue eyes.

But she and I are nothing alike. Because she is not me. She is not... *us*.

She is free. She is normal. She has a house, and a dog, and a family. *My* family, actually. Because she has Lauren. And Lauren, and Nick, and Chek were all I ever had to begin with. And ever since Nick sent Lauren to live with Sasha, I have been missing something. Missing her, of course. But it was more than that.

And then, when Check died, I was missing another something. Him, of course, but again, it was so much more than that. Because all I had left was Nick.

And now I find that I need more Nick.

More, and more, and *more* Nick.

But now *she's* here.

She's going to make her claim and demand her parts. Little parts at first. But then more, and more, and more parts until there's nothing left for me. No leftovers, even. She will get Lauren and Nick and I will have no one.

I'm just about to break away and run. Just get in my truck and drive. For days, and days, and days. Maybe I'll never stop. I'll drive west until I run out of road, then go south until I come to the end of the world. I'll disappear. I'll leave them alone. They don't need me. I'm just baggage. I'm just—

The screen door slaps behind me and Nick and I turn to find Merc on the stoop behind us. "Sash." This single word just a little bit hesitant. "So glad you could come."

"Is this what you wanted my opinion on?" Sasha is annoyed when she motions to Nick.

"Yes. But there's more to it than that." Merc and Nick lock eyes for a moment. "A lot more, actually."

This is when I notice that Harrison has exited the plane and is walking down the driveway towards us, looking like he'd rather be anywhere but here.

"Fine." Sasha shrugs. "I'm here. So fuck it. Tell me everything."

Merc nods his head towards Harrison. "Let's talk in private."

She doesn't argue. No one argues. Sasha Cherlin turns her back to Nick and me, and she and Merc meet up with Harrison halfway down the driveway, then they walk back towards the plane.

"Follow me." Nick still has a hold of my hand, so when he starts walking, I go with him. He says nothing, just leads me towards the field of sunflowers. It's late in the day now. The sun is almost gone. But a little bit of orange glow lingers like a halo over the top of the tall flowers.

We enter the field and this is when I realize I have no shoes on. But it's a good thing. The dirt is thick and soft. It's special dirt. Cared-for dirt. Dirt filled with everything a little seed needs to survive and grow big. It's late summer so the sunflowers are tall now, much taller than me. The gorgeous yellow heads kiss Nick's shoulders as we push past row, after row. They leave behind little dots of orange and black. A clue, I think. But I'm not sure what mystery we're solving. We turn into another row and suddenly the whole sky is lit up red before me. And it's such a beautiful contrast over the golden sunflowers—so, so, *so* fuckin' pretty—I might cry over it.

But then the words are there.

My words whispering in my ear.

My kisses with Nick.

Flawless, marvelous, divine, sensational.
Heavenly, powerful, glorious, delightful.

Nick stops on the edge of the sunflowers and I see that we have come to a clearing. Everything about the now feels like a fantasy. Like I'm in someone's storybook and this is the perfect ending. Nick looks over his shoulder at me, smiling. He says, "I made this

304

for us. Years ago, actually. I never let them plant anything here, but I make them cut the grass so it's short and soft."

Then he pulls me into the clearing with him and we take a moment to spin in place, staring up at the sky.

I'm lost, I think.

And it's so weird. Because wasn't I just found a few hours ago?

Gorgeous, the words say.

Gorgeous, gorgeous, gorgeous, they insist.

But it's not. Not really, is it?

Because I'm not the last Wild Child, am I?

I am not the last of anything.

I'm a whole new *miserable* beginning.

CHAPTER TWENTY-FOUR

Sasha is shaking when she reaches for the cup of tea that Harrison brewed while she was facing her worst nightmare. Shaking hard enough that some of the liquid spills over the side of the private-jet-approved bone china cup when she raises it to her mouth.

"Are you OK?" Harrison asks.

It should be me asking. I should not have brought her here. What the hell was I thinking?

"Fine." Sasha sets the cup down on the little matching saucer and the two pieces of porcelain clatter together for a moment until they settle. Then Sasha smooths out an imaginary wrinkle in her tank top, takes a deep breath, and looks right at me. "What the fuck, Merc?"

"I should've told you—"

"I told him it was a bad idea—"

"I specifically said I do not want to know!"

We're all talking at the same time so for a couple seconds the inside of the little jet feels like chaos. But once we get out all our initial complaints and confessions—for me, at least—we linger in another heavy silence.

Sasha turns her back to me and walks over to the closest window. Movement catches my attention and I watch as Nick Tate leads Wendy Gale into a field of tall sunflowers until they both disappear. Sasha turns back and crosses her arms. "I cannot believe you brought me here."

"This whole thing has gotten complicated." I'm on the verge of begging her to cut me a break.

"Yeah. Because Merc here kidnapped Nick Tate's *girlfriend*, mentally fucked her over for a few days, and then dangled her situation in front of him until he caved. This is a complete shit show and I am against all of it! But I'm not in charge, so whatever!"

Harrison turns, walks into the cockpit, and closes the little door. I would like to think it's because he wants to give us privacy, but that's definitely not why he just walked out.

He is blaming me.

"Fine." I throw up my hands. "It's all my fault. I'm a big ol' dick. And I have now earned the blame for every bad thing that happens to us for the next ten years. I accept that. But I don't have a choice and once you hear the story, maybe you won't agree with me, but at least you'll understand."

Sasha lets out a long exhale. Then she slips into a seat and points to the other one across the table. "Sit then. Tell me everything. Jax is gonna be pissed. He still works for the FBI, Merc! We're not supposed to know this kind of shit!"

I sit, lean back into the luxurious leather seat, and put my hands out in a mea culpa gesture. "OK. I get it.

I fucked up. But does that mean you don't want to hear my story or—"

"Of course I want to hear the fucking story!"

We both laugh. "It's really not my fault, Sasha. You sent me on this job."

"Job? It wasn't a job!"

"Fuck yeah, it was. Adam Boucher wants me to unfuck Donovan Couture, Sasha. That's one hundred percent the description of a fucking job!"

She narrows her eyes at me. "So it's my fault?"

"Yep."

She turns her head away and stares at the sunflower field. But I catch a small smile.

"Listen, it's a can of fucking worms, OK? And you're the one who gave me Wendy's name."

She turns back to me. "Because I didn't think you were stupid enough to *kidnap* her."

"I tracked her for a couple days and decided she's pretty dangerous."

"No shit, Sherlock. She's a seasoned professional Company Zero girl assassin!"

I nod. "Yeah. She's pretty good too." I pull aside some of my very thick dark hair and show Sasha the gash on my skull. "She was wearing a spiked bracelet. Fucking thing needed seven stitches. And I had to do that myself. In the mirror. Do you have any idea how hard it is to stitch up the side of your head in a mirror?"

Sasha scoffs. "You're lucky to be alive. What the hell were you thinking? And she's his *girlfriend?*"

Sasha is good, but not good enough to hide the feelings that come out with that question. "I don't know if she's his girlfriend. But she's something to him."

"Something important. Obviously." And again, she looks at the sunflower field where Nick and Wendy disappeared. She snaps out of it and looks me in the eyes. "Tell me everything."

So I tell her. "When I left Fort Collins I stopped by that tattoo shop on my way out of town and talked to that pink-haired girl."

"Belinda."

"Yep. Her."

"Why?"

"Because remember how she just appeared out of nowhere right before that Kansas shit went down?"

Sasha's face goes dark. Not pale. Thinking about Kansas right now is making her angry, not sad. "No. I don't really remember that. I was a little busy back then trying to outrun the FBI."

"Well, she did appear out of nowhere. I didn't make a big deal, of course, because it wasn't my business. I'm not really connected to those Vaughn brothers, so what the fuck do I care, right?"

Sasha shrugs. "OK."

"So I go in to the tattoo shop and she recognizes me. Maybe we don't hang out or anything, but she's seen me around at various holiday parties and whatnot. And I ask her about a girl named Wendy. And she says, 'Creepy Wendy?' And I say, 'Maaaaybeee?' And she says, 'Last I heard she was working for Tony Dumas's cousin-brother-in-law, Zach.'"

Sasha smiles. "Cousin-brother-in-law?"

"It actually makes sense."

She waves a hand. "Yes. I know who Zach is."

"So I go down to Key West where this Zach guy lives and park in front of his house. And I wasn't there ten minutes scoping shit out when he appears, walks over to my car, and says, 'I think I know you.'"

"What did you say?"

"We argued about that a bit."

Sasha chuckles.

"But turns out, he did know me. At least, *of* me, OK? And then he says, 'Nick Tate,' Sasha. Nick Tate used my name as a threat back when Cabal Island was going down."

Sasha makes a face. "What the hell is Cabal Island?"

I point at her. "That's what I said. And he said that while you were doing Kansas, they—like thousands of 'thems'—were all down in the Caribbean fucking shit up for the Company elites and they call this operation Cabal Island."

"So Nick was there?"

"He was there."

"But he was with me—" She stops. Because of course, Nick was not with her.

"That was his brother, Santos."

"His brother?" Her voice is low now. Almost a whisper. And then she's silent for a moment and I can almost hear all the wheels inside her head spinning around as she puts this all together. "I knew that wasn't him." She looks up at me. "I fucking *knew*. That *wasn't* him. I told Jax that when he took me to that FBI safehouse. I know you never saw it, but he had thousands of pictures, Merc. Of this guy who looked just like Nick *if* you erased all the crazy drug-lord tattoos and facial scars. I fucking *knew* that wasn't him."

"It wasn't him."

311

"Then what happened?"

"Well, this Zach guy was actually pretty helpful. He said I was a legend, that he'd been dying to meet me—"

"Merc. No one cares about your legendary status. What happened next?"

"He knew Creepy Wendy and after I promised not to hurt her, he told me about her stomping grounds so I could go look for her."

"So you lied to him."

"I didn't hurt her."

"You kidnapped her."

"And drugged her. And... got inside her mind. But I was on a new mission now, right?"

"Find Nick Tate."

"And here we are."

"Why am I here again?"

"I need your advice. Because OK, I found Nick. That's cool, I guess. I can get over the betrayal if you can. But"—I point at her—"if you want to stay angry, I'm on your side. I will hate that fucker until the day he dies."

She waves a hand at me. "Whatever. What do you want to ask me, Merc? I want to go home."

"This Donovan thing."

"You're gonna do it?"

"I think I have to—"

"You don't have to, Merc. If you're not comfortable getting involved, then just say no. I will tell Adam that I did my best."

"It's not quite that simple anymore."

"Why not?"

"Because I have since learned, from both Creepy Wendy—"

"Don't call her that. She's a grown woman. No grown woman wants to be called Creepy Wendy."

"Sorry. I have since learned from both *Gwendolyn* and Nicholas"—she scoffs at me—"that there is... could be... maybe a problem."

"What kind of problem?"

"With the girls."

Sasha sits up. "What do you mean?"

"I would like to preface this with the disclaimer that we don't actually know if any of this shit is true—"

"What *shit*, Merc?"

"That guy Donovan? He's... twisted."

"Yeah, I know. Carter."

"Right. Carter. Well, according to Nicholas Tate—" She smiles. She can't help it. I'm quite funny when I want to be. "He says that Carter had some breeding program going and that he's been making Zero girls for the last fifteen years."

"OK."

"And Nicholas says that Carter is the father of my girls and has placed a trigger inside them. That he made them like Indie, Sasha. That one day my sweet girls will go off the rails the way that girl did. Which can't be true, right? I mean, Daphne is such a good kid. She is, Sash. You know her. You've seen her. None of my girls are a problem. They're perfect. And Daphne is almost sixteen and this Donovan guy is what? Thirty?"

"Hmm."

I expect Sasha to agree with me immediately. Surely this asshole has not been fathering children since he was a teenager. Even for the Company, that's fucked up. But she dithers. "What do you mean, hmm? I'm right, right? There's no way some stupid teenager took over this bizarre sci-fi breeding program and started making assassins."

"Well. I can't say for sure, and here's why. Donovan, and Carter by proxy, was not a normal kid. He was some kind of child genius. He went to medical school when he was fifteen. Medical school, Merc. Which means he was in regular university when he was like twelve. So yeah. It's unlikely that what Nick said is entirely true. He claims he never lied to me, and if I had any leftover fucks to hand out to him and wanted to think this over thoroughly, I'd probably have to agree with that. But I think we have to assume that there is some nugget of truth in what Nick told you. Even if most of what he said ends up being flawed information."

I let out a long breath and look out the window. "So it's entirely possible that my girls came from this psycho's program and he put a trigger inside them?"

"I think the part about the Zero program is accurate. They were part of that. But whether or not Carter fathered them or had the time to mess with their heads? That's another story. Especially for Lily, right? She was so small when you got her."

"I need to find out. I can't just walk away from this. And I have another problem too. I—" But I can't get the words out.

"You what? Don't make me wait for it, Merc. What?"

"I kinda… miss this stuff."

"What?"

314

"I mean, if I meet these people, and do this job... I'm not sure I'll be able to stop. I retired early. I've been a good father and husband for almost a whole decade now. I kept everyone safe. But if this turns out to be true—if these assholes like Carter are still out there and not in control—then I have to do something about it. I can't walk away from that."

Sasha sighs. "Well. You were right. You did have a damn good reason for bringing me here today."

I nod and lean back in my seat.

But she doesn't even know the half of it yet. And I'm not ready to tell her the rest.

I'm not ready to admit that I might want to save Carter Couture so I can get this shit done. And I'm certainly not going to tell her Nick and I might be teaming up against Adam in the near future.

All that shit is just... need-to-know.

And right now, she doesn't need to know.

CHAPTER TWENTY-FIVE

I say the words as we spin slowly in a circle of sunflowers. It is sweet, beautiful, perfect, and whole. It is everlasting, transcendent, exceptional, and extraordinary. It is remarkable, exquisite, priceless, and sublime. It is flawless, marvelous, divine, and sensational. It is heavenly, powerful, glorious, and delightful.

It is lovely.

It is majestic.

It is gorgeous.

And it is misery.

But I wouldn't change a thing.

Wendy Gale isn't the kind of girl you let go of. I think I've made my point on that. And maybe you don't agree—whatever. I give no fucks what anyone else thinks about what I am doing. I did this and I take full responsibility.

Wendy is saying the words too. We repeat them over and over. Her voice is small and low like it was back in the beginning. We spin one more time and then

I stop and she stops with me. Her eyes are distant as they look up at the sky.

Indie got a lot of things right about us, but she missed all the critical things that make us... *us*.

I'm not saying what we do in the sunflowers is the most important part about who and what Wendy and I are, because that would diminish how I feel about her. But the sunflowers are up there with us being curious travelers, lost wanderers, and professional killers.

But what we do in the sunflowers makes us a team.

And here's the thing, OK? It's not an excuse. I'm not defending myself. I don't think I have anything to defend, but... here's the thing.

I will do *anything* for her.

Anything.

I will literally blow up the entire fucking planet to save Wendy Gale.

Letting go has never been an option.

And when I found that book she stole from that library all those years ago, when she was just a child who barely knew anything about herself, I made a decision right then and there.

Look at what she scribbled on those pages.

Read it yourself.

Ten Zeroes, they go on a hunt in the night.
They run, and they scream, and they kick, and they bite.
But the island is small and the danger is great.
So the Zeroes give in and live out their fate.

They rounded us up and put us in pens.
They gave us all numbers and sold us to men.
They taught us to fight and be wicked and wild.

They split us apart to get rid of the child.

I am what's left of the girl left behind.
I am strong, and skilled, and cunning, and wise.
I will never be weak, I will never deny
That work is my life and my master my prize.

I have words for her words and here they are:
Nasty, foul, disgusting, and rank.
Obscene, revolting, indecent, and vile.
Sick, repulsive, loathsome, and gross.
I could go on, and on, and on.
But I won't. There's no point.
I know what she is.
I know what she can do.
But I also know I can *fix her.*
So that's what I did.
Wouldn't you have done the same thing?

When I found that book, I made a choice. And when she showed up at her cabin on her seventeenth birthday—seventeen days after her life *imploded*—I knew what I had to do.

She wanted a cure, so I would be her cure.

I am her cure.

CHAPTER TWENTY-SIX

"We're not driving to Louisiana. What the fuck is wrong with you people?" This is a serious question I'm asking. "We have a jet, Nick. Right out there in your fucking front yard. Why the hell would we waste an entire day and drive thirteen hundred miles when we can get there in two hours?"

"First of all"—Nick holds up a finger—"we need to go back to Mount Pleasant."

"Fuck that," I growl. "No."

"Yes," Nick insists. "My truck is still in Mount Pleasant."

"Who cares? I'm not giving in on the drive, but if I were to give in, why the fuck would we need two trucks?"

"Because this is how Wendy and I do things, OK? We're leaving here in Wendy's truck, we're driving to Mount Pleasant so I can pick up my truck, and then we'll split up—"

"Fuck you." I laugh. "Do you think I'm stupid? Let me guess, you and Wendy get in your truck and Sasha, Harrison, and I get in Wendy's truck—"

"I'm not going," Harrison says.

We all stop the conversation to look at Harrison. "What?" I ask.

"I'm not going," he says. "I'm going home, Merc. I'm too old for this shit. So maybe Nick's idea is a good one."

I let out a long breath of frustration as I look over at Sasha. We're all sitting at Nick's backyard picnic table. It's late now. Dark and no moon. But there's a whole line of citronella candles in the middle of the table, so everyone's face is flickering with flames. Sasha shrugs, and we're so close, her shoulder bumps against mine.

"It's probably for the best," Nick says. He's talking to Harrison. Then he looks across the table at me. "And no. You and I can drive in my truck and Sasha and Wendy can drive in hers."

I don't know that I fully understand the deep connection these two killers have with their fucking vehicles, but whatever. If Harrison's out—and it sounds like he is—then we really don't have a choice. My truck is back in Fort Collins, so… "Whatever," I huff. Then I look at Sasha again. "Is this all OK with you?"

I'm talking about her riding with Wendy, but I think Sasha is more worried about being stuck with Nick. "Sure." She smiles at Wendy, who is sitting across the table next to Nick. "I'm sure Wendy and I have enough in common to fill a two-day road trip."

And this makes me think about spending all that time with Nick.

I groan because it's gonna be horrible.

Sasha pats my arm as she reads my mind. "You'll live."

After an uncomfortable sleep on Nick's floor—Harrison took the couch, Sasha stayed in the jet, and Nick and Wendy took the only bedroom with a bed—I wake just as the sun is rising. We say goodbye to Harrison, pile into Wendy's truck, and start our ten-hour drive to Mount Pleasant.

Nick and Wendy trade places driving while Sasha and I doze in the back.

Pretty much no one says anything and we stay the night at the hotel. Sash and I get separate rooms, but Wendy and Nick stay together.

They are a team, I realize. And I guess I knew this, but I didn't understand the extent of their connection. They are a couple and they do couple things. Like speak without words. They shoot each other those *looks*.

So I spend all of the day-two drive thinking about that.

Nick isn't chatty, so I'm grateful for that. He doesn't prompt me for small talk. In fact, he pays more attention to Wendy—who is in a whole other vehicle—than he does to me. So this gives me a lot of time to think.

Thinking can be good. But overthinking is almost never going to get you where you need to go.

So lots of what-ifs begin creeping into my mind as we head south. And we're just starting to get to that part of Louisiana where you don't dare pull over to the side of the road because the vegetation could be hiding any number of weird bayou predators when it hits me.

Something is wrong with this entire... what to call it? Encounter? Job? Mission? Take your pick. And here's how I know something is wrong:

I got to thinking about the image board where all us dangerous types hang out to get intel. And then I started thinking about how that anonymous person misdirected the diggers away from Sasha and on to Nick. I don't ask him about this even though that would probably make the last couple hours of this nearly intolerable drive go faster, because I don't want to tip him off.

He was that guy. I know it. I feel this in my gut and you don't get as far as I have in this fucked-up shadow world without listening to your gut.

Fine. I understand that move. Distraction, right?

Look here, not there. Follow me, not her.

Mistakes always happen when you're looking the other way.

I knew this.

But even though you know things, when you're in the middle of a PSYOP it's almost inevitable that you lose your way—even if it's just for a few moments as you stop, calm yourself down, and put the pieces together.

I lost my way here with good ol' Nick Tate.

Because he did the oldest trick in the book on me again.

Look here, not there.

Look at Adam, look at Carter, look at Donovan, look at your girls, look at Sasha.

Look at all the things.

But whatever you do, Merc... do not look at Wendy.

CHAPTER TWENTY-SEVEN

They call it Old Home, a leftover bit of grandeur from the old days. It's surrounded on three sides by a lake and the winding, sandy banks of the Old Pearl River. I have never been here, but I've relentlessly spied on it over the past several years with high-altitude drones equipped with night vision.

That night vision didn't do it justice because when I follow Wendy's truck down the long Spanish oak-lined driveway I almost lose my breath when the house comes into view.

The pecan trees, lush, geometric gardens, and sunset-lit lake are just the icing on the cake that is the mansion. I suddenly feel less of a person for having grown up on a superyacht. For wanting to call a swim platform 'home' when Adam Boucher grew up here.

Beyond the house are the infamous woods. Filled with snakes, and gators, and probably even panthers. The entire place smells like... earth. Deep, rich, dark dirt. But not the kind I have up in Nebraska. This earth is overflowing with other things. Magic, maybe.

"Wow." Merc is craning his neck to get a better look at things. "I was expecting something over the top, but this—"

He doesn't finish his sentence. He doesn't need to.

There are already four trucks in the driveway when we pull up, but don't you worry. There's room enough for ten more vehicles after we pull in next to them.

Off to the left is a shop that looks like a barn. A man comes out wearing a welding apron and shielding his eyes from the sun glare. McKay. Core McKay. Infamous Zero-girl trainer and constant confidant to Adam. But I barely get a look at him before my attention is pulled over to a little girl on the massive front porch.

A little *blonde* girl.

I stare at her as an old, familiar feeling rushes through my body.

Then a blonde woman appears. Indie. And I give the little girl a name. Magnolia. So very, *very* Southern, that name.

There is a moment of heavy hesitation as Indie and I stare at each other through the windshield. She could be Wendy—even after their very different upbringings, they are still that alike.

It's unsettling.

But then the screen door slaps closed behind Indie and Adam appears behind her.

He could be me. Even after our very different upbringings, we are still that alike.

No, I caution myself internally. My eyes are brown. His are not.

Like there was some kind of cue, we all get out of the trucks at the same time. Wendy walks around the back of my truck, coming up behind me to take my hand. But that silence is back and we all just… stare at each other for a good ten seconds.

Finally, Adam says, "Wendy, would you like to introduce us?"

Of course he says that.

Six Degrees of Wendy Gale.

She is what connects us, not me.

Wendy lets go of my hand, walks over to Adam, leans up on her tiptoes, and plants a kiss on his cheek. "Long time."

Adam is only looking at me when he answers. "Too long, Wen."

Wendy turns back to her little band of… whatever we are, and smiles. "Adam, this is Nick. I'm sure you've met though, right?"

"No," I say. "We actually haven't."

"Of course," Adam says. "That was your *brother*."

Wendy is a professional. She's been around more egocentric dangerous men than she could ever hope to count, so she slides right into the other introductions. "Well, that's McKay." She points to him as he walks around our little troop and stands at the bottom of the stairs with his arms crossed like he's some kind of badass bodyguard. Which he is, I suppose.

Wendy grabs Indie's hand and pulls her in for a hug. Indie hugs her back, and they don't cut it short, either. They take their hello seriously. Wendy has her back to me so at first I don't realize they're talking, but then I catch Indie's lips moving as they whisper greetings, or secrets, or, hell, threats for all I know.

But probably not threats, because Wendy is smiling a real smile—it's sad, so it's real—when she turns back to us and says, "And that's Maggie."

Maggie beams her smile right at me. "Nick. Nick. Nick." She says it like maybe she's trying out my name the way any normal kid might. But then again, maybe she's just committing my face to memory so she can kill me later.

"Where's Nathan?" I ask. He's the only one, aside from Wendy, who I know up close and personal.

"He's across the lake right now. We're building a house over there."

We all turn in unison to glance over at the wooden frame of a future lake house. There is no sign of Nathan St. James, but we all pretend he's over there.

"And you know Sasha." Adam and Sasha exchange a look. It is neither friendly nor filled with animosity. It's tentative. Like they are old acquaintances, but they were both really hoping they'd never have to see or speak to each other again.

"Sasha. How very nice to finally see you again. It's been a very long time."

"We might as well have never met." There's no heat in Sasha's tone, but her words have an edge. "That's how far away I am from that little girl who owes you this debt."

Adam looks her up and down, not actually leering at her—I highly doubt Adam Boucher is interested in Sasha that way—but it's definitely a once-over. "I would have to agree. You are nothing like that girl I once knew."

"And that's Merc." Wendy shrugs like her part in this is over now.

Adam walks over to Merc and extends his hand. "It is a pleasure to finally meet you, Merrick."

I huff and Adam shoots me a sideways glance. "What?"

I put up both hands. "Nothin'." But silently I find it pretentious that Adam, and only Adam, has the nerve to call Merc by his given name when most of the world doesn't even know that moniker exists.

But then again, did I really expect Adam Boucher to invite us into his home without having the upper hand in some way?

Maybe not even just some ways, but all the ways?

Merc takes offense to the unauthorized familiarity, but has enough sense not to say anything. I might not have seen this man in almost twenty years, but he's a lot easier to read than he thinks.

He shakes Adam's hand, but doesn't say anything back.

"Well," Indie says, "that's that. Come on, Wendy. I wanna show you your room."

And then that *is* that. Because both Indie and Maggie grab Wendy by the hand and lead her inside. Wendy doesn't look back at me and I'm proud of her for that.

"Come on," McKay says, nodding his head in the direction of Merc and Sasha. "I'll show you your rooms."

McKay takes the porch steps three at a time and Adam falls in next to him as they head for the door.

Merc, Sasha, and I all look at each other for a moment, then we shrug and follow.

When we get inside McKay says, "Sasha and Merc, you two are down this way." He points to a doorway on the other side of the large formal living room. There are enough windows in this place to see that the doorway leads to a breezeway that separates the two wings of the mansion. Merc and Sasha follow him and then disappear.

But I'm distracted by the chatter of girls and the sound of feet thumping on old wooden floors above my head and look at the ceiling.

"Indie made a place for you and Wendy on the third floor," Adam says. "You must've made quite an impression on her when you talked."

I redirect my attention back to Adam Boucher and I'm taken aback for a moment. It's fucking freaky how alike we are. "Why do ya say that?"

Adam nods his head to the upstairs. "She made me drive her into New Orleans yesterday to buy an AC unit for the third-floor bedroom. And while we were gone, she made McKay fix it up."

"Oh." I look up the long, grand staircase and relax a little. "That was nice of her."

"Wasn't really for you, I don't think. She likes Wendy." Then he narrows his eyes at me. "We all like Wendy."

"That we do," I agree.

"Why are you here, Nick?"

"You wanted Merc, I delivered you Merc."

"You brought me Merc, Sasha Cherlin, Wendy Gale, and yourself."

"So? You want me to leave or something?"

"Not at all. I'm more curious than ever."

He's *Southern.* I mean, I always knew this, but his accent seems different now that we're actually face to face in his very, very, *very* Southern mansion. A little thicker, maybe. Not that noticeable, still barely there. But it's disconcerting. Like I don't know him.

"I just want you to know," Adam continues, "that I will not tolerate any fuckery of any kind when it comes to Donovan. If you interfere—"

"I'm not here to interfere."

"Good." He lets out a breath and nods his head to the stairs. "Then why don't you join me for a drink by the pool. I'm sure everyone else will find their way to us when it's appropriate."

"What about Donovan?"

"What about him?"

"Aren't we gonna like… look in on the guy? He's the whole reason we're here."

Adam squints his eyes at me again. "He's the reason Merc is here. Why you are here, well, that's still up for debate."

I plead no contest with my hands. "A drink it is, then."

I follow him down a hallway, through a large chef's kitchen attached to a massive floor-to-ceiling-window lined family room, and duck past sheer curtains billowing in the breeze that cover an open French door. We find ourselves on the pool deck. It's a gorgeous pool. This entire property is much, *much* more than I expected it to be and I once again find myself comparing our lives.

We are so very alike, but all the things around us are so very different.

"So." Adam leads me over to a wet bar underneath a large pergola. "You and Wendy. How's that work?"

"How's what work?"

I expect Adam to serve up some kind of pretentious whiskey. I expect crystal glasses. I expect him to be a lot like my father, I realize. So when he reaches into a fridge and pulls out two silver cans of Ghost in the Machine, I am forced to take a second look at what seems like my lifelong nemesis.

I take the can and nod my head in thanks. We pop them open, drink, and then we both turn to look at the thick, encroaching woods on the other side of the massive, immaculate pool.

"So. You and Wendy, huh?" Adam tries again. "What's that like?"

"What's it *like*?" I side-eye him. "It's lovely, Adam."

"She's very young."

"So?"

"You're, what? The same age I am, right?"

"I guess."

"And Wendy is the same age as Indie, right?"

"I... couldn't even tell ya."

"There's like half a year difference between them. But it's easy enough to see that they come from the same crop."

I let out a breath. "I would appreciate it if you didn't talk about my wife that way."

Adam's laugh is so loud, a whole flock of birds squawk and take flight from the thick canopy of trees. "*Wife*?"

I take a casual drink of my beer and caution myself to be cool. "That's right. You heard me."

"When did this happen?"

"Last New Year's."

"Well." Adam turns his body so he can face me. "I'm hurt that I wasn't invited to the celebration."

"It was a private affair."

"I expect it was."

Seconds tick off in silence and I can practically hear the wheels grinding inside Adam's head. He's not sure of me now. Maybe he had some reason cooked up for why I was suddenly so involved in his life. Maybe he sees past the whole Sasha phone call.

But I doubt it.

He has no idea what I'm doing here.

"Can I ask you something?"

I shrug. "I might not answer, but whatever."

"Why?"

"Why what?"

"Why Wendy?"

"Why not Wendy? No." I put up a hand before he can speak. I should let this go, but I can't. I should let him think anything he wants about Wendy and me, but I won't. I'm going to set him straight. "I love her, Adam. And I hope you don't doubt that because it would be unfortunate if anything happened to her at any point in the future. I will *destroy* everything in front of me if it comes down to protecting Wendy."

"Whoa, whoa, whoa. Hold on there. You're touchy tonight, Nick. I wouldn't dream of harming a single hair on Wendy Gale's head. She is a valued member of my team."

"I understand that. But this needs to be said." I pause to look him in the eyes. "Because there will be no second chance. Wendy might have been a valued employee in your *organization*"—I practically sneer that word—"but she is mine now, do you understand me?"

"Perfectly. If anyone should ever hurt... *our* Wendy, trust me"—he tilts his chin up like he's superior to me—"I would be the first in line to deliver retribution. She is one of *us*."

"One of *us*," I agree.

Adam smiles. "Exactly. Us, Nick. Us. We are all on the same team."

I hold my can of beer up and knock it against his. "That we are."

But it's not the team he thinks.

I am on Team Wendy and regardless of what Adam Boucher thinks, there is no room for him and his ilk with us.

"So. What have you been up to all these years, Nick? Keeping busy, I'm sure."

"You know what I've been up to. Nathan St. James lives here, and he's far more *us* than I am. Where is he, Adam?"

Adam actually has the gall to look around. Like Nathan is hiding in the bushes and we just misplaced him. "Oh, he's lurking somewhere."

"Building that house across the lake, maybe."

"Maybe." Adam smiles. "But back to you. Tell me more."

I almost laugh. "I haven't told anything, so how could I tell you more?"

"Is this how it's gonna be then?"

"If you mean the cat-and-mouse game?" I shrug. "I can't see any way around it, can you?"

Adam turns to face me. He's not that far away. And even though we're like *exactly* the same height and build, we didn't have the same training growing up. We are very different in all the ways that matter. But that doesn't mean he's not formidable. He did have that brain injury, courtesy of Indie. But he was an assassin, after all. Not rank and file, which is what I would call Nathan. So Adam Boucher is not a man you underestimate. And I don't.

He says, "Why are you *here*, Nick?"

"I'm delivering your PSYOPS agent, as requested."

Adam's eyes narrow down into tiny slits as he parses my words, trying his best to read between the lines. "Merc?"

My heart flutters a little at his question. "Who else?"

He cocks his head to the side like he's genuinely perplexed. "Are you lying to me, Nick Tate?"

"I do not lie."

He barks out a laugh. Same way Sasha did.

And this kinda pisses me off. "Name one time I lied to you."

"Well..." But he falters.

"I have never lied to you. I have only withheld my truth. And my truth, Adam Boucher, has nothing to do with you."

"Doesn't it?"

"It does not."

"Well, I find that very interesting."

"And why's that?"

"Because I was down in a graveyard not more than a month ago and do you know what I was doing there?"

"I wouldn't even know where to start guessing."

"I was digging up my brother's grave."

I don't know what to say to that, so I stutter. "I… I… I'm sorry to hear the sad news about your brother."

"Is that a joke?"

"No. I didn't even realize you had a brother."

Adam smiles and points at me. "Nor I you."

I have to chuckle. "Yeah. I guess that's a little bit weird."

"Is that *all* it is?"

"Adam. I feel like you're leading me around in circles. What are you trying to say that you can't seem to spit out?"

He studies me for a moment, that small smile growing bigger as the seconds tick off. "You really don't know, do you?"

I am truly confused and his clutter of words is knocking me off my game. I have no fucking idea what Adam is getting at. This is not good because I'm playing like seventeen games in my head at the moment—all those balls in the air, all those secrets flying around, tryin' their best to surface—and this bizarre conversation will not be what ruins the tail end of an eight-year plan.

"Well? Are you gonna tell me?"

"What do you do again?"

I decide I'm just gonna give him what he wants. He already knows. I'm sure Nathan has told him everything. "I kill Zero girls. Is that the information you're fishing for? Because Indie's not on the list and neither is her daughter."

"*My* daughter," Adam says. And everything about his tone has changed. "She's *my* daughter too."

"I thought—"

"Not biological, you idiot. But that girl is mine. Same way Wendy is yours, I guess."

"Not the same, but—"

"Anyway," Adam cuts me off. "No, sir. That was not the information I was fishing for. But it's a start, at least."

"Shouldn't we just concentrate on Donavan?"

"Oh"—Adam looks over his shoulder at the house—"don't you worry about Donovan. I'm sure McKay and Merc are working the details out as we speak."

And then something hits me. A sudden realization. A full illumination of what he just did.

He separated us and I didn't even realize it. Indie took Wendy to debrief her. And McKay took Merc and Sasha to debrief them.

"This is about me," I say.

"You sound so surprised."

"What the fuck? Is Donovan even alive?"

"Oh, everything you heard about Donovan is true. And I do appreciate your help in that regard, but that's not really why you're here, is it, Nick? Why don't we cut out the bullshit and get to the point? Why. Are you here?"

Why am I here?

He wants to know why I'm here?

I'm here because eight years ago I found a book in the back of my truck, a book that was filled with desperate hopelessness, and I decided then and there that I would not allow this girl to grow up just so she could die.

I was going to fix her.

I was going to *cure* her.

I went to Chek first. I told him what I wanted to do. I showed him the book. But Chek wasn't interested. His line of thinking was… if it ain't broke, don't fix it.

But Wendy *was* broke. She had been shattered long before Chek saved her. And it was just a matter of time before there were so many cracks, we wouldn't be able to put her back together again.

Every good little Zero girl needs a handler.

That's Chek. That's Adam.

But if you want them to grow up sane, they need more than just a man to keep them in line.

They need a McKay.

They need a Donovan.

I was Wendy's McKay.

I was Wendy's Donovan.

And seventeen days after Chek died, on Wendy Gale's seventeenth birthday, I knew she was at her breaking point. She was not gonna come back from what happened to Chek.

No. If I'm only talking in my head, then I should at least be honest with myself.

Wendy was not gonna come back from the realization that *she* was the one who killed Chek that day Cabal Island was going down.

She killed him.

She didn't arrive at the cabin on her seventeenth birthday alone. She was with me.

So I did what I had to do.

I went into her head.

I twisted it all up, wrung it all out, and then smoothed it all over.

Her. Cure.

I am the cure.

Because Merc isn't the last functioning Company-trained PSYOPS agent left in the world.

He's not even Company, but even if he were, *he is no me.*

I'm am the last fully-sanctioned, fully-trained Company PSYOPS left in this world.

Me.

And Wendy Gale really is sweet, beautiful, perfect, and whole. She is everlasting, transcendent, exceptional, and extraordinary. She is remarkable, exquisite, priceless, and sublime. She is flawless, marvelous, divine, and sensational. She is heavenly, powerful, glorious, and delightful.

She is lovely.

She is majestic.

She is gorgeous.

And she is… miserable.

She is a piece of gorgeous misery and I cannot bear it.

"Not gonna answer me?"

I snap back to the present and find Adam waiting on an answer.

"That's fine," Adam says. "I already know why you're here."

"Look." I huff. "I did my best, OK? She killed him, Adam. She was the one who killed him. And no one knew what to do with her. No one but me. *Me*, Adam. *Me*. So they let her go. They let her just get in that fucking truck and drive. And do you know where I found her?" I feel like I might cry. So I pause and take a deep breath, then swallow hard and continue. "She left a message for me on the board. It was just one message. And I was eleven hours late in seeing it because I wasn't thinking clearly. I didn't look. I should've, I get that. But I didn't. And I can't change it. I found her at my house, Adam. Standing in my sunflower field. She was a mess. A fuckin' mess. She knew she killed him, but there was a war going on in her mind. She was crazy. You have to understand, right? You know what it's like. Haven't you ever found Indie like this? So yeah, I did it. I went inside her head and rearranged things and—"

"Hold. The fuck. On." Adam holds up his hand and just stares at me. "What the hell are you talking about?"

"What?"

"What are you talking about? Are you telling me that you... what? PSYOPed *Wendy*?"

"What?"

"Is that what you just said?"

"You said you already knew why I was here."

"I thought you were here..." It takes him a moment, but then he lets out a long breath and closes his eyes. "You're here for *Carter*."

I snap out of my crazed and desperate rant and focus. "Wait. Why did *you* think I was here?"

"Because you're my missing dead *brother*, dude."

"*What?*"

There is a long silence as each of us takes our time coming to terms with what the other just said. And then, before we can discuss it further, everyone is back.

Wendy appears with Indie and Maggie, the three of them laughing like normal girls.

Merc and Sasha appear with McKay, also looking settled and, if not happy, at the very least at ease.

Even Nathan appears. He jokes around with Wendy like this is just some planned family reunion.

Adam and I just stand there, facing each other.

So many questions running through our minds.

And then, because we are who we are, we say nothing.

Welcome to the End of Book Shit! This is the part of the book where I get to say anything I want about the story you just read or listened to. It's never edited so if you see a typo, just chill, man. It's 2021. I don't need that kind of *pressure*.

Speaking of. Oh, man. 2021. We thought 2020 was fucking crazy? 2021 was like, Hold my beer, bitches. And let's face it—2022 is just Groundhog Day at this point.

But seriously, tho. It was a pretty good for me career-wise. I have nothing to complain about. But the world? Yeah. The fucking world has gone insane. I feel like I'm living in one of my books. Like Bossy Brothers Johnny, or Spencer. Hell, let's face it. We're in the

Company. And I just kinda have to laugh about it even though none a single bit of it is funny.

2022 is my ten-year author anniversary. I started writing my first fiction book on January 1, 2012. In September of that year, I released that book. And then two weeks later I released the second one. Two weeks after that, I released book 3. So by the end of 2012—one year—I had put out three books and was already working on book four of that series.

But I started out writing science fiction thrillers. Those were all my Junco books. I would not start writing romance until February 2014. That was Tragic and that's where this whole Company world started.

People often ask me where I get my ideas. This is the number one question people have for me. Number two is—what happened to you? Why are you like this?

Truth be told—I was raised by a single mother and she was pretty boring. She wasn't a stripper, she didn't drink or do drugs, and she always worked two jobs.

Now. With that said. My aunt—my mother's sister? Yeah. I think she was supposed to be my mother. Because she and I were like peas in a pod. But not the good kind of peas. Which is dumb. There are no good peas. Peas are gross. She was the one who was married to the professional poker player I mention in Bossy Bride. Mind you, this was back before there was professional poker like we know and love today. In fact, it wasn't professional, let's just call it mob and all under the table.

So she was colorful. And my father, he's still alive so let's just call him unconventional.

And I'm one of those fearless people. Not the courageous kind, but the clueless kind. But I kind of think that's a good thing. Whenever I reach a goal I always look back and think—Man, I'm so fucking glad I was so clueless when I started this stupid journey, because fuck this shit. I would've never done it if I had known.

I'm just really—stupidly—confident that if I put my mind to it, I can conquer shit. Because if I really want something I turn in to one of those tunnel-vision, goal-oriented assholes who does nothing but race towards that finish line.

The next most popular question I get is do I ever run out of ideas. You'd be surprised how many people ask me this.

My farrier, who is coming tomorrow, BTW. And BBTW, he's writing a book about being a farrier and he's actually a pretty good writer, so when he puts that book up on sale, I'm gonna promote the fuck out it. Anyway, he asked me this question the last time he was here trimming the donkeys.

But I don't really understand this question. It's kinda like asking a surgeon—so... do you ever fail at this whole surgeon thing? i.e. Do you ever kill them?

I'm a hundred percent positive that surgeons kill people all the time. It's kind of the nature of the biz. But the answer for me is NO. No. I *never* run out of ideas. Ever. Like, I have twenty-seven fucking stories in my head right now just waiting for me to have time to write them. I'm a fucking writer. It's my job.

Sometimes I get stuck in a story though. Everyone gets stuck in a story. I'm gonna talk about that in a bit.

But the third most popular question is how do I keep it all straight. They often say they think my office has a whole wall of pictures and notes with strings or lines connecting all the related pieces.

You know the scene. There's a serial killer on the loose the crazy detective who is always right, but no one ever believes them because they take lithium twice a day, is gonna solve this murder mystery by posting pics and newspaper clippings and connecting all the dots. (Yep. Just like that room in Bossy Jesse.)

Sadly, no. As fun as it sounds, I don't do that. I don't keep what's called a story bible that holds the whole thing together for me. If I write anything down it's scribbled on the back of a note or put into an email that I send myself with a title in code that I only know how to decipher, except it wasn't a code, it was a typo. So I can't ever find it.

I'm just not an organized person at all. I lose everything. But you know what I don't lose? My head. That's why I keep that shit up there. My head is always right where it's supposed to be.

Oh my God. I just thought about something. Did you ever watch that series on Netflix called Lock and Key? They have a key that allows you to go inside someone's head and see how they organize their memories.

You know what my head looks like?

That lithium detective's office wall.

Because I'm gonna be honest with you. Not only do I NOT keep any kind of filing system about my stories, I don't even plan them. I just make it up as I go.

None of this was planned.

Not a single book.

I might've known where it was headed when I started a few of them. And I usually do have an ending in mind. But all those words between chapter one and chapter end, yeah. I'm not sure I even know where that all comes from.

I have talked to many author friends about this idea creation stuff. Asking them—where do they get their ideas. Where does the story come from? Some of them tell me how they plot a book, which I give no fucks about. If you're plotting out your entire story, our words don't come from the same place. And it could be that these writers are just... not lying, I'm not sure I would call it lying. But not able to understand where the words *really* come from.

And I'm talking about *writers* here. Not people who vomit words onto pages and call it a story.

Writers know they have no fucking clue where this shit comes from. Because all writers have written books—maybe one, maybe a hundred—and they get to the end and they say, Wow. I don't know where that came from. I don't feel like I wrote it. I feel like it just came out of me.

The entire Junco series is like that for me. From beginning to end. It looks NOTHING like the book I set out to write. There were a few things that made it all the way to the end, but the purpose of those things were completely different.

And I often look back on that series and think... I didn't write that. It wasn't me. That's how detached I am from that whole process of creating that story and those people in those places.

And don't get me wrong. I *did* the research. I had books, and books, and books of research for that story. I'm the one who sat down at the keyboard every night and typed for hours, and hours, and hours.

But I didn't come up with that story.

It just poured out.

Most of the time, when I was done writing for the night, I would just stop and look at it and think… what the fuck? Like how did these people get so real? How did these places get so real I can see them in my head like I've been there?

But you can't think about it for very long because you will never get that answer. People think Julie, it's just you, bitch. Your mind did that.

OK. It did. Because that's the logical explanation.

But creation isn't logical. It just isn't.

It's the same way for the Company. If someone asks me about a scene from one of my books, I immediately picture the place where it happened. Every word I write takes place somewhere. And I can tell you what the temperature was outside that day. I can tell you what furniture was in the room. I know the road they were traveling. I see it all in my head.

So all this Company stuff? I didn't really write this story, it just came out and this is what we got.

I came up with the characters. I came up with their names, their jobs, the kind of car they drive. But none of these books were what I set out to do when I wrote Tragic.

I never once said, "I think I'll write books about assassins who work for a global shadow government and want to take it down from the inside." That thought never happened.

What really happened was that I said, "I want to write about a little girl who kills people."

And twenty-seven books later, this is literally where we ended up.

People who don't write probably think this whole "muse" thing is a joke. Or it's just... some weird part of our imaginations. Creative people are overly dramatic and moody, right? We're difficult. We love the spotlight or we are reclused.

But the muse is a real thing for artists, and writers, and other creators. There is a "zone" out there filled with ideas, and stories, and visions. It's like a river. Constantly flowing. And we creative people, we just reach into that current and pluck things out.

And then we put it into our work.

It's mine, I guess. I'm the one who plucked it. I'm the one who rescued it from the endless river of stories. But did I come up with it?

There are lots of days when I think... not really.

You can believe it or not, but this is how it happens.

Most of these stories... I didn't plot this shit, OK? I just didn't. I sat down, reached into the river, plucked out what I could, and I put it down on paper.

When I write a book it's like a movie in my head and I'm just an observer.

Which leads me to this really intriguing thought exercise — what happens to the deleted words and scenes?

I'll tell you what happens - it fucks with my spatial awareness inside the story, that's what happens. What do I mean by that? I mean... I have already pictured that scene. I have already been in that space, as that character. I have already lived it. (so to speak).

So if I delete words, I'm deleting parts of the character's life. I'm deleting part of their world.

It probably sounds a bit crazy, but that's how it feels. I have to wipe my mind of that scene and start imagining it all over again. Which is not that easy to do, so I don't do it often.

And this brings me to my point, I guess.

My fans are awesome but not every reader is a fan. So I got some comments about how long it took me to write the last two books in this series.

But here's why it took so long: I started Gorgeous Misery at least seven times. I got as far as forty-five thousand words one of those times. And I threw them all out. I have seven folders called Gorgeous Misery on various computers. All with different variations of file names.

And the characters and the story, and the places in those drafts, they were all part of the story. And then they got deleted and they weren't.

So that really fucked with me.

And then, we have Nick Tate.

Nick. Fucking. Tate.

I love him. He's definitely one of my favorites. But at this point in time—chapter one of Gorgeous Misery—I have to account for TWENTY YEARS OF HIS LIFE, people.

Talk about a challenge.

I wanted to tell you everything. I wanted you to have all the stories. I wanted you to live all those days with Lauren with me. I wanted to take you on every job he did with Wendy. I wanted to tell you every word.

But that's not a story. That's barfing words.

So I had to choose. Which parts need to be told to get through the fourth book.

And after seven drafts, and throwing out nearly seventy-five thousand words, this is where we landed.

This is Nick Tate's bizarre love story.

And it's a lot of things, but normal isn't one of them.

But what did you expect?

It's Nick Tate.

While I was writing this story I was, of course, thinking a lot about Merc. And that story—Meet Me in the Dark—how *necessary* it was. How you had to have Sydney's story before you could ever begin to understand what kind of people we're dealing with.

Meet Me in the Dark is my darkest book. And I never went that dark again—Not even Sick Heart is as dark at Meet Me in the Dark.

But it was *necessary*.

That's how I feel about Gorgeous Misery. It's not hearts and flowers, but it's necessary. And it *is* a love story. It's a love story about a man who just want to save his girl.

That's it.

That's all it is.

All the other stuff plays out in Lovely Darkness.

And I promise, when you get to the last page… it all falls into place.

353

Thank you for reading, thank you for reviewing, and I'll see you in the next book.

Julie
December 13, 2021

P.S. – After I wrote this, I was like… didn't I make notes about what I wanted to say in this EOBS? Of course, I did. And none of this crazy shit was on that list, Julie!

So I went and looked, and yeah. ALL of this crazy shit was on my list. :)

See! Up in the head, people. Up in the head.

:)

If you want the complete Company story you should read the books in the order below. I made some notes about which characters first show up where, if you're just looking for a specific Company storyline.

Rook and Ronin Series

The entire Company beginnings start in this series. But each series is its own entry point. You can jump in and read them out of order as long as you follow the specific series reading order.

Tragic
Manic
Panic
Ford – Sasha Cherlin (age 12) and Merc first appear here
Spencer – James Fenici first appears here – Five is born

The Company - Rook & Ronin Spin-off – new entry point into the series

The Company – James and Vincent Fenici age 28, Sasha Cherlin age 13, Nick and Harper Tate age 18. This is the **full story of the "Santa Barbara Incident"** where Adam and Donovan's fathers die.

Meet Me In The Dark – Merc, Sasha Cherlin age 21, Sydney Channing (Company Girl like Indie and Sasha)

Three, Two, One – STANDALONE BOOK – Jax Barlow first appears

Wasted Lust – Sasha Cherlin, age 24, with Jax Barlow.

Nick Tate, age 29, plays a major role and the rest of the Company characters also show back up.

First appearance of Angelica Fenici and "other Adam".

Wasted Lust takes place DURING Creeping Beautiful. Specifically when Indie is 15 years old and the "Company falls" and when Nick meets Adam in Daphne, Alabama.

The Mister Series – Rook & Ronin/Company
Spin-off – new entry point into the series

Mr. Perfect

Mr. Romantic – First appearance of the Silver Society – i.e. The Company

Mr. Corporate – First appearance of "Five"

Mr. Mysterious – Spencer's daughters

Mr. Match – All the Rook & Ronin Kids come back to play.

Mr. Five (or just Five) – Ford's son and Spencer's daughter

Mr. & Mrs. – Ford and Spencer show back up with all the kids

The Bossy Brothers Series
Rook & Ronin/Company Spin-off – new entry
point into the series

In to Her – STANDALONE BOOK – Logan first appears

Bossy Brothers: Jesse – First appearance of The Way – i.e. The Company

Bossy Brothers: Joey

Bossy Brothers: Johnny – Logan shows back up Indie first appears at age 14, Chek's first appearance

Bossy Bride: Jesse and Emma – Chek and Wendy mentioned

Bossy Brothers: Alonzo – Chek and Wendy mentioned

Creeping Beautiful – Rook & Ronin and Company Spin-off – new entry point into the series

The complete story of Nick Tate, James and Vincent Fenici, "Wendy", "Chek", Indie Anna Accorsi, Adam Boucher, Donovan and Carter Couture, Core McKay, and Nathan St. James.

Creeping Beautiful (book 1)
Pretty Nightmare (book 2)
Gorgeous Misery (book 3)
Lovely Darkness (book 4)

ABOUT THE AUTHOR

JA Huss *never wanted* to be a writer and she still dreams of that elusive career as an astronaut. She originally went to school to become an equine veterinarian but soon figured out they keep horrible hours and decided to go to grad school instead. That Ph.D. wasn't all it was cracked up to be (and she really sucked at the whole scientist thing), so she dropped out and got a M.S. in forensic toxicology just to get the whole thing over with as soon as possible.

After graduation she got a job with the state of Colorado as their one and only hog farm inspector and spent her days wandering the Eastern Plains shooting the shit with farmers.

After a few years of that, she got bored. And since she was a homeschool mom and actually does love science, she decided to write science textbooks and make online classes for other homeschool moms.

She wrote more than two hundred of those workbooks and was the number one publisher at the online homeschool store many times, but eventually she covered every science topic she could think of and ran out of shit to say.

So in 2012 she decided to write fiction instead. That year she released her first three books and started a career that would make her a New York Times bestseller and land her on the USA Today Bestseller's List twenty-one times in the next five years.

In May 2018 MGM Television bought the TV and film rights for five of her books in the Rook & Ronin and Company series' and in March 2019 they offered her and her writing partner, Johnathan McClain, a script deal to write a pilot for a TV show.

Her books have sold millions of copies all over the world, the audio version of her semi-autobiographical book, Eighteen, was nominated for a Voice Arts Award and an Audie Award in 2016 and 2017 respectively, her audiobook, Mr. Perfect, was nominated for a Voice Arts Award in 2017, and her audiobook, Taking Turns, was nominated for an Audie Award in 2018. In 2019 her book, Total Exposure, was nominated for a Romance Writers of America RITA Award.

She lives on a ranch in Central Colorado with her family.